S0-AIY-904

A Fanciful Correspondence

Dear Mr. Lincoln:

The very best letter I can write in the half-hour before the carriage will be at the door to take me to Mrs. Braddon's dance shall be yours tonight. I am sitting here in the library, arrayed in my smartest, newest, whitest, silkiest gown, with a string of pearls which Uncle James gave me today about my throat — the dear, glistening, sheeny things! And I am looking forward to the "dances and delight" of the evening with keen anticipation.

You asked me in your last letter if I did not sometimes grow weary of my endless round of dances and dinners and social functions. No, no, never! I enjoy every one of them, every minute of them. I love life and its bloom and brilliancy; I love meeting new people; I love the ripple of music, the hum of laughter and conversation. Every morning when I awaken the new day seems to me to be a good fairy who will bring me some beautiful gift of joy. . . .

ACROSS THE MILES

L. M. Montgomery

Across the Miles

TALES OF CORRESPONDENCE

edited by Rea Wilmshurst

BANTAM BOOKS
NEW YORK · TORONTO · LONDON · SYDNEY · AUCKLAND

RL 6.5, age 010 and up

ACROSS THE MILES

A Bantam Book / published by arrangement with
McClelland & Stewart Inc.
PRINTING HISTORY
McClelland & Stewart Inc. edition published 1995
Bantam edition published April 1997

The Starfire logo is a registered trademark of Bantam Books,
a division of Bantam Doubleday Dell Publishing Group, Inc.
Registered in U.S. Patent and Trademark Office and elsewhere.

"Anne of Green Gables" is a trademark and a Canadian official mark
of the Anne of Green Gables Licensing Authority Inc., which is
owned by the heirs of L. M. Montgomery and the Province of Prince
Edward Island and located in Charlottetown, Prince Edward Island.

All rights reserved.
Compilation, Introduction, and edited text copyright © 1995 by
David Macdonald, Ruth Macdonald, and Rea Wilmshurst.
Cover art copyright © 1995 by Laurie McGaw.
No part of this book may be reproduced or transmitted in any
form or by any means, electronic or mechanical, including
photocopying, recording, or by any information storage and
retrieval system, without permission in writing from the publisher.
For information address: McClelland & Stewart Inc.,
481 University Avenue, Toronto, Ontario M5G 2E9.

If you purchased this book without a cover you should be aware
that this book is stolen property. It was reported as "unsold and
destroyed" to the publisher and neither the author nor the
publisher has received any payment for this "stripped book."

ISBN: 0-553-57103-6

Published simultaneously in the United States and Canada

Bantam Books are published by Bantam Books, a division of Bantam
Doubleday Dell Publishing Group, Inc. Its trademark, consisting
of the words "Bantam Books" and the portrayal of a rooster, is
Registered in U.S. Patent and Trademark Office and in other
countries. Marca Registrada. Bantam Books, 1540 Broadway, New
York, New York 10036.

PRINTED IN THE UNITED STATES OF AMERICA

0 9 8 7 6 5 4 3 2 1

OPM

Contents

Introduction

IN MONTGOMERY'S DAY, at least before the advent of the telephone, letters (and messages passed by word of mouth) were the sole means of communication between people who lived at a distance from each other. Letter-writing was a cultivated skill, honed by another nineteenth-century pastime, keeping a journal. The stories in *Across the Miles* bear witness to the importance these writing forms played in ordinary people's lives, as they corresponded with loved ones and expressed themselves through their journals.

The epistolary novel – one written entirely in the form of letters – has a long and distinguished history in English literature; the best known example is probably Richardson's *Clarissa*. Montgomery herself attempted the form in *Anne of Windy Poplars*, which is made up largely of Anne's letters to Gilbert before their marriage while she is principal of Summerside High School and he is getting his medical degree. The letters allow us to listen in as Anne tells the man she loves her reactions to people and events in her new surroundings. In some of the tales in this collection Montgomery similarly establishes her characters through their letters, and those letters form the major part of the text. In other tales it may be a written note or invitation that precipitates the action.

In still other stories, it is through the pages of a journal that the story unfolds. The convention of eavesdropping on a personal journal gives an author the chance to write a first-person narration as the action is occurring, providing both immediacy and intimacy. Because she kept a journal for most of her life, Montgomery was familiar with the form and comfortable with the convention. (And her own journals have revealed a darker side to Montgomery that few of her faithful readers had been aware of.) Montgomery wrote about half of *Rilla of Ingleside* as entries in Rilla's war-diary, her "old hotch-potch of a journal," inviting readers to feel even closer to Rilla by reading over her shoulder, sympathizing with her problems and predicaments, her joys and fears, through the years of World War I.

Can there be many young women who have not, at some time, kept a journal, even if it fell by the wayside within a few months? Like Beatrice, in "The Understanding of Sister Sara," who says, "I began this journal last New Year's – wrote two entries in it and then forgot all about it." Beatrice picks up her journal again when she needs a place in which to pour out her heart, because her sister Sara seems so unsympathetic, but in the process she reveals her own self-absorption. Cornelia Marshall mentions the beginning of her diary-keeping career too: "Aunt Jemima gave me this diary for a Christmas present," but she doesn't feel the need to unburden her heart: "I'm not a bit sentimental and I never have time for soul outpourings." Still, she confesses later, "It is rather good to have a diary to pour out your woes in when you feel awfully bad and have no one to sympathize with you," and later yet makes another discovery: "I've found out what diaries are for . . . to work off blue moods in" ("The Growing Up of Cornelia").

Written invitations, sent by hand or by post, were, especially in the days before the telephone, the proper way of arranging a social gathering, even among intimates and for relatively informal occasions. Grace Seeley receives a written invitation to the college prom in "The Jest That Failed," and a last-minute invitation, such as the one Nan sends Florrie Hamilton to ask her to come for a visit the same afternoon, is a written note, taken to the post office in the morning and picked up at noon ("A Fortunate Mistake").

When young men left home to seek their fortunes at the turn of the century, letters were the only way for the folks back home to keep in touch with them. When Anna refuses to write to Gilbert, who has gone out west to earn money to pay off the mortgage on his parents' home, her sister Alma writes instead, pretending that the letters come from Anna. She is able to practise this deception because she runs the post office. L. M. Montgomery once said that if she and her grandmother had not run the Cavendish post office, she might never have persisted in her attempts to be published. It would have been embarrassing for her to have had local gossips, kept informed by the village post-master or -mistress (always at the centre of village life), commenting upon her many submissions and rejections. As it was, she was able to keep her secret until, in her own idiom, "success crowned her efforts." Like Montgomery, Alma is able to keep her secret by being post-mistress. Of course, when Gilbert returns Alma has to face the consequences ("Anna's Love Letters").

The west was full of young men like Gilbert, and many of them were comforted by letters from home. But if they were alone in the world, with no fond friends or relatives to write to them, it was much harder for them to keep up their spirits, so they sometimes sought a correspondence with a stranger. Montgomery herself exchanged literary letters with two men through much of her life, meeting G. B. Macmillan only once, on her honeymoon in Scotland, and Ephraim Weber (who lived on the prairies) never. When, in "A Correspondence and a Climax," John Lincoln asks through a newspaper column for a penpal, he begins to receive letters from Sidney Richmond, apparently a young socialite in the east, and they correspond for four years. Her letters make a great difference in his life, but his unexpected decision to come east to visit causes Sidney great consternation. Another widely separated pair exchange letters between P.E.I. and Vancouver. They too meet after years of letter writing ("The Girl and the Photograph").

Montgomery illustrates the importance of the sympathy that can be conveyed on paper in "The Letters." Wealthy, middle-aged Isobel Shirley begins to receive anonymous letters of comfort and encouragement after the death of her father leaves her alone in the world. The letters sustain and enliven her, though she is unable to respond: "After every letter there was something new for me to hunt out and learn and assimilate, until my old narrow mental attitude had so broadened and deepened, sweeping out into circles of thought I had never known or imagined, that I hardly knew myself." She is finally so involved that she writes answers, though they have to be kept locked in her desk, undelivered: "Safe in the belief that the mysterious friend to whom it was written would never see it, I wrote with a perfect freedom and a total lack of self-consciousness that I could never have attained otherwise." Both Isobel Shirley and an unnamed school-master in another story keep their letters secret, and in both stories the climax comes when the letters are finally sent and read. The schoolmaster, too, writes more easily because he intends never to send his letters: "And it was because she never was to see them that he dared to write them, straight out of his full heart, taking the exquisite pleasure of telling her what he never could permit himself to tell her face to face" ("The Schoolmaster's Letters").

As readers of Volume Four of this series (*After Many Days*) know, Montgomery believed that the passage of time might often bring about a change that would result in a person's hap-piness, or that some significant piece of information might be revealed after years of misunderstanding. Not surprisingly, then, letters whose delivery is long delayed play a significant part in several of these tales. When her long-dead brother's letter finally comes to Mary Isabel it is fifteen years late, but it is not too late to change her life ("The Revolt of Mary Isabel"). And when sweet but embittered Miss Sally is given the letter her long-ago sweetheart was prevented from sending her, her attitude to life and marriage changes completely ("Miss Sally's Letter"). Some letters from the past are discovered in unusual places, and their appearance changes the lives or fortunes of the finders: the old yellowed letter Claude and Philippa use to mend their kite has important repercussions for the Leete family ("Our Runaway Kite"); Patty and Carry's financial problems are solved when they find the letter and gift Aunt Caroline hid for them three years earlier ("Aunt Caroline's Silk Dress"). Yet another document, though not a letter, keeps its secret for years until two acts of generosity reveal its hiding place ("The Promissory Note").

In most of Montgomery's stories people live in their own homes, but in this collection there is one scene set in a boarding house, a feature of life that was much commoner in Montgomery's day than it is now. Students living away from home, single men or women who had not yet or could not afford to set up housekeeping on their own, and old people conserving slim resources would rent a room in a large house where the proprietress provided furniture, linens, and meals. Montgomery used her personal experience of "boarding-out" while at college in Halifax in both *Anne of Green Gables*, when Anne goes to Charlottetown for her year of teacher training, and *Anne of the Island*, when Anne and Priscilla board for a year before setting up house in "Patty's Place." When a grey and rainy day depresses all the inhabitants of Mrs. Plunkett's boarding house, including Cyrilla Blair and her two roommates, "Cyrilla's Inspiration," in an unexpected epistolary form, brings a pleasant conclusion to the miserable day.

Cyrilla and her friends are happy at least in having each other to keep themselves cheery, but a girl in another story, Grace Seeley, lives by herself: ". . . she rented a little unfurnished room and cooked her own meals over an oil stove" ("The Jest That Failed"). To her snobbish classmates this is intolerable and they do their best to embarrass her by sending her an invitation to the senior prom in the name of the most eligible man at the college. Their false values are displayed by Montgomery clearly and unsparingly; she has an eye for this sort of thing and probably suffered from it herself as a young country girl in the city. "The Jest That Failed" concerns schoolgirl unpleasantness, but boys are not immune to the same disease. In "The Old Fellow's Letter" two boys forge a love-letter in their mathematics professor's name to one of the loveliest girls in town to pay the professor back for some imagined offence. The letter does not have the effect they had hoped for, however, and neither does the false invitation to Grace.

Besides writing for her characters, Montgomery shows them in their everyday lives, and her style is often at its most colourful when dealing with those who are less educated. Here is Mrs. Emory, (whose favourite expression is "Dear life and heart!"), surprised to see her boarder up early: "What on earth is the matter, Mr. Murray? You ain't sick now surely? I told you them pond fogs was p'isen after night!" ("At Five O'Clock in the Morning"). "Aunt Susanna's Birthday Celebration" is told in the first person, as spoken by an old woman to a young girl; the story is full of the freshness of direct speech. And here is a man-on-campus describing the town beauty: "She was all togged out in some new fall duds, and I guess she'd come out to show them off. They were brownish, kind of, and she'd a spanking hat on with feathers and things in it. Her hair was shining under it, all purply-black, and she looked sweet enough to eat" ("The Old Fellow's Letter"). This story is full of such slangy, breezy writing, showing Montgomery deftly capturing the speech patterns of the young male animal.

Whether they are described by an omniscient narrator or

in the first-person musings of a journal, Montgomery's lovers are most often handsome or beautiful, and in sketching them she draws on a vein of rich phrases. In this collection we meet the woman Murray sees milking cows: "her profile . . . was perfect, and the colouring of the oval cheek and the beautiful curve of the chin were something to adore" ("At Five O'Clock in the Morning"), and the girl Curtis meets in the woods: "With that face before my eyes I thought only of its purity and sweetness, of the lovely soul and rich mind looking out of the great, greyish-blue eyes which, in the dimness of the pine shadows, looked almost black" ("The Girl and the Photograph"). Montgomery's picture of an "old-maid" of forty has charming details: Mary Isabel has "little rings of dark hair" which, though brushed straight back faithfully "a dozen times a day" keep creeping down, "kinking defiance to Louisa," her martinet older sister. The curls and her "wood-brown eyes" play havoc with the heart of the middle-aged doctor next door ("The Revolt of Mary Isabel").

In addition to making people live for us, Montgomery's ability to describe the world of nature is one of her most striking characteristics. Whether or not she mentions Prince Edward Island specifically, readers know that her home inspired many of her descriptions, and *Across the Miles* has many telling and vivid examples. The seaside at sunset: "bays that were like great cups of sapphire brimming over with ruby wine for gods to drain, on headlands that were like amethyst, on wide sweeps of sea that were blue and far and mysterious" ("The Schoolmaster's Letters"). Dawn: "Overhead, the sky was a vast, high-sprung arch of unstained crystal. Down over the sand dunes, where the pond ran out into the sea, was a great arc of primrose smitten through with auroral crimsonings" ("At Five O'Clock in the Morning"). Autumn: "the slim wild cherry trees were bronzing under the autumn frosts," and the light from a red maple was "streaming in through the open door behind her, staining her light house-dress and mellowing the golden sheen of her hair" ("Anna's Love Letters"). November: "It was a stormy, unrestful sunset, gleaming angrily through the dark fir boughs that were now and again tossed suddenly and distressfully in a fitful gust of wind. Below, in the garden, it was quite dark, and I could only see dimly the dead leaves that were whirling and dancing uncannily over the roseless paths" ("The Letters").

Throughout these stories Montgomery's people put pen to paper and we see how their writings affect their lives; significant portions of those lives unreel before us, and we are caught up in the enchantment provided by a master storyteller. In a world just past the time of quill pens, but well before the advent of the disposable ballpoint, the written word supplies personal and intimate information and a letter is an important event. Montgomery's cast of characters ranges widely, from the poor but ambitious student Grace Seeley to the rich but lonely Isobel Shirley, from the "unholy imp" Link Houseman to the poor country doctor Jack Willoughby and his millionaire rival Gus Sinclair. Montgomery's tone can be serious or playful; her tales may be about love or everyday life; the setting may be a poor cottage or a society mansion. But always her stories open up for us a world we have lost, a world of old-fashioned values and concerns, a world we enter into gladly, sure that there we will find people, places, and plots to amuse, charm, and move us.

Rea Wilmshurst
October 1994

A Correspondence and
a Climax

A T sunset Sidney hurried to her room to take off the soiled and faded cotton dress she had worn while milking. She had milked eight cows and pumped water for the milk-cans afterward in the fag-end of a hot summer day. She did that every night, but tonight she had hurried more than usual because she wanted to get her letter written before the early farm bedtime. She had been thinking it out while she milked the cows in the stuffy little pen behind the barn. This monthly letter was the only pleasure and stimulant in her life. Existence would have been, so Sidney thought, a dreary, unbearable blank without it.

She cast aside her milking-dress with a thrill of distaste that tingled to her rosy fingertips. As she slipped into her blue-print afternoon dress her aunt called to her from below. Sidney ran out to the dark little entry and leaned over the stair railing. Below in the kitchen there was a hubbub of laughing, crying, quarrelling children, and a reek of bad tobacco smoke drifted up to the girl's disgusted nostrils.

Aunt Jane was standing at the foot of the stairs with a lamp in one hand and a year-old baby clinging to the other. She was a big shapeless woman with a round good-natured face – cheerful and vulgar as a sunflower was Aunt Jane at all times and occasions.

"I want to run over and see how Mrs. Brixby is this evening, Siddy, and you must take care of the baby till I get back."

Sidney sighed and went downstairs for the baby. It never would have occurred to her to protest or be petulant about it. She had all her aunt's sweetness of disposition, if she resembled her in nothing else. She had not grumbled because she had to rise at four that morning, get breakfast, milk the cows, bake bread, prepare seven children for school, get dinner, preserve twenty quarts of strawberries, get tea, and milk the cows again. All her days were alike as far as hard work and dullness went, but she accepted them cheerfully and uncomplainingly. But she did resent having to look after the baby when she wanted to write her letter.

She carried the baby to her room, spread a quilt on the floor for him to sit on, and gave him a box of empty spools to play with. Fortunately he was a phlegmatic infant, fond of staying in one place, and not given to roaming about in search of adventures; but Sidney knew she would have to keep an eye on him, and it would be distracting to literary effort.

She got out her box of paper and sat down by the little table at the window with a small kerosene lamp at her elbow. The room was small – a mere box above the kitchen which Sidney shared with two small cousins. Her bed and the cot where the little girls slept filled up almost all the available space. The furniture was poor, but everything was neat – it was the only neat room in the house, indeed, for tidiness was no besetting virtue of Aunt Jane's.

Opposite Sidney was a small muslined and befrilled toilet-table, above which hung an eight-by-six-inch mirror, in which Sidney saw herself reflected as she devoutly hoped other people did not see her. Just at that particular angle one eye appeared to be as large as an orange, while the other was the size of a pea, and the mouth zigzagged from ear to ear. Sidney hated that mirror as virulently as she could hate anything. It seemed to her to typify all that was unlovely in her life. The mirror of existence into which her fresh young soul had looked for twenty years gave back to her wistful gaze just such distortions of fair hopes and ideals.

Half of the little table by which she sat was piled high with books – old books, evidently well read and well-bred books, classics of fiction and verse every one of them, and all bearing on the flyleaf the name of Sidney Richmond, thereby meaning not the girl at the table, but her college-bred young father who had died the day before she was born. Her mother had died the day after, and Sidney thereupon had come into the hands of good Aunt Jane, with those books for her dowry, since nothing else was left after the expenses of the double funeral had been paid.

One of the books had Sidney Richmond's name printed on the title-page instead of written on the flyleaf. It was a thick little volume of poems, published in his college days – musical, unsubstantial, pretty little poems, every one of which the girl Sidney loved and knew by heart.

Sidney dropped her pointed chin in her hands and looked dreamily out into the moonlit night, while she thought her letter out a little more fully before beginning to write. Her big brown eyes were full of wistfulness and romance; for Sidney was romantic, albeit a faithful and understanding acquaintance with her father's books had given to her romance refinement and reason, and the delicacy of her own nature had imparted to it a self-respecting bias.

Presently she began to write, with a flush of real excitement on her face. In the middle of things the baby choked on a small twist spool and Sidney had to catch him up by the heels and hold him head downward until the trouble was ejected. Then she had to soothe him, and finally write the rest of her letter holding him on one arm and protecting the epistle from the grabs of his sticky little fingers. It was certainly letter-writing under difficulties, but Sidney seemed to deal with them mechanically. Her soul and understanding were elsewhere.

Four years before, when Sidney was sixteen, still calling herself a schoolgirl by reason of the fact that she could be spared to attend school four months in the winter when work was slack, she had been much interested in the "Maple Leaf" department of the Montreal weekly her uncle took. It was a page given over to youthful Canadians and filled with their contributions in the way of letters, verses, and prize essays. Noms de plume were signed to these, badges were sent to those who joined the Maple Leaf Club, and a general delightful sense of mystery pervaded the department.

Often a letter concluded with a request to the club members to correspond with the writer. One such request went from Sidney under the pen-name of "Ellen Douglas." The girl was lonely in Plainfield; she had no companions or associates such as she cared for; the Maple Leaf Club represented all that her life held of outward interest, and she longed for something more.

Only one answer came to "Ellen Douglas," and that was forwarded to her by the long-suffering editor of "The Maple Leaf." It was from John Lincoln of the Bar N Ranch, Alberta. He wrote that, although his age debarred him from membership in the club (he was twenty, and the limit was eighteen), he read the letters of the department with much interest, and often had thought of answering some of the requests for correspondents. He never had done so, but "Ellen Douglas's" letter was so interesting that he had decided to write to her. Would she be kind enough to correspond with him? Life on the Bar N, ten miles from the outposts of civilization, was lonely. He was two years out from the east, and had not yet forgotten to be homesick at times.

Sidney liked the letter and answered it. Since then they had written to each other regularly. There was nothing sentimental, hinted at or implied, in the correspondence. Whatever the faults of Sidney's romantic visions were, they did not tend to precocious flirtation. The Plainfield boys, attracted by her beauty and repelled by her indifference and aloofness, could have told that. She never expected to meet John Lincoln, nor did she wish to do so. In the correspondence itself she found her pleasure.

John Lincoln wrote breezy accounts of ranch life and adventures on the far western plains, so alien and remote from snug, humdrum Plainfield life that Sidney always had the sensation of crossing a gulf when she opened a letter from the Bar N. As for Sidney's own letter, this is the way it read as she wrote it:

"The Evergreens," Plainfield.

Dear Mr. Lincoln:

The very best letter I can write in the half-hour before the carriage will be at the door to take me to Mrs. Braddon's dance shall be yours tonight. I am sitting here in the library, arrayed in my smartest, newest, whitest, silkiest gown, with a string of pearls which Uncle James gave me today about my throat – the dear, glistening, sheeny things! And I am looking forward to the "dances and delight" of the evening with keen anticipation.

You asked me in your last letter if I did not sometimes grow weary of my endless round of dances and dinners and social functions. No, no, never! I enjoy every one of them, every minute of them. I love life and its bloom and brilliancy; I love meeting new people; I love the ripple of music, the hum of laughter and conversation. Every morning when I awaken the new day seems to me to be a good fairy who will bring me some beautiful gift of joy.

The gift she gave me today was my sunset gallop on my grey mare Lady. The thrill of it is in my veins yet. I distanced the others who rode with me and led the homeward canter alone, rocking along a dark, gleaming road, shadowy with tall firs and pines, whose balsam made all the air resinous around me. Before me was a long valley filled with purple dusk, and beyond it meadows of sunset and great lakes of saffron and rose where a soul might lose itself in colour. On my right was the harbour, silvered over with a rising moon. Oh, it was all glorious – the clear air with its salt-sea tang, the aroma of the pines, the laughter of my friends behind me, the spring and rhythm of Lady's grey satin body beneath me! I wanted to ride on so forever, straight into the heart of the sunset.

Then home and to dinner. We have a houseful of guests at present – one of them an old statesman with a massive silver head, and eyes that have looked into people's thoughts so long that you have an uncanny feeling that they can see right through your soul and read motives you dare not avow even to yourself. I was terribly in awe of him at first, but when I got acquainted with him I found him charming. He is not above talking delightful nonsense even to a girl. I sat by him at dinner, and he talked to me – not nonsense, either, this time. He told me of his political contests and diplomatic battles; he was wise and witty and whimsical. I felt as if I were drinking some rare, stimulating mental wine. What a privilege it is to meet such men and take a peep through their wise eyes at the fascinating game of empire-building!

I met another clever man a few evenings ago. A lot of us went for a sail on the harbour. Mrs. Braddon's house party came too. We had three big white boats that skimmed down the moonlit channel like great white sea birds. There was another boat far across the harbour, and the people in it were singing. The music drifted over the water to us, so sad and sweet and beguiling that I could have cried for very pleasure. One of Mrs. Braddon's guests said to me:

"That is the soul of music with all its sense and earthliness refined away."

I hadn't thought about him before – I hadn't even caught his name in the general introduction. He was a tall, slight man, with a worn, sensitive face and iron-grey hair – a quiet man who hadn't laughed or talked. But he began to talk to me then, and I forgot all about the others. I never had listened to anybody in the least like him. He talked of books and music, of art and travel. He had been all over the world, and had seen everything everybody else had seen and everything they hadn't too, I think. I seemed to be looking into an enchanted mirror where all my own dreams and ideals were reflected back to me, but made, oh, so much more beautiful!

On my way home after the Braddon people had left us somebody asked me how I liked Paul Moore! The man I had been talking with was Paul Moore, the great novelist! I was almost glad I hadn't known it while he was talking to me – I should have been too awed and reverential to have really enjoyed his conversation. As it was, I had contradicted him twice, and he had laughed and liked it. But his books will always have a new meaning to me henceforth, through the insight he himself has given me.

It is such meetings as these that give life its sparkle for me. But much of its abiding sweetness comes from my friendship with Margaret Raleigh. You will be weary of my rhapsodies over her. But she is such a rare and wonderful woman; much older then I am, but so young in heart and soul and freshness of feeling! She is to me mother and sister and wise, clear-sighted friend. To her I go with all my perplexities and hopes and triumphs. She has sympathy and understanding for my every mood. I love life so much for giving me such a friendship!

This morning I wakened at dawn and stole away to the shore before anyone else was up. I had a delightful run-away. The long, low-lying meadows between "The Evergreens" and the shore were dewy and fresh in that first light, that was as fine and purely tinted as the heart of one of my white roses. On the beach the water was purring in little blue ripples, and, oh, the sunrise out there beyond the harbour! All the eastern Heaven was abloom with it. And there was a wind that came dancing and whistling up the channel to replace the beautiful silence with a music more beautiful still.

The rest of the folks were just coming downstairs when I got back to breakfast. They were all yawny, and some were grumpy, but I had washed my being in the sunrise and felt as blithesome as the day. Oh, life is so good to live!

Tomorrow Uncle James's new vessel, the *White Lady*, is to be launched. We are going to make a festive occasion of it, and I am to christen her with a bottle of cobwebby old wine.

But I hear the carriage, and Aunt Jane is calling me. I had a great deal more to say – about your letter, your big "round-up" and your tribulations with your Chinese cook – but I've only time now to say goodbye. You wish me a lovely time at the dance and a full programme, don't you?

Yours sincerely,
Sidney Richmond.

Aunt Jane came home presently and carried away her sleeping baby. Sidney said her prayers, went to bed, and slept soundly and serenely.

She mailed her letter the next day, and a month later an answer came. Sidney read it as soon as she left the post office, and walked the rest of the way home as in a nightmare, staring straight ahead of her with wide-open, unseeing brown eyes.

John Lincoln's letter was short, but the pertinent paragraph of it burned itself into Sidney's brain. He wrote:

I am going east for a visit. It is six years since I was home, and it seems like three times six. I shall go by the C.P.R., which passes through Plainfield, and I mean to stop off for a day. You will let me call and see you, won't you? I shall have to take your permission for granted, as I shall be gone before a letter from you can reach the Bar N. I leave for the east in five days, and shall look forward to our meeting with all possible interest and pleasure.

Sidney did not sleep that night, but tossed restlessly about or cried in her pillow. She was so pallid and hollow-eyed the next morning that Aunt Jane noticed it, and asked her what the matter was.

"Nothing," said Sidney sharply. Sidney had never spoken sharply to her aunt before. The good woman shook her head. She was afraid the child was "taking something."

"Don't do much today, Siddy," she said kindly. "Just lie around and take it easy till you get rested up. I'll fix you a dose of quinine."

Sidney refused to lie around and take it easy. She swallowed the quinine meekly enough, but she worked fiercely all day, hunting out superfluous tasks to do. That night she slept the sleep of exhaustion, but her dreams were unenviable and the awakening was terrible.

Any day, any hour, might bring John Lincoln to Plainfield. What should she do? Hide from him? Refuse to see him? But he would find out the truth just the same; she would lose his friendship and respect just as surely. Sidney trod the way of the transgressor, and found that its thorns pierced to bone and marrow. Everything had come to an end – nothing was left to her! In the untried recklessness of twenty untempered years she wished she could die before John Lincoln came to Plainfield. The eyes of youth could not see how she could possibly live afterward.

SOME DAYS LATER a young man stepped from the C.P.R. train at Plainfield station and found his way to the one small hotel the place boasted. After getting his supper he asked the proprietor if he could direct him to "The Evergreens."

Caleb Williams looked at his guest in bewilderment. "Never heerd o' such a place," he said.

"It is the name of Mr. Conway's estate – Mr. James Conway," explained John Lincoln.

"Oh, Jim Conway's place!" said Caleb. "Didn't know that was what he called it. Sartin I kin tell you whar' to find it. You see that road out thar'? Well, just follow it straight along for a mile and a half till you come to a blacksmith's forge. Jim Conway's house is just this side of it on the right – back from the road a smart piece and no other handy. You can't mistake it."

John Lincoln did not expect to mistake it, once he found it; he knew by heart what it appeared like from Sidney's description: an old stately mansion of mellowed brick, covered with ivy and set back from the highway amid fine ancestral trees, with a pine-grove behind it, a river to the left, and a harbour beyond.

He strode along the road in the warm, ruddy sunshine of early evening. It was not a bad-looking road at all; the farmsteads sprinkled along it were for the most part snug and wholesome enough; yet somehow it was different from what he had expected it to be. And there was no harbour or glimpse of distant sea visible. Had the hotel-keeper made a mistake? Perhaps he had meant some other James Conway.

Presently he found himself before the blacksmith's forge. Beside it was a rickety, unpainted gate opening into a snake-fenced lane feathered here and there with scrubby little spruces. It ran down a bare hill, crossed a little ravine full of young white-stemmed birches, and up another bare hill to an equally bare crest where a farmhouse was perched – a farmhouse painted a stark, staring yellow and the ugliest thing in farmhouses that John Lincoln had ever seen, even among the log shacks of the west. He knew now that he had been misdirected, but as there seemed to be nobody about the forge he concluded that he had better go to the yellow house and inquire within. He passed down the lane and over the little rustic bridge that spanned the brook. Just beyond was another home-made gate of poles.

Lincoln opened it, or rather he had his hand on the hasp of twisted withes which secured it, when he was suddenly arrested by the apparition of a girl, who flashed around the curve of young birch beyond and stood before him with panting breath and quivering lips.

"I beg your pardon," said John Lincoln courteously, dropping the gate and lifting his hat. "I am looking for the house of Mr. James Conway – 'The Evergreens.' Can you direct me to it?"

"That is Mr. James Conway's house," said the girl, with the tragic air and tone of one driven to desperation and an impatient gesture of her hand toward the yellow nightmare above them.

"I don't think he can be the one I mean," said Lincoln perplexedly. "The man I am thinking of has a niece, Miss Richmond."

"There is no other James Conway in Plainfield," said the girl. "This is his place – nobody calls it 'The Evergreens' but myself. I am Sidney Richmond."

For a moment they looked at each other across the gate, sheer amazement and bewilderment holding John Lincoln mute. Sidney, burning with shame, saw that this stranger was exceedingly good to look upon – tall, clean-limbed, broad-shouldered, with clear-cut bronzed features and a chin and eyes that would have done honour to any man. John Lincoln, among all his confused sensations, was aware that this slim, agitated young creature before him was the loveliest thing he ever had seen, so lithe was her figure, so glossy and dark and silken her bare, wind-ruffled hair, so big and brown and appealing her eyes, so delicately oval her flushed cheeks. He felt that she was frightened and in trouble, and he wanted to comfort and reassure her. But how could she be Sidney Richmond?

"I don't understand," he said perplexedly.

"Oh!" Sidney threw out her hands in a burst of passionate protest. "No, and you never will understand – I can't make you understand."

"I don't understand," said John Lincoln again. "Can you be Sidney Richmond – the Sidney Richmond who has written to me for four years?"

"I am."

"Then, those letters –"

"Were all lies," said Sidney bluntly and desperately. "There was nothing true in them – nothing at all. This is my home. We are poor. Everything I told you about it and my life was just imagination."

"Then why did you write them?" he asked blankly. "Why did you deceive me?"

"Oh, I didn't mean to deceive you! I never thought of such a thing. When you asked me to write to you I wanted to, but I didn't know what to write about to a stranger. I just couldn't write you about my life here, not because it was hard, but it was so ugly and empty. So I wrote instead of the life I wanted to live – the life I did live in imagination. And when once I had begun, I had to keep it up. I found it so fascinating, too! Those letters made that other life seem real to me. I never expected to meet you. These last four days since your letter came have been dreadful to me. Oh, please go away and forgive me if you can! I know I can never make you understand how it came about."

Sidney turned away and hid her burning face against the cool white bark of the birch tree behind her. It was worse than she had even thought it would be. He was so handsome, so manly, so earnest-eyed! Oh, what a friend to lose!

John Lincoln opened the gate and went up to her. There was a great tenderness in his face, mingled with a little kindly, friendly amusement.

"Please don't distress yourself so, Sidney," he said, unconsciously using her Christian name. "I think I do understand. I'm not such a dull fellow as you take me for. After all, those letters were true – or, rather, there was truth in them. You revealed yourself more faithfully in them than if you had written truly about your narrow outward life."

Sidney turned her flushed face and wet eyes slowly toward him, a little smile struggling out amid the clouds of woe. This young man was certainly good at understanding. "You – you'll forgive me then?" she stammered.

"Yes, if there is anything to forgive. And for my own part, I am glad you are not what I have always thought you were. If I had come here and found you what I expected, living in such a home as I expected, I never could have told you or even thought of telling you what you have come to mean to me in these lonely years during which your letters have been the things most eagerly looked forward to. I should have come this evening and spent an hour or so with you, and then have gone away on the train tomorrow morning, and that would have been all.

"But I find instead just a dreamy romantic little girl, much like my sisters at home, except that she is a great deal cleverer. And as a result I mean to stay a week at Plainfield and come to see you every day, if you will let me. And on my way back to the Bar N I mean to stop off at Plainfield again for another week, and then I shall tell you something more – something it would be a little too bold to say now, perhaps, although I could say it just as well and truly. All this if I may. May I, Sidney?"

He bent forward and looked earnestly into her face.

Sidney felt a new, curious, inexplicable thrill at her heart. "Oh, yes – I suppose so," she said shyly.

"Now, take me up to the house and introduce me to your Aunt Jane," said John Lincoln in satisfied tone.

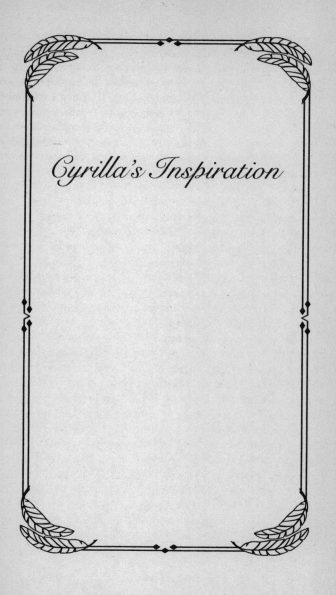

Cyrilla's Inspiration

T was a rainy Saturday afternoon and all the boarders at Mrs. Plunkett's were feeling dull and stupid, especially the Normal School girls on the third floor, Cyrilla Blair and Carol Hart and Mary Newton, who were known as The Trio, and shared the big front room together.

They were sitting in that front room, scowling out at the weather. At least, Carol and Mary were scowling. Cyrilla never scowled; she was sitting curled up on her bed with her Greek grammar, and she smiled at the rain and her grumbling chums as cheerfully as possible.

"For pity's sake, Cyrilla, put that grammar away," moaned Mary. "There is something positively uncanny about a girl who can study Greek on Saturday afternoons – at least, this early in the term."

"I'm not really studying," said Cyrilla, tossing the book away. "I'm only pretending to. I'm really just as bored and lonesome as you are. But what else is there to do? We can't stir outside the door; we've nothing to read; we can't make candy since Mrs. Plunkett has forbidden us to use the oil stove in our room; we'll probably quarrel all round if we sit here in idleness; so I've been trying to brush up my Greek verbs by way of keeping out of mischief. Have you any better employment to offer me?"

"If it were only a mild drizzle we might go around and see the Patterson girls," sighed Carol. "But there is no venturing out in such a downpour. Cyrilla, you are supposed to be the brainiest one of us. Prove your claim to such pre-eminence by thinking of some brand-new amusement, especially suited to rainy afternoons. That will be putting your grey matter to better use than squandering it on Greek verbs out of study limits."

"If only I'd got a letter from home today," said Mary, who seemed determined to persist in gloom. "I wouldn't mind the weather. Letters are such cheery things – especially the letters my sister writes. They're so full of fun and nice little news. The reading of one cheers me up for the day. Cyrilla Blair, what is the matter? You nearly frightened me to death!"

Cyrilla had bounded from her bed to the centre of the floor, waving her Greek grammar wildly in the air.

"Girls, I have an inspiration!" she exclaimed.

"Good! Let's hear it," said Carol.

"Let's write letters – rainy-day letters – to everyone in the house," said Cyrilla. "You may depend all the rest of the folks under Mrs. Plunkett's hospitable roof are feeling more or less blue and lonely too, as well as ourselves. Let's write them the jolliest, nicest letters we can compose and get Nora Jane to take them to their rooms. There's that pale little sewing girl, I don't believe she ever gets letters from anybody, and Miss Marshall, I'm sure *she* doesn't, and poor old Mrs. Johnson, whose only son died last month, and the new music teacher who came yesterday, a letter of welcome to her – and old Mr. Grant, yes, and Mrs. Plunkett too, thanking her for all her kindness to us. You know she has been awfully nice to us in spite of the oil stove ukase. That's six – two apiece. Let's do it, girls."

Cyrilla's sudden enthusiasm for her plan infected the others.

"It's a nice idea," said Mary, brightening up. "But who's to write to whom? I'm willing to take anybody but Miss Marshall. I couldn't write a line to her to save my life. She'd be horrified at anything funny or jokey and our letters will have to be mainly nonsense – nonsense of the best brand, to be sure, but still nonsense."

"Better leave Miss Marshall out," suggested Carol. "You know she disapproves of us anyhow. She'd probably resent a letter of the sort, thinking we were trying to play some kind of joke on her."

"It would never do to leave her out," said Cyrilla decisively. "Of course, she's a bit queer and unamiable, but, girls, think of thirty years of boarding-house life, even with the best of Plunketts. Wouldn't that sour anybody? You know it would. You'd be cranky and grumbly and disagreeable too, I dare say. I'm really sorry for Miss Marshall. She's had a very hard life. Mrs. Plunkett told me all about her one day. I don't think we should mind her biting little speeches and sharp looks. And anyway, even if she is really as disagreeable as she sometimes seems to be, why, it must make it all the harder for her, don't you think? So she needs a letter most of all. I'll write to her, since it's my suggestion. We'll draw lots for the others."

Besides Miss Marshall, the new music teacher fell to Cyrilla's share. Mary drew Mrs. Plunkett and the dressmaker, and Carol drew Mrs. Johnson and old Mr. Grant. For the next two hours the girls wrote busily, forgetting all about the rainy day, and enjoying their epistolary labours to the full. It was dusk when all the letters were finished.

"Why, hasn't the afternoon gone quickly after all!" exclaimed Carol. "I just let my pen run on and jotted down any good working idea that came into my head. Cyrilla Blair, that big fat letter is never for Miss Marshall! What on earth did you find to write her?"

"It wasn't so hard when I got fairly started," said Cyrilla, smiling. "Now, let's hunt up Nora Jane and send the letters around so that everybody can read his or hers before tea-time. We should have a choice assortment of smiles at the table instead of all those frowns and sighs we had at dinner."

Miss Emily Marshall was at that moment sitting in her little back room, all alone in the dusk, with the rain splashing drearily against the windowpanes outside. Miss Marshall was feeling as lonely and dreary as she looked – and as she had often felt in her life of sixty years. She told herself bitterly that she hadn't a friend in the world – not even one who cared enough for her to come and see her or write her a letter now and then. She thought her boarding-house acquaintances disliked her and she resented their dislike, without admitting to herself that her ungracious ways were responsible for it. She smiled sourly when little ripples of laughter came faintly down the hall from the front room where The Trio were writing their letters and laughing over the fun they were putting into them.

"If they were old and lonesome and friendless they wouldn't see much in life to laugh at, I guess," said Miss Marshall bitterly, drawing her shawl closer about her sharp shoulders. "They never think of anything but themselves and if a day passes that they don't have 'some fun' they think it's a fearful thing to put up with. I'm sick and tired of their giggling and whispering."

In the midst of these amiable reflections Miss Marshall heard a knock at her door. When she opened it there stood Nora Jane, her broad red face beaming with smiles.

"Please, Miss, here's a letter for you," she said.

"A letter for me!" Miss Marshall shut her door and stared at the fat envelope in amazement. Who could have written it? The postman came only in the morning. Was it some joke, perhaps? Those giggling girls? Miss Marshall's face grew harder as she lighted her lamp and opened the letter suspiciously.

"Dear Miss Marshall," it ran in Cyrilla's pretty girlish writing, "we girls are so lonesome and dull that we have decided to write rainy-day letters to everybody in the house just to cheer ourselves up. So I'm going to write to you just a letter of friendly nonsense."

Pages of "nonsense" followed, and very delightful nonsense it was, for Cyrilla possessed the happy gift of bright and easy letter-writing. She commented wittily on all the amusing episodes of the boarding-house life for the past month; she described a cat-fight she had witnessed from her window that morning and illustrated it by a pen-and-ink sketch of the belligerent felines; she described a lovely new dress her mother had sent her from home and told all about the class party to which she had worn it; she gave an account of her vacation camping trip to the mountains and pasted on one page a number of small snapshots taken during the outing; she copied a joke she had read in the paper that morning and discussed the serial story in the boarding-house magazine which all the boarders were reading; she wrote out the directions for a new crocheted tidy her sister had made – Miss Marshall had a mania for crocheting; and she finally wound up with "all the good will and good wishes that Nora Jane will consent to carry from your friend, Cyrilla Blair."

Before Miss Marshall had finished reading that letter she had cried three times and laughed times past counting. More tears came at the end – happy, tender tears such as Miss Marshall had not shed for years. Something warm and sweet and gentle seemed to thrill to life within her heart. So those girls were not such selfish, heedless young creatures as she had supposed! How kind it had been in Cyrilla Blair to think of her and write so to her. She no longer felt lonely and neglected. Her whole sombre world had been brightened to sunshine by that merry friendly letter.

Mrs. Plunkett's table was surrounded by a ring of smiling faces that night. Everybody seemed in good spirits in spite of the weather. The pale little dressmaker, who had hardly uttered a word since her arrival a week before, talked and laughed quite merrily and girlishly, thanking Cyrilla unreservedly for her "jolly letter." Old Mr. Grant did not grumble once about the rain or the food or his rheumatism and he told Carol that she might be a good letter writer in time if she looked after her grammar more carefully – which, from Mr. Grant, was high praise. All the others declared that they were delighted with their letters – all except Miss

Marshall. She said nothing, but later on, when Cyrilla was going upstairs, she met Miss Marshall in the shadows of the second landing.

"My dear," said Miss Marshall gently, "I want to thank you for your letter. I don't think you can realize just what it has meant to me. I was so – so lonely and tired and discouraged. It heartened me right up. I – I know you have thought me a cross and disagreeable person. I'm afraid I have been, too. But – but – I shall try to be less so in future. If I can't succeed all at once don't mind me because, under it all, I shall always be your friend. And I mean to keep your letter and read it over every time I feel myself getting bitter and hard again."

"Dear Miss Marshall, I'm so glad you liked it," said Cyrilla frankly. "We're all your friends and would be glad to be chummy with you. Only we thought perhaps we bothered you with our nonsense."

"Come and see me sometimes," said Miss Marshall with a smile. "I'll try to be 'chummy' – perhaps I'm not yet too old to learn the secret of friendliness. Your letter has made me think that I have missed much in shutting all young life out from mine as I have done. I want to reform in this respect if I can."

When Cyrilla reached the front room she found Mrs. Plunkett there.

"I've just dropped in, Miss Blair," said that worthy woman, "to say that I dunno as I mind your making candy once in a while if you want to. Only do be careful not to set the place on fire. Please be *particularly* careful not to set it on fire."

"We'll try," promised Cyrilla with dancing eyes. When the door closed behind Mrs. Plunkett the three girls looked at each other.

"Cyrilla, that idea of yours was a really truly inspiration," said Carol solemnly.

"I believe it was," said Cyrilla, thinking of Miss Marshall.

Miss Sally's Letter

ISS Sally peered sharply at Willard Stanley, first through her gold-rimmed glasses and then over them. Willard continued to look very innocent. Joyce got up abruptly and went out of the room.

"So you have bought that queer little house with the absurd name?" said Miss Sally.

"You surely don't call Eden an absurd name," protested Willard.

"I do – for a house. Particularly such a house as that. Eden! There are no Edens on earth. And what are you going to do with it?"

"Live in it."

"Alone?"

Miss Sally looked at him suspiciously.

"No. The truth is, Miss Sally, I am hoping to be married in the fall and I want to fix up Eden for my bride."

"Oh!" Miss Sally drew a long breath, partly it seemed of relief and partly of triumph, and looked at Joyce, who had returned, with an expression that said, "I told you so"; but Joyce, whose eyes were cast down, did not see it.

"And," went on Willard calmly, "I want you to help me fix it up, Miss Sally. I don't know much about such things and you know everything. You will be able to tell me just what to do to make Eden habitable."

Miss Sally looked as pleased as she ever allowed herself to look over anything a man suggested. It was the delight of her heart to plan and decorate and contrive. Her own house was a model of comfort and good taste, and Miss Sally was quite ready for new worlds to conquer. Instantly Eden assumed importance in her eyes. She might be sorry for the misguided bride who was rashly going to trust her life's keeping to a man, but she would see, at least, that the poor thing should have a decent place to begin her martyrdom in.

"I'll be pleased to help you all I can," she said graciously.

Miss Sally could speak very graciously when she chose, even to men. You would not have thought she hated them, but she did. In all sincerity, too. Also, she had brought her niece up to hate and distrust them. Or, she had tried to do so. But at times Miss Sally was troubled with an uncomfortable suspicion that Joyce did not hate and distrust men quite as thoroughly as she ought. The suspicion had recurred several times this summer since Willard Stanley had come to take charge of the biological station at the harbour. Miss Sally did not distrust Willard on his own account. She merely distrusted him on principle and on Joyce's account. Nevertheless, she was rather nice to him. Miss Sally, dear, trim, dainty Miss Sally, with her snow-white curls and her big girlish black eyes, couldn't help being nice, even to a man.

Willard had come a great deal to Miss Sally's. If it were Joyce he were after Miss Sally blocked his schemes with much enjoyment. He never saw Joyce alone – that Miss Sally knew of, at least – and he did not make much apparent headway. But now all danger was removed, Miss Sally thought. He was going to be married to somebody else, and Joyce was safe.

"Thank you," said Willard. "I'll come up tomorrow afternoon, and you and I will take a prowl about Eden and see what must be done. I'm ever so much obliged, Miss Sally."

"I wonder who he is going to marry," said Miss Sally, careless of grammar, after he had gone. "Poor, poor girl!"

"I don't see why you should pity her," said Joyce, not looking up from her embroidery. There was just the merest tremor in her voice. Miss Sally looked at her sharply.

"I pity any woman who is foolish enough to marry," she said solemnly. "No man is to be trusted, Joyce – no man. They are all ready to break a trusting woman's heart for the sport of it. Never you allow any man the chance to break yours, Joyce. I shall never consent to your marrying anybody, so mind you don't take any such notion into your head. There oughtn't to be any danger, for I have instilled correct ideas on this subject into you from childhood. But girls are such fools. I know, because I was one myself once."

"Of course, I would never marry without your consent, Aunt Sally," said Joyce, smiling faintly but affectionately at her aunt. Joyce loved Miss Sally with her whole heart. Everybody did who knew her. There never was a more lovable creature than this pretty little old maid who hated the men so bitterly.

"That's a good girl," said Miss Sally approvingly. "I own that I have been a little afraid that this Willard Stanley was coming here to see you. But my mind is set at rest on that point now, and I shall help him fix up his doll house with a clear conscience. Eden, indeed!"

Miss Sally sniffed and tripped out of the room to hunt up a furniture catalogue. Joyce sighed and let her embroidery slip to the floor.

"Oh, I'm afraid Willard's plan won't succeed," she murmured. "I'm afraid Aunt Sally will never consent to our marriage. And I can't and won't marry him unless she does, for she would never forgive me and I couldn't bear that. I wonder what makes her so bitter against men. She is so sweet and loving, it seems simply unnatural that she should have such a feeling so deeply rooted in her. Oh, what will she say when she finds out – dear little Aunt Sally? I couldn't bear to have her angry with me."

The next day Willard came up from the harbour and took Miss Sally down to see Eden. Eden was a tiny, cornery, gabled grey house just across the road and down a long, twisted windy lane, skirting the edge of a beech wood. Nobody had lived in it for four years, and it had a neglected, out-at-elbow appearance.

"It's rather a box of a place, isn't it?" said Willard slowly. "I'm afraid she will think so. But it is all I can afford just now. I dream of giving her a palace some day, of course. But we'll have to begin humbly. Do you think anything can be made of it?"

Miss Sally was busily engaged in sizing up the possibilities of the place.

"It is pretty small," she said meditatively. "And the yard is small too – and there are far too many trees and shrubs all messed up together. They must be thinned out – and that paling taken down. I think a good deal can be done with it. As for the house – well, let us see the inside."

Willard unlocked the door and showed Miss Sally over the place. Miss Sally poked and pried and sniffed and wrinkled her forehead, and finally stood on the stairs and delivered her ultimatum.

"This house can be done up very nicely. Paint and paper will work wonders. But I wouldn't paint it outside. Leave it that pretty silver weather-grey and plant vines to run over it. Oh, we'll see what we can do. Of course it is small – a kitchen, a dining room, a living room, and two bedrooms. You won't want anything stuffy. You can do the painting yourself, and I'll help you hang the paper. How much money can you spend on it?"

Willard named the sum. It was not a large one.

"But I think it will do," mused Miss Sally. "We'll *make* it do. There's such satisfaction getting as much as you possibly can out of a dollar, and twice as much as anybody else would get. I enjoy that sort of thing. This will be a game, and we'll play it with a right good will. But I do wish you would give the place a sensible name."

"I think Eden is the most appropriate name in the world," laughed Willard. "It will be Eden for me when she comes."

"I suppose you tell her all that and she believes it," said Miss Sally sarcastically. "You'll both find out that there is a good deal more prose than poetry in life."

"But we'll find it out *together*," said Willard tenderly.

"Won't that be worth something, Miss Sally? Prose, rightly written and read, is sometimes as beautiful as poetry."

Miss Sally deigned no reply. She carefully gathered up her grey silken skirts from the dusty floor and walked out. "Get Christina Bowes to come up tomorrow and scrub this place out," she said practically. "We can go to town and select paint and paper. I should like the dining room done in pale green and the living room in creamy tones, ranging from white to almost golden brown. But perhaps my taste won't be hers."

"Oh, yes, it will," said Willard with assurance. "I am quite certain she will like everything you like. I can never thank you enough for helping me. If you hadn't consented I should have had to put it into the hands of some outsider whom I couldn't have helped at all. And I *wanted* to help. I wanted to have a finger in everything, because it is for her, you see, Miss Sally. It will be such a delight to fix up this little house, knowing that she is coming to live in it."

"I wonder if you really mean it," said Miss Sally bitterly. "Oh, I dare say you think you do. But *do* you? Perhaps you do. Perhaps you are the exception that proves the rule."

This was a great admission for Miss Sally to make.

For the next two months Miss Sally was happy. Even Willard himself was not more keenly interested in Eden and its development. Miss Sally did wonders with his money. She was an expert at bargain hunting, and her taste was excellent. A score of times she mercilessly nipped Willard's suggestions in the bud. "Lace curtains for the living room – never! They would be horribly out of place in such a house. You don't want curtains at all – just a frill is all that quaint window needs, with a shelf above it for a few bits of pottery. I picked up a love of a brass platter in town yesterday – got it for next to nothing from that old Jew who would really rather *give* you a thing than suffer you to escape without taking something. Oh, I know how to manage them."

"You certainly do," laughed Willard. "It amazes me to see how far you can stretch a dollar."

Willard did the painting under Miss Sally's watchful eye, and they hung the paper together. Together they made trips to town or junketed over the country in search of furniture and dishes of which Miss Sally had heard. Day by day the little house blossomed into a home, and day by day Miss Sally's interest in it grew. She began to have a personal affection for its quaint rooms and their adornments. Moreover, in spite of herself, she felt a growing interest in Willard's bride. He never told her the name of the girl he hoped to bring to Eden, and Miss Sally never asked it. But he talked of her a great deal, in a shy, reverent, tender way.

"He certainly seems to be very much in love with her," Miss Sally told Joyce one evening when she returned from Eden. "I would believe in him if it were possible for me to believe in a man. Anyway, she will have a dear little home. I've almost come to love that Eden house. Why don't you come down and see it, Joyce?"

"Oh, I'll come some day – I hope," said Joyce lightly. "I think I'd rather not see it until it is finished."

"Willard is a nice boy," said Miss Sally suddenly. "I don't think I ever did him justice before. The finer qualities of his character come out in these simple, homely little doings and tasks. He is certainly very thoughtful and kind. Oh, I suppose he'll make a good husband, as husbands go. But he doesn't know the first thing about managing. If his wife isn't a good manager, I don't know what they'll do. And perhaps she won't like the way we've done up Eden. Willard says she will, of course, because he thinks her perfection. But she may have dreadful taste and want the lace curtains and that nightmare of a pink rug Willard admired, and I dare say she'd rather have a new flaunting set of china with rosebuds on it than that dear old dull blue I picked up for a mere song down at the Aldenbury auction. I stood in the rain for two mortal hours to make sure of it, and it was really worth all that Willard has spent on the dining room put together. It will break my heart if she sets to work altering Eden. It's simply perfect as it is – though I suppose I shouldn't say it."

IN ANOTHER WEEK Eden was finished. Miss Sally stood in the tiny hall and looked about her.

"Well, it is done," she said with a sigh. "I'm sorry. I have enjoyed fixing it up tremendously, and now I feel that my occupation is gone. I hope you are satisfied, Willard."

"Satisfied is too mild a word, Miss Sally. I am delighted. I knew you could accomplish wonders, but I never hoped for *this*. Eden is a dream – the dearest, quaintest, sweetest little home that ever waited for a bride. When I bring her here – oh, Miss Sally, do you know what that thought means to me?"

Miss Sally looked curiously at the young man. His face was flushed and his voice trembled a little. There was a far-away shining look in his eyes as if he saw a vision.

"I hope you and she will be happy," said Miss Sally slowly. "When will she be coming, Willard?"

The flush went out of Willard's face, leaving it pale and determined.

"That is for her – and you – to say," he answered steadily.

"Me!" exclaimed Miss Sally. "What have I to do with it?"

"A great deal – for unless you consent she will never come here at all."

"Willard Stanley," said Miss Sally, with ominous calm, "who is the girl you mean to marry?"

"The girl I *hope* to marry is Joyce, Miss Sally. Wait – don't say anything till you hear me out." He came close to her and caught her hands in a boyish grip. "Joyce and I have loved each other ever since we met. But we despaired of winning your consent, and Joyce will not marry me without it. I thought if I could get you to help me fix up my little home that you might get so interested in it – and so well acquainted with me – that you would trust me with Joyce. Please do, Miss Sally. I love her so truly and I know I can make her happy. If you don't, Eden shall never have a mistress. I'll shut it up, just as it is, and leave it sacred to the dead hope of a bride that will never come to it."

"Oh, you wouldn't," protested Miss Sally. "It would be a shame – such a dear little house – and after all the trouble I've taken. But you have tricked me – oh, you men couldn't be straightforward in anything –"

"Wasn't it a fair device for a desperate lover, Miss Sally?" interrupted Willard. "Oh, you mustn't hold spite because of it, dear. And you will give me Joyce, won't you? Because if you don't, I really will shut up Eden forever."

Miss Sally looked wistfully around her. Through the open door on her left she saw the little living room with its quaint, comfortable furniture, its dainty pictures and adornments. Through the front door she saw the trim, velvet-swarded little lawn. Upstairs were two white rooms that only wanted a woman's living presence to make them jewels. And the kitchen on which she had expended so much thought and ingenuity – the kitchen furnished to the last detail, even to the kindling in the range and the match Willard had laid ready to light it! It gave Miss Sally a pang to think of that altar fire never being lighted. It was really the thought of the kitchen that finished Miss Sally.

"You've tricked me," she said again reproachfully. "You've tricked me into loving this house so much that I cannot bear the thought of it never living. You'll have to have Joyce, I suppose. And I believe I'm glad that it isn't a stranger who is to be the mistress of Eden. Joyce won't hanker after pink rugs and lace curtains. And her taste in china is the same as mine. In one way it's a great relief to my mind. But it's a fearful risk – a fearful risk. To think that you may make my dear child miserable!"

"You know you don't think that I will, Miss Sally. I'm not really such a bad fellow, now, am I?"

"You are a man – and I have no confidence whatever in men," declared Miss Sally, wiping some very real tears from her eyes with a very unreal sort of handkerchief – one of the cobwebby affairs of lace her daintiness demanded.

"Miss Sally, why have you such a rooted distrust of men?" demanded Willard curiously. "Somehow, it seems so foreign to your character."

"I suppose you think I am a perfect crank," said Miss Sally, sighing. "Well, I'll tell you why I don't trust men. I have a very good reason for it. A man broke my heart and embittered my life. I've never spoken about it to a living soul, but if you want to hear about it, you shall."

Miss Sally sat down on the second step of the stairs and tucked her wet handkerchief away. She clasped her slender white hands over her knee. In spite of her silvery hair and the little lines on her face she looked girlish and youthful. There was a pink flush on her cheeks, and her big black eyes sparkled with the anger her memories aroused in her.

"I was a young girl of twenty when I met him," she said, "and I was just as foolish as all young girls are – foolish and romantic and sentimental. He was very handsome and I thought him – but there, I won't go into that. It vexes me to recall my folly. But I loved him – yes, I did, with all my heart – with all there was of me to love. He made me love him. He deliberately set himself to win my love. For a whole summer he flirted with me. I didn't know he was flirting – I thought him in earnest. Oh, I was such a little fool – and so happy. Then – he went away. Went away suddenly without even a word of goodbye. But he had been summoned home by his father's serious illness, and I thought he would write – I waited – I hoped. I never heard from him – never saw him again. He had tired of his plaything and flung it aside. That is all," concluded Miss Sally passionately. "I never trusted any man again. When my sister died and gave me her baby, I determined to bring the dear child up safely, training her to avoid the danger I had fallen into. Well, I've failed. But perhaps it will be all right – perhaps there are some men who are true, though Stephen Merritt was false."

"Stephen – who?" demanded Willard abruptly. Miss Sally coloured.

"I didn't mean to tell you his name," she said, getting up. "It was a slip of the tongue. Never mind – forget it and him. He was not worthy of remembrance – and yet I do remember him. I can't forget him – and I hate him all the more for it – for having entered so deeply into my life that I could not cast him out when I knew him unworthy. It is humiliating. There – let us lock up Eden and go home. I suppose you are dying to see Joyce and tell her your precious plot has succeeded."

Willard did not appear to be at all impatient. He had relapsed into a brown study, during which he let Miss Sally lock up the house. Then he walked silently home with her. Miss Sally was silent too. Perhaps she was repenting her confidence – or perhaps she was thinking of her false lover. There was a pathetic droop to her lips, and her black eyes were sad and dreamy.

"Miss Sally," said Willard at last, as they neared her house, "had Stephen Merritt any sisters?"

Miss Sally threw him a puzzled glance.

"He had one – Jean Merritt – whom I disliked and who disliked me," she said crisply. "I don't want to talk of her – she was the only woman I ever hated. I never met any of the other members of his family – his home was in a distant part of the state."

Willard stayed with Joyce so brief a time that Miss Sally viewed his departure with suspicion. This was not very lover-like conduct.

"I dare say he's like all the rest – when his aim is attained the prize loses its value," reflected Miss Sally pessimistically. "Poor Joyce – poor child! But there – there isn't a single inharmonious thing in his house – that is one comfort. I'm so thankful I didn't let Willard buy those brocade chairs he wanted. They would have given Joyce the nightmare."

Meanwhile, Willard rushed down to the biological station and from there drove furiously to the station to catch the evening express. He did not return until three days later, when he appeared at Miss Sally's, dusty and triumphant.

"Joyce is out," said Miss Sally.

"I'm glad of it," said Willard recklessly. "It's you I want to see, Miss Sally. I have something to show you. I've been all the way home to get it."

From his pocketbook Willard drew something folded and creased and yellow that looked like a letter. He opened it carefully and, holding it in his fingers, looked over it at Miss Sally.

"My grandmother's maiden name was Jean Merritt," he said deliberately, "and Stephen Merritt was my great-uncle. I never saw him – he died when I was a child – but I've heard my father speak of him often."

Miss Sally turned very pale. She passed her cobwebby handkerchief across her lips and her hand trembled. Willard went on.

"My uncle never married. He and his sister Jean lived together until her late marriage. I was not very fond of my grandmother. She was a selfish, domineering woman – very unlike the grandmother of tradition. When she died everything she possessed came to me, as my father, her only child, was then dead. In looking over a box of old papers I found a letter – an old love letter. I read it with some interest, wondering whose it could be and how it came among Grandmother's private letters. It was signed 'Stephen,' so that I guessed my great-uncle had been the writer, but I had no idea who the Sally was to whom it was written, until the other day. Then I knew it was you – and I went home to bring you your letter –

the letter you should have received long ago. Why you did not receive it I cannot explain. I fear that my grandmother must have been to blame for that – she must have intercepted and kept the letter in order to part her brother and you. In so far as I can I wish to repair the wrong she has done you. I know it can never be repaired – but at least I think this letter will take the bitterness out of the memory of your lover."

He dropped the letter in Miss Sally's lap and went away.

Pale, Miss Sally picked it up and read it. It was from Stephen Merritt to "dearest Sally," and contained a frank, manly avowal of love. Would she be his wife? If she would, let her write and tell him so. But if she did not and could not love him, let her silence reveal the bitter fact; he would wish to spare her the pain of putting her refusal into words, and if she did not write he would understand that she was not for him.

When Willard and Joyce came back into the twilight room they found Miss Sally still sitting by the table, her head leaning pensively on her hand. She had been crying – the cob-webby handkerchief lay beside her, wrecked and ruined for-ever – but she looked very happy.

"I wonder if you know what you have done for me," she said to Willard. "But no – you can't know – you can't realize it fully. It means everything to me. You have taken away my humiliation and restored to me my pride of womanhood. He really loved me – he was not false – he was what I believed him to be. Nothing else matters to me at all now. Oh, I am very happy – but it would never have been if I had not con-sented to give you Joyce."

She rose and took their hands in hers, joining them.

"God bless you, dears," she said softly. "I believe you will be happy and that your love for each other will always be true and faithful and tender. Willard, I give you my dear child in perfect trust and confidence."

With her yellowed love letter clasped to her heart, and a raptured shining in her eyes, Miss Sally went out of the room.

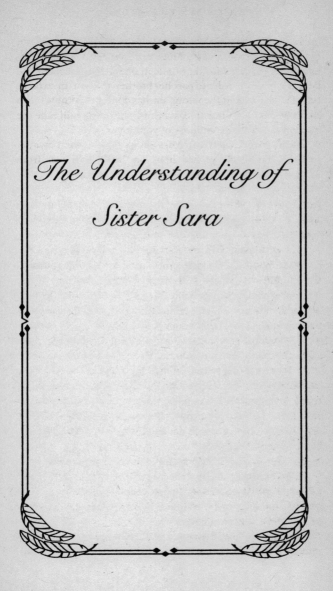

The Understanding of
Sister Sara

JUNE First.

I began this journal last New Year's – wrote two entries in it and then forgot all about it. I came across it today in a rummage – Sara insists on my cleaning things out thoroughly every once in so long – and I'm going to keep it up. I feel the need of a confidant of some kind, even if it is only an inanimate journal. I have no other. And I cannot talk my thoughts over with Sara – she is so unsympathetic.

Sara is a dear good soul and I love her as much as she will let me. I am also very grateful to her. She brought me up when our mother died. No doubt she had a hard time of it, poor dear, for I never was easily brought up, perversely preferring to come up in my own way. But Sara did her duty unflinchingly and – well, it's not for me to say that the result does her credit. But it really does, considering the material she had to work with. I'm a bundle of faults as it is, but I tremble to think what I would have been if there had been no Sara.

Yes, I love Sara, and I'm grateful to her. But she doesn't understand me in the least. Perhaps it is because she is so much older than I am, but it doesn't seem to me that Sara could really ever have been young. She laughs at things I consider the most sacred and calls me a romantic girl, in a tone of humorous toleration. I am chilled and thrown back on myself, and the dreams and confidences I am bubbling over with have no outlet. Sara couldn't understand – she is so practical. When I go to her with some beautiful thought I have found in a book or poem she is quite likely to say, "Yes, yes, but I noticed this morning that the braid was loose on your skirt, Beatrice. Better go and sew it on before you forget again. 'A stitch in time saves nine.'"

When I come home from a concert or lecture, yearning to talk over the divine music or the wonderful new ideas with her, she will say, "Yes, yes, but are you sure you didn't get your feet damp? Better go and change your stockings, my dear. 'An ounce of prevention is worth a pound of cure.'"

So I have given up trying to talk things over with Sara. This old journal will be better.

Last night Sara and I went to Mrs. Trent's musicale. I had to sing and I had the loveliest new gown for the occasion. At first Sara thought my old blue dress would do. She said we must economize this summer and told me I was entirely too extravagant in the matter of clothes. I cried about it after I went to bed. Sara looked at me very sharply the next morning without saying anything. In the afternoon she went uptown and bought some lovely pale yellow silk organdie. She made it up herself – Sara is a genius at dressmaking – and it was the prettiest gown at the musicale. Sara wore her old grey silk made over. Sara doesn't care anything about dress, but then she is forty.

Walter Shirley was at the Trents'. The Shirleys are a new family here; they moved to Atwater two months ago. Walter is the oldest son and has been at college in Marlboro all winter so that nobody here knew him until he came home a fortnight ago. He is very handsome and distinguished-looking and everybody says he is so clever. He plays the violin just beautifully and has such a melting, sympathetic voice and the loveliest deep, dark, inscrutable eyes. I asked Sara when we came home if she didn't think he was splendid.

"He'd be a nice boy if he wasn't rather conceited," said Sara.

After that it was impossible to say anything more about Mr. Shirley.

I am glad he is going to be in Atwater all summer. We have so few really nice young men here; they go away just as soon as they grow up and those who stay are just the muffs. I wonder if I shall see Mr. Shirley soon again.

June Thirtieth.

It does not seem possible that it is only a month since my last entry. It seems more like a year – a delightful year. I can't believe that I am the same Beatrice Mason who wrote then. And I am not, either. She was just a simple little girl, knowing nothing but romantic dreams. I feel that I am very much changed. Life seems so grand and high and beautiful. I want to be a true noble woman. Only such a woman could be worthy of – of – a fine, noble man. But when I tried to say something like this to Sara she replied calmly:

"My dear child, the average woman is quite good enough for the average man. If she can cook his meals decently and keep his buttons sewed on and doesn't nag him he will think that life is a pretty comfortable affair. And that reminds me, I saw holes in your black lace stockings yesterday. Better go and darn them at once. 'Procrastination is the thief of time.'"

Sara cannot understand.

Blanche Lawrence was married yesterday to Ted Martin. I thought it the most solemn and sacred thing I had ever listened to – the marriage ceremony, I mean. I had never thought much about it before. I don't see how Blanche could care anything for Ted – he is so stout and dumpy, with shallow blue eyes and a little pale moustache. I must say I do not like fair men. But there is no doubt that he and Blanche love each other devotedly and that fact sufficed to make the service very beautiful to me – those two people pledging each other to go through life together, meeting its storm and sunshine hand in hand, thinking joy the sweeter because they shared it, finding sorrow sacred because it came to them both.

When Sara and I walked home from the church Sara said, "Well, considering the chances she has had, Blanche Lawrence hasn't done so well after all."

"Oh, Sara," I cried, "she has married the man she loves

and who loves her. What better is there to do? I thought it beautiful."

"They should have waited another year at least," said Sara severely. "Ted Martin has only been practising law for a year, and he had nothing to begin with. He can't have made enough in one year in Atwater to justify him in setting up house-keeping. I think a man ought to be ashamed of himself to take a girl from a good home to an uncertainty like that."

"Not if she loved him and was willing to share the uncertainty," I said softly.

"Love won't pay the butcher's bill," said Sara with a sniff, "and landlords have an unfeeling preference for money over affection. Besides, Blanche is a mere child, far too young to be burdened with the responsibilities of life."

Blanche is twenty – two years older than I am. But Sara talks as if I were a mere infant.

July Thirtieth.

Oh, I am so happy! I wonder if there is another girl in the world as happy as I am tonight. No, of course there cannot be, because there is only one Walter!

Walter and I are engaged. It happened last night when we were sitting out in the moonlight under the silver maple on the lawn. I cannot write down what he said – the words are too sacred and beautiful to be kept anywhere but in my own heart forever and ever as long as I live. And I don't remember just what I said. But we understood each other perfectly at last.

Of course Sara had to do her best to spoil things. Just as Walter had taken my hand in his and bent forward with his splendid earnest eyes just burning into mine, and my heart was beating so furiously, Sara came to the front door and called out, "Beatrice! Beatrice! Have you your rubbers on? And don't you think it is too damp out there for you in that heavy dew? Better come into the house, both of you. Walter has a cold now."

"Oh, we'll be in soon, Sara," I said impatiently. But we didn't go in for an hour, and when we did Sara was cross; and after Walter had gone she told me I was a very silly girl to be so reckless of my health and risk getting pneumonia loitering out in the dew with a sentimental boy.

I had had some vague thoughts of telling Sara all about my new happiness, for it was so great I wanted to talk it over with somebody, but I couldn't after that. Oh, I wish I had a mother! She could understand. But Sara cannot.

Walter and I have decided to keep our engagement a secret for a month – just our own beautiful secret unshared by anyone. Then before he goes back to college he is going to tell Sara and ask her consent. I don't think Sara will refuse it exactly. She really likes Walter very well. But I know she will be horrid and I just dread it. She will say I am too young and that a boy like Walter has no business to get engaged until he is through college and that we haven't known each other long enough to know anything about each other and that we are only a pair of romantic children. And after she has said all this and given a disapproving consent she will begin to train me up in the way a good housekeeper should go, and talk to me about table linen and the best way to manage a range and how to tell if a chicken is really a chicken or only an old hen. Oh, I know Sara! She will set the teeth of my spirit on edge a dozen times a day and rub all the bloom off my dear, only, little romance with her horrible practicalities. I know one must learn about those things of course and I do want to make Walter's home the best and dearest and most comfortable spot on earth for him and be the very best little wife and housekeeper I can be when the time comes. But I want to dream my dreams first and Sara will wake me up so early to realities.

This is why we determined to keep one month sacred to ourselves. Walter will graduate next spring – he is to be a doctor – and then he intends to settle down in Atwater and work up a practice. I am sure he will succeed for everyone likes him so much. But we are to be married as soon as he is through college because he has a little money of his own – enough to set up housekeeping in a modest way with care and economy. I know Sara will talk about risk and waiting and all that just as she did in Ted Martin's case. But then Sara does not understand.

Oh, I am so happy! It almost frightens me – I don't see how anything so wonderful can last. But it will last, for nothing can ever separate Walter and me, and as long as we are together and love each other this great happiness will be mine. Oh, I want to be so good and noble for his sake. I want to make life "one grand sweet song." I have gone about the house today feeling like a woman consecrated and set apart from other women by Walter's love. Nothing could spoil it, not even when Sara scolded me for letting the preserves burn in the kettle because I forgot to stir them while I was planning out our life together. Sara said she really did not know what would happen to me some day if I was so careless and forgetful. But then, Sara does not understand.

August Twentieth.

It is all over. Life is ended for me and I do not know how I can face the desolate future. Walter and I have quarrelled and our engagement is broken. He is gone and my heart is breaking.

I hardly know how it began. I'm sure I never meant to flirt with Jack Ray. I never did flirt with him either, in spite of Walter's unmanly accusations. But Walter has been jealous of Jack all summer, although he knew perfectly well he needn't be, and two nights ago at the Morley dance poor Jack seemed so dull and unhappy that I tried to cheer him up a little and be kind to him. I danced with him three times and sat out another dance just to talk with him in a real sisterly fashion. But Walter was furious and last night when he came up he said horrid things – things no girl of any spirit could endure, and things he could never have said to me if he had really cared one bit for me. We had a frightful quarrel and when I saw plainly that Walter no longer loved me I told him that he was free and that I never wanted to see him again and that I hated him. He glared at me and said that I should have my wish – I never should see him again and he hoped he would never again meet such a faithless, fickle girl. Then he went away and slammed the front door.

I cried all night, but today I went about the house singing. I would not for the world let other people know how Walter has treated me. I will hide my broken heart under a smiling face bravely. But, oh, I am so miserable! Just as soon as I am old enough I mean to go away and be a trained nurse. There is nothing else left in life for me. Sara does not suspect that anything is wrong and I am so thankful she does not. She would not understand.

September Sixth.

Today I read this journal over and thought I would burn it, it is so silly. But on second thought I concluded to keep it as a reminder of how blind and selfish I was and how good Sara is. For I am happy again and everything is all right, thanks to Sara. The very day after our quarrel Walter left Atwater. He did not have to return to college for three weeks, but he went to visit some friends down in Charlotteville and I heard – Mollie Roach told me – Mollie Roach was always wild about Walter herself – that he was not coming back again, but would go right on to Marlboro from Charlotteville. I smiled squarely at Mollie as if I didn't care a particle, but I can't describe how I felt. I knew then that I had really been hoping that something would happen in three weeks to make our quarrel up. In a small place like Atwater people in the same set can't help meeting. But Walter had gone and I should never see him again, and what was worse I knew he didn't care or he wouldn't have gone.

I bore it in silence for three weeks, but I will shudder to the end of my life when I remember those three weeks. Night before last Sara came up to my room where I was lying on my bed with my face in the pillow. I wasn't crying – I couldn't cry. There was just a dreadful dull ache in everything. Sara sat down on the rocker in front of the window and the sunset light came in behind her and made a sort of nimbus round her head, like a motherly saint's in a cathedral.

"Beatrice," she said gently, "I want to know what the trouble is. You can't hide it from me that something is wrong. I've noticed it for some time. You don't eat anything and you cry all night – oh, yes, I know you do. What is it, dear?"

"Oh, Sara!"

I just gave a little cry, slipped from the bed to the floor, laid my head in her lap, and told her everything. It was such a relief, and such a relief to feel those good motherly arms around me and to realize that here was a love that would never fail me no matter what I did or how foolish I was. Sara heard me out and then she said, without a word of reproach or contempt, "It will all come out right yet, dear. Write to Walter and tell him you are sorry."

"Sara, I never could! He doesn't love me any longer – he said he hoped he'd never see me again."

"Didn't you say the same to him, child? He meant it as little as you did. Don't let your foolish pride keep you miserable."

"If Walter won't come back to me without my asking him he'll never come, Sara," I said stubbornly.

Sara didn't scold or coax any more. She patted my head and kissed me and made me bathe my face and go to bed. Then she tucked me in just as she used to do when I was a little girl.

"Now, don't cry, dear," she said, "it will come right yet."

Somehow, I began to hope it would when Sara thought so, and anyhow it was such a comfort to have talked it all over with her. I slept better than I had for a long time, and it was seven o'clock yesterday morning when I woke to find that it was a dull grey day outside and that Sara was standing by my bed with her hat and jacket on.

"I'm going down to Junction Falls on the 7:30 train to see Mr. Conway about coming to fix the back kitchen floor," she said, "and I have some other business that may keep me for some time, so don't be anxious if I'm not back till late. Give the bread a good kneading in an hour's time and be careful not to bake it too much."

That was a dismal day. It began to rain soon after Sara left and it just poured. I never saw a soul all day except the milkman, and I was really frantic by night. I never was so glad of anything as when I heard Sara's step on the verandah. I flew to the front door to let her in – and there was Walter all dripping wet – and his arms were about me and I was crying on the shoulder of his mackintosh.

I only guessed then what I knew later on. Sara had heard from Mrs. Shirley that Walter was going to Marlboro that day without coming back to Atwater. Sara knew that he must change trains at Junction Falls and she went there to meet him. She didn't know what train he would come on so she went to meet the earliest and had to wait till the last, hanging around the dirty little station at the Falls all day while it poured rain, and she hadn't a thing to eat except some fancy biscuits she had bought on the train. But Walter came at last on the 7:50 train and there was Sara to pounce on him. He told me afterwards that no angel could have been so beautiful a vision to him as Sara was, standing there on the wet platform with her tweed skirt held up and a streaming umbrella over her head, telling him he must come back to Atwater because Beatrice wanted him to.

But just at the moment of his coming I didn't care how he

had come or who had brought him. I just realized that he was there and that was enough. Sara came in behind him. Walter's wet arms were about me and I was standing there with my thin-slippered feet in a little pool of water that dripped from his umbrella. But Sara never said a word about colds and dampness. She just smiled, went on into the sitting-room, and shut the door. Sara understood.

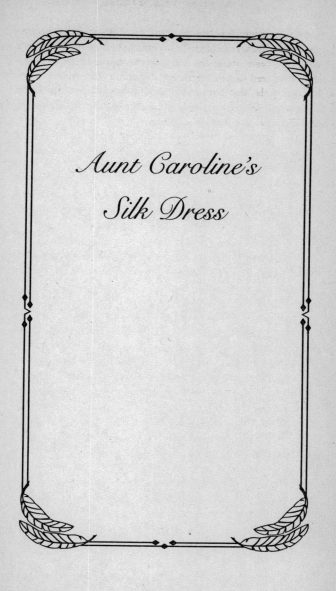

Aunt Caroline's
Silk Dress

ATTY came in from her walk to the post office with cheeks finely reddened by the crisp air. Carry surveyed her with pleasure. Of late Patty's cheeks had been entirely too pale to please Carry, and Patty had not had a very good appetite. Once or twice she had even complained of a headache. So Carry had sent her to the office for a walk that night, although the post office trip was usually Carry's own special constitutional, always very welcome to her after a weary day of sewing on other people's pretty dresses.

Carry never sewed on pretty dresses for herself, for the simple reason that she never had any pretty dresses. Carry was twenty-two – and feeling forty; her last pretty dress had been when she was a girl of twelve, before her father had died. To be sure, there was the silk organdie Aunt Kathleen had sent her, but that was fit only for parties, and Carry never went to any parties.

"Did you get any mail, Patty?" she asked unexpectantly. There was never much mail for the Lea girls.

"Yes'm," said Patty briskly. "Here's the *Weekly Advocate*, and a patent medicine almanac with all your dreams expounded, *and* a letter for Miss Carry M. Lea. It's postmarked Enfield, and has a suspiciously matrimonial look. I'm sure it's an invitation to Chris Fairley's wedding. Hurry up and see, Caddy."

Carry, with a little flush of excitement on her face, opened her letter. Sure enough, it contained an invitation "to be present at the marriage of Christine Fairley."

"How jolly!" exclaimed Patty. "Of course you'll go, Caddy. You'll have a chance to wear that lovely organdie of yours at last."

"It was sweet of Chris to invite me," said Carry. "I really didn't expect it."

"Well, I did. Wasn't she your most intimate friend when she lived in Enderby?"

"Oh, yes, but it is four years since she left, and some people might forget in four years. But I might have known Chris wouldn't. Of course I'll go."

"And you'll make up your organdie?"

"I shall have to," laughed Carry, forgetting all her troubles for a moment, and feeling young and joyous over the prospect of a festivity. "I haven't another thing that would do to wear to a wedding. If I hadn't that blessed organdie I couldn't go, that's all."

"But you have it, and it will look lovely made up with a tucked skirt. Tucks are so fashionable now. And there's that lace of mine you can have for a bertha. I want you to look just right, you see. Enfield is a big place, and there will be lots of grandees at the wedding. Let's get the last fashion sheet and pick out a design right away. Here's one on the very first page that would be nice. You could wear it to perfection, Caddy – you're so tall and slender. It wouldn't suit a plump and podgy person like myself at all."

Carry liked the pattern, and they had an animated discussion over it. But, in the end, Carry sighed, and pushed the sheet away from her, with all the brightness gone out of her face.

"It's no use, Patty. I'd forgotten for a few minutes, but it's all come back now. I can't think of weddings and new dresses, when the thought of that interest crowds everything else out. It's due next month – fifty dollars – and I've only ten saved up. I can't make forty dollars in a month, even if I had any amount of sewing, and you know hardly anyone wants sewing done just now. I don't know what we shall do. Oh, I suppose we can rent a couple of rooms in the village and *exist* in them. But it breaks my heart to think of leaving our old home."

"Perhaps Mr. Kerr will let us have more time," suggested

Patty, not very hopefully. The sparkle had gone out of her face too. Patty loved their little home as much as Carry did.

"You know he won't. He has been only too anxious for an excuse to foreclose, this long time. He wants the land the house is on. Oh, if I only hadn't been sick so long in the summer – just when everybody had sewing to do. I've tried so hard to catch up, but I couldn't." Carry's voice broke in a sob.

Patty leaned over the table and patted her sister's glossy dark hair gently.

"You've worked too hard, dearie. You've just gone to skin and bone. Oh, I know how hard it is! I can't bear to think of leaving this dear old spot either. If we could only induce Mr. Kerr to give us a year's grace! I'd be teaching then, and we could easily pay the interest and some of the principal too. Perhaps he will if we both go to him and coax very hard. Anyway, don't worry over it till after the wedding. I want you to go and have a good time. You never have good times, Carry."

"Neither do you," said Carry rebelliously. "You never have anything that other girls have, Patty – not even pretty clothes."

"'Deed, and I've lots of things to be thankful for," said Patty cheerily. "Don't you fret about me. I'm vain enough to think I've got some brains anyway, and I'm a-meaning to do something with them too. Now I think I'll go upstairs and study this evening. It will be warm enough there tonight, and the noise of the machine rather bothers me."

Patty whisked out, and Carry knew she should go to her sewing. But she sat a long while at the table in dismal thought. She was so tired, and so hopeless. It had been such a hard struggle, and it seemed now as if it would all come to naught. For five years, ever since her mother's death, Carry had supported herself and Patty by dressmaking. They had been a hard five years of pinching and economizing and going without, for Enderby was only a small place, and there were two other dressmakers. Then there was always the mortgage to devour everything. Carry had kept it at bay till now, but at last she was conquered. She had had typhoid fever in the spring and had not been able to work for a long time. Indeed, she had gone to work before she should. The doctor's bill was yet unpaid, but Dr. Hamilton had told her to take her time. Carry knew she would not be pressed for that, and next year Patty would be able to help her. But next year would be too late. The dear little home would be lost then.

When Carry roused herself from her sad reflections, she saw a crumpled note lying on the floor. She picked it up and absently smoothed it out. Seeing Patty's name at the top she was about to lay it aside without reading it, but the lines were few, and the sense of them flashed into Carry's brain. The note was an invitation to Clare Forbes's party! The Lea girls had known that the Forbes girls were going to give a party, but they had not expected that Patty would be invited. Of course, Clare Forbes was in Patty's class at school and was always very nice and friendly with her. But then the Forbes set was not the Lea set.

Carry ran upstairs to Patty's room. "Patty, you dropped this on the floor. I couldn't help seeing what it was. Why didn't you tell me Clare had invited you?"

"Because I knew I couldn't go, and I thought you would feel badly over that. Caddy, I wish you hadn't seen it."

"Oh, Patty, I *do* wish you could go to the party. It was so sweet of Clare to invite you, and perhaps she will be offended if you don't go – she won't understand. Clare Forbes isn't a girl whose friendship is to be lightly thrown away when it is offered."

"I know that. But, Caddy dear, it is impossible. I don't think that I have any foolish pride about clothes, but you know it is out of the question to think of going to Clare Forbes's party in my last winter's plaid dress, which is a good two inches too short and skimpy in proportion. Putting my own feelings aside, it would be an insult to Clare. There, don't think any more about it."

But Carry did think about it. She lay awake half the night wondering if there might not be some way for Patty to go to that party. She knew it was impossible, unless Patty had a new dress, and how could a new dress be had? Yet she did so want Patty to go. Patty never had any good times, and she was studying so hard. Then, all at once, Carry thought of a way by which Patty might have a new dress. She had been tossing restlessly, but now she lay very still, staring with wide-open eyes at the moonlit window, with the big willow boughs branching darkly across it. Yes, it was a way, but could she? *Could* she? Yes, she could, and she would. Carry buried her face in her pillow with a sob and a gulp. But she had decided what must be done, and how it must be done.

"Are you going to begin on your organdie today?" asked Patty in the morning, before she started for school.

"I must finish Mrs. Pidgeon's suit first," Carry answered. "Next week will be time enough to think about my wedding garments."

She tried to laugh and failed. Patty thought with a pang that Carry looked horribly pale and tired – probably she had worried most of the night over the interest. "I'm so glad she's going to Chris's wedding," thought Patty, as she hurried down the street. "It will take her out of herself and give her something nice to think of for ever so long."

Nothing more was said that week about the organdie, or the wedding, or the Forbes's party. Carry sewed fiercely, and sat at her machine for hours after Patty had gone to bed. The night before the party she said to Patty, "Braid your hair tonight, Patty. You'll want it nice and wavy to go to the Forbes's tomorrow night."

Patty thought that Carry was actually trying to perpetrate a weak joke, and endeavoured to laugh. But it was a rather dreary laugh. Patty, after a hard evening's study, felt tired and discouraged, and she was really dreadfully disappointed about the party, although she wouldn't have let Carry suspect it for the world.

"You're going, you know," said Carry, as serious as a judge, although there was a little twinkle in her eyes.

"In a faded plaid two inches too short?" Patty smiled as brightly as possible.

"Oh, no. I have a dress all ready for you." Carry opened the wardrobe door and took out – the loveliest girlish dress of creamy organdie, with pale pink roses scattered over it, made with the daintiest of ruffles and tucks, with a bertha of soft creamy lace, and a girdle of white silk. "This is for you," said Carry.

Patty gazed at the dress with horror-stricken eyes. "Caroline Lea, *that is your organdie!* And you've gone and made it up for *me*! Carry Lea, what are you going to wear to the wedding?"

"Nothing. I'm not going."

"You are – you must – you shall. I won't take the organdie."

"You'll have to now, because it's made to fit you. Come, Patty dear, I've set my heart on your going to that party. You mustn't disappoint me – you *can't*, for what good would it do? I can never wear the dress now."

Patty realized that. She knew she might as well go to the party, but she did not feel much pleasure in the prospect. Nevertheless, when she was ready for it the next evening, she couldn't help a little thrill of delight. The dress was so pretty, and dainty, and becoming.

"You look sweet," exclaimed Carry admiringly. "There, I hear the Browns' carriage. Patty, I want you to promise me this – that you'll not let any thought of me, or my not going to the wedding, spoil your enjoyment this evening. I gave you the dress that you might have a good time, so don't make my gift of no effect."

"I'll try," promised Patty, flying downstairs, where her next-door neighbours were waiting for her.

At two o'clock that night Carry was awakened to see Patty bending over her, flushed and radiant. Carry sat sleepily up. "I hope you had a good time," she said.

"I had – oh, I had – but I didn't waken you out of your hard-earned slumbers at this wee sma' hour to tell you that. Carry, I've thought of a way for you to go to the wedding. It just came to me at supper. Mrs. Forbes was sitting opposite to me, and her dress suggested it. You must make over Aunt Caroline's silk dress."

"Nonsense," said Carry, a little crossly; even sweet-tempered people are sometimes cross when they are wakened up for – as it seemed – nothing.

"It's good plain sense. Of course, you must make it over and –"

"Patty Lea, you're crazy. I wouldn't dream of wearing that hideous thing. Bright green silk, with huge yellow brocade flowers as big as cabbages all over it! I think I see myself in it."

"Caddy, listen to me. You know there's enough of that black lace of mother's for the waist, and the big black lace shawl of Grandmother Lea's will do for the skirt. Make it over –"

"A plain slip of the silk," gasped Carry, her quick brain seizing on all the possibilities of the plan. "*Why* didn't I think of it before? It will be just the thing, the greens and yellow will be toned down to a nice shimmer under the black lace. And I'll make cuffs of black velvet with double puffs above – and just cut out a wee bit at the throat with a frill of lace and a band of black velvet ribbon around my neck. Patty Lea, it's an inspiration."

Carry was out of bed by daylight the next morning and, while Patty still slumbered, she mounted to the garret, and took Aunt Caroline's silk dress from the chest where it had lain forgotten for three years. Carry held it up at arm's length, and looked at it with amusement.

"It is certainly ugly, but with the lace over it it will look very different. There's enough of it, anyway, and that skirt is stiff enough to stand alone. Poor Aunt Caroline, I'm afraid I wasn't particularly grateful for her gift at the time, but I really am now."

Aunt Caroline, who had given the dress to Carry three years before, was an old lady of eighty, the aunt of Carry's father. She had once possessed a snug farm but in an evil hour she had been persuaded to deed it to her nephew, Edward Curry, whom she had brought up. Poor Aunt Caroline had lived to regret this step, for everyone in Enderby knew that Edward Curry and his wife had repaid her with ingratitude and greed.

Carry, who was named for her, was her favourite grand-niece and often went to see her, though such visits were coldly received by the Currys, who always took especial care never to leave Aunt Caroline alone with any of her relatives. On one occasion, when Carry was there, Aunt Caroline had brought out this silk dress.

"I'm going to give this to you, Carry," she said timidly. "It's a good silk, and not so very old. Mr. Greenley gave it to me for a birthday present fifteen years ago. Maybe you can make it over for yourself."

Mrs. Edward, who was on duty at the time, sniffed disagreeably, but she said nothing. The dress was of no value in her eyes, for the pattern was so ugly and old-fashioned that none of her smart daughters would have worn it. Had it been otherwise, Aunt Caroline would probably not have been allowed to give it away.

Carry had thanked Aunt Caroline sincerely. If she did not care much for the silk, she at least prized the kindly motive behind the gift. Perhaps she and Patty laughed a little over it as they packed it away in the garret. It was so very ugly, but

Carry thought it was sweet of Aunt Caroline to have given her something. Poor old Aunt Caroline had died soon after, and Carry had not thought about the silk dress again. She had too many other things to think of, this poor worried Carry.

After breakfast Carry began to rip the skirt breadths apart. Snip, snip, went her scissors, while her thoughts roamed far afield – now looking forward with renewed pleasure to Christine's wedding, now dwelling dolefully on the mortgage. Patty, who was washing the dishes, knew just what her thoughts were by the light and shadow on her expressive face.

"Why! – what?" exclaimed Carry suddenly. Patty wheeled about to see Carry staring at the silk dress like one bewitched. Between the silk and the lining which she had just ripped apart was a twenty-dollar bill, and beside it a sheet of letter paper covered with writing in a cramped angular hand, both secured very carefully to the silk.

"Carry Lea!" gasped Patty.

With trembling fingers Carry snipped away the stitches that held the letter, and read it aloud.

"My dear Caroline," it ran, "I do not know when you will find this letter and this money, but when you do it belongs to you. I have a hundred dollars which I always meant to give you because you were named for me. But Edward and his wife do not know I have it, and I don't want them to find out. They would not let me give it to you if they knew, so I have thought of this way of getting it to you. I have sewed five twenty-dollar bills under the lining of this skirt, and they are all yours, with your Aunt Caroline's best love. You were always a good girl, Carry, and you've worked hard, and I've given Edward enough. Just take this money and use it as you like.

"Aunt Caroline Greenley."

"Carry Lea, are we both dreaming?" gasped Patty.

With crimson cheeks Carry ripped the other breadths apart, and there were the other four bills. Then she slipped down in a little heap on the sofa cushions and began to cry – happy tears of relief and gladness.

"We can pay the interest," said Patty, dancing around the room, "and get yourself a nice new dress for the wedding."

"Indeed I won't," said Carry, sitting up and laughing through her tears. "I'll make over this dress and wear it out of gratitude to the memory of dear Aunt Caroline."

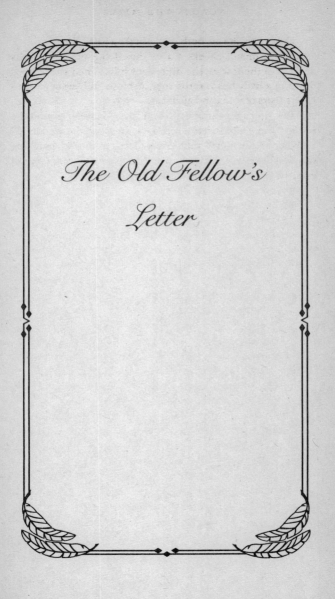

The Old Fellow's

Letter

UGGLES and I were down on the Old Fellow. It doesn't matter why and, since in a story of this kind we must tell the truth no matter what happens – or else where is the use of writing a story at all? – I'll have to confess that we had deserved all we got and that the Old Fellow did no more than his duty by us. Both Ruggles and I see that now, since we have had time to cool off, but at the moment we were in a fearful wax at the Old Fellow and were bound to hatch up something to get even with him.

Of course, the Old Fellow had another name, just as Ruggles has another name. He is principal of the Frampton Academy – the Old Fellow, not Ruggles – and his name is George Osborne. We have to call him Mr. Osborne to his face, but he is the Old Fellow everywhere else. He is quite old – thirty-six if he's a day, and whatever possessed Sylvia Grant – but there, I'm getting ahead of my story.

Most of the Cads like the Old Fellow. Even Ruggles and I like him on the average. The girls are always a little provoked at him because he is so shy and absent-minded, but when it comes to the point, they like him too. I heard Emma White say once that he was "so handsome"; I nearly whooped. Ruggles was mad because he's gone on Em. For the idea of calling a thin, pale, dark, dreamy-looking chap like the Old Fellow "handsome" was more than I could stand without guffawing. Em probably said it to provoke Ruggles; she couldn't really have thought it. "Micky," the English professor, now – if she had called him handsome there would have been some sense in it. He is splendid: big six-footer with magnificent muscles, red cheeks, and curly yellow hair. I can't see how he can be contented to sit down and teach mushy English literature and poetry and that sort of thing. It would have been more in keeping with the Old Fellow. There was a rumour running at large in the Academy that the Old Fellow wrote poetry, but he ran the mathematics and didn't make such a foozle of it as you might suppose, either.

Ruggles and I meant to get square with the Old Fellow, if it took all the term; at least, we said so. But if Providence hadn't sent Sylvia Grant walking down the street past our boarding house that afternoon, we should probably have cooled off before we thought of any working plan of revenge.

Sylvia Grant did go down the street, however. Ruggles, hanging halfway out of the window as usual, saw her, and called me to go and look. Of course I went. Sylvia Grant was always worth looking at. There was no girl in Frampton who could hold a candle to her when it came to beauty. As for brains, that is another thing altogether. My private opinion is that Sylvia hadn't any, or she would never have preferred – but there, I'm getting on too fast again. Ruggles should have written this story; he can concentrate better.

Sylvia was the Latin professor's daughter; she wasn't a Cad girl, of course. She was over twenty and had graduated from it two years ago, but she was in all the social things that went on in the Academy; and all the unmarried professors, except the Old Fellow, were in love with her. Micky had it the worst, and we had all made up our minds that Sylvia would marry Micky. He was so handsome, we didn't see how she could help it. I tell you, they made a dandy-looking couple when they were together.

Well, as I said before, I toddled to the window to have a look at the fair Sylvia. She was all togged out in some new fall duds, and I guess she'd come out to show them off. They were brownish, kind of, and she'd a spanking hat on with feathers and things in it. Her hair was shining under it, all purply-black, and she looked sweet enough to eat. Then she saw Ruggles and me and she waved her hand and laughed, and her big blackish-blue eyes sparkled; but she hadn't been laughing before, or sparkling either.

I'd thought she looked kind of glum, and I wondered if she and Micky had had a falling out. I rather suspected it, for at the Senior Prom, three nights before, she had hardly looked at Micky, but had sat in a corner and talked to the Old Fellow. He didn't do much talking; he was too shy, and he looked mighty uncomfortable. I thought it kind of mean of Sylvia to torment him so, when she knew he hated to have to talk to girls, but when I saw Micky scowling at the corner, I knew she was doing it to make him jealous. Girls won't stick at anything when they want to provoke a chap; I know it to my cost, for Jennie Price – but that has nothing to do with this story.

Just across the square Sylvia met the Old Fellow and bowed. He lifted his hat and passed on, but after a few steps he turned and looked back; he caught Sylvia doing the same thing, so he wheeled and came on, looking mighty foolish. As he passed beneath our window Ruggles chuckled fiendishly.

"I've thought of something, Polly," he said – my name is Paul. "Bet you it will make the Old Fellow squirm. Let's write a letter to Sylvia Grant – a love letter – and sign the Old Fellow's name to it. She'll give him a fearful snubbing, and we'll be revenged."

"But who'll write it?" I said doubtfully. "I can't. You'll have to, Ruggles. You've had more practice."

Ruggles turned red. I know he writes to Em White in vacations.

"I'll do my best," he said, quite meekly. "That is, I'll compose it. But you'll have to copy it. You can imitate the Old Fellow's handwriting so well."

"But look here," I said, an uncomfortable idea striking me, "what about Sylvia? Won't she feel kind of flattish when she finds out he didn't write it? For of course he'll tell her. We haven't anything against her, you know."

"Oh, Sylvia won't care," said Ruggles serenely. "She's the sort of girl who can take a joke. I've seen her eyes shine over tricks we've played on the professors before now. She'll just laugh. Besides, she doesn't like the Old Fellow a bit. I know from the way she acts with him. She's always so cool and stiff when he's about, not a bit like she is with the other professors."

Well, Ruggles wrote the letter. At first he tried to pass it off on me as his own composition. But I know a few little things, and one of them is that Ruggles couldn't have made up that letter any more than he could have written a sonnet. I told him so, and made him own up. He had a copy of an old letter that had been written to his sister by her young man. I suppose Ruggles had stolen it, but there is no use inquiring too closely into these things. Anyhow, that letter just filled the bill. It was beautifully expressed. Ruggles's sister's young man must have possessed lots of ability. He was an English professor, something like Micky, so I suppose he was extra good at it. He started in by telling her how much he loved her, and what an angel of beauty and goodness he had always thought her; how unworthy he felt himself of her and how little hope he had that she could ever care for him; and he wound up by imploring her to tell him if she could possibly love him a little bit and all that sort of thing.

I copied the letter out on heliotrope paper in my best imitation of the Old Fellow's handwriting and signed it, "Yours devotedly and imploringly, George Osborne." Then we mailed it that very evening.

The next evening the Cad girls gave a big reception in the Assembly Hall to an Academy alumna who was visiting the Greek professor's wife. It was the smartest event of the term and everybody was there – students and faculty and, of course, Sylvia Grant. Sylvia looked stunning. She was all in white, with a string of pearls about her pretty round throat and a couple of little pink roses in her black hair. I never saw her so smiling and bright; but she seemed quieter than usual, and avoided poor Micky so skilfully that it was really a pleasure to watch her. The Old Fellow came in late, with his tie all crooked, as it always was; I saw Sylvia blush and nudged Ruggles to look.

"She's thinking of the letter," he said.

Ruggles and I never meant to listen, upon my word we didn't. It was pure accident. We were in behind the flags and palms in the Modern Languages Room, fixing up a plan how to get Em and Jennie off for a moonlit stroll in the grounds – these things require diplomacy I can tell you, for there are always so many other fellows hanging about – when in came Sylvia Grant and the Old Fellow arm in arm. The room was quite empty, or they thought it was, and they sat down just on the other side of the flags. They couldn't see us, but we could see them quite plainly. Sylvia still looked smiling and happy, not a bit mad as we had expected, but just kind of shy and radiant. As for the Old Fellow, he looked, as Em White would say, as Sphinx-like as ever. I'd defy any man alive to tell from the Old Fellow's expression what he was thinking about or what he felt like at any time.

Then all at once Sylvia said softly, with her eyes cast down, "I received your letter, Mr. Osborne."

Any other man in the world would have jumped, or said, "My letter!!!" or shown surprise in some way. But the Old Fellow has a nerve. He looked sideways at Sylvia for a moment and then he said kind of drily, "Ah, did you?"

"Yes," said Sylvia, not much above a whisper. "It – it surprised me very much. I never supposed that you – you cared for me in that way."

"Can you tell me how I could help caring?" said the Old Fellow in the strangest way. His voice actually trembled.

"I – I don't think I would tell you if I knew," said Sylvia, turning her head away. "You see – I don't want you to help caring."

"Sylvia!"

You never saw such a transformation as came over the Old

Fellow. His eyes just blazed, but his face went white. He bent forward and took her hand.

"Sylvia, do you mean that you – you actually care a little for me, dearest? Oh, Sylvia, do you mean that?"

"Of course I do," said Sylvia right out. "I've always cared – ever since I was a little girl coming here to school and breaking my heart over mathematics, although I hated them, just to be in your class. Why – why – I've treasured up old geometry exercises you wrote out for me just because you wrote them. But I thought I could never make you care for me. I was the happiest girl in the world when your letter came today."

"Sylvia," said the Old Fellow, "I've loved you for years. But I never dreamed that you could care for me. I thought it quite useless to tell you of my love – before. Will you – can you be my wife, darling?"

At this point Ruggles and I differ as to what came next. He asserts that Sylvia turned square around and kissed the Old Fellow. But I'm sure she just turned her face and gave him a look and then he kissed her.

Anyhow, there they both were, going on at the silliest rate about how much they loved each other and how the Old Fellow thought she loved Micky and all that sort of thing. It was awful. I never thought the Old Fellow or Sylvia either could be so spooney. Ruggles and I would have given anything on earth to be out of that. We knew we'd no business to be there and we felt as foolish as flatfish. It was a tremendous relief when the Old Fellow and Sylvia got up at last and trailed away, both of them looking idiotically happy.

"Well, did you ever?" said Ruggles.

It was a girl's exclamation, but nothing else would have expressed his feelings.

"No, I never," I said. "To think that Sylvia Grant should be sweet on the Old Fellow when she could have Micky! It passes comprehension. Did she – did she really promise to marry him, Ruggles?"

"She did," said Ruggles gloomily. "But, I say, isn't that Old Fellow game? Tumbled to the trick in a jiff; never let on but what he wrote the letter; never will let on, I bet. Where does the joke come in, Polly, my boy?"

"It's on us," I said, "but nobody will know of it if we hold our tongues. We'll have to hold them anyhow, for Sylvia's sake, since she's been goose enough to go and fall in love with the Old Fellow. She'd go wild if she ever found out the letter was a hoax. We have made that match, Ruggles. He'd never have got up enough spunk to tell her he wanted her, and she'd probably have married Micky out of spite."

"Well, you know the Old Fellow isn't a bad sort after all," said Ruggles, "and he's really awfully gone on her. So it's all right. Let's go and find the girls."

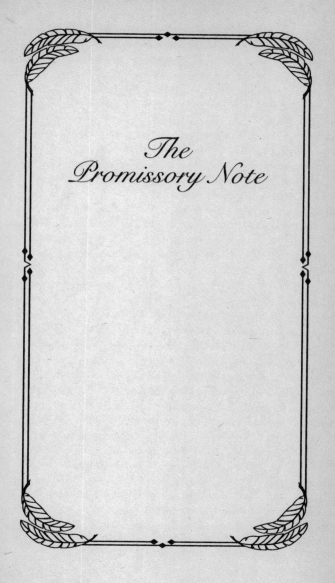

*The
Promissory Note*

RNEST Duncan swung himself off the platform of David White's store and walked whistling up the street. Life seemed good to Ernest just then. Mr. White had given him a rise in salary that day, and had told him that he was satisfied with him. Mr. White was not easy to please in the matter of clerks, and it had been with fear and trembling that Ernest had gone into his store six months before. He had thought himself fortunate to secure such a chance. His father had died the preceding year, leaving nothing in the way of worldly goods except the house he had lived in. For several years before his death he had been unable to do much work, and the finances of the little family had dwindled steadily. After his father's death Ernest, who had been going to school and expecting to go to college, found that he must go to work at once instead to support himself and his mother.

If George Duncan had not left much of worldly wealth behind him, he at least bequeathed to his son the interest of a fine, upright character and a reputation for honesty and integrity. None knew this better than David White, and it was on this account that he took Ernest as his clerk, over the heads of several other applicants who seemed to have a stronger "pull."

"I don't know anything about *you*, Ernest," he said bluntly. "You're only sixteen, and you may not have an ounce of real grit or worth in you. But it will be a queer thing if your father's son hasn't. I knew him all his life. A better man never lived nor, before his accident, a smarter one. I'll give his son a chance, anyhow. If you take after your dad you'll get on all right."

Ernest had not been in the store very long before Mr. White concluded, with a gratified chuckle, that he did take after his father. He was hard-working, conscientious, and obliging. Customers of all sorts, from the rough fishermen who came up from the harbour to the old Irishwomen from the back country roads, liked him. Mr. White was satisfied. He was beginning to grow old. This lad had the makings of a good partner in him by and by. No hurry; he must serve a long apprenticeship first and prove his mettle; no use spoiling him by hinting at future partnerships before need was. That would all come in due time. David White was a shrewd man.

Ernest was unconscious of his employer's plans regarding him; but he knew that he stood well with him and, much to his surprise, he found that he liked the work, and was beginning to take a personal interest and pleasure in the store. Hence, he went home to tea on this particular afternoon with buoyant step and smiling eyes. It was a good world, and he was glad to be alive in it, glad to have work to do and a dear little mother to work for. Most of the folks who met him smiled in friendly fashion at the bright-eyed, frank-faced lad. Only old Jacob Patterson scowled grimly as he passed him, emitting merely a surly grunt in response to Ernest's greeting. But then, old Jacob Patterson was noted as much for his surliness as for his miserliness. Nobody had ever heard him speak pleasantly to anyone; therefore his unfriendliness did not at all dash Ernest's high spirits.

"I'm sorry for him," the lad thought. "He has no interest in life save accumulating money. He has no other pleasure or affection or ambition. When he dies I don't suppose a single regret will follow him. Father died a poor man, but what love and respect went with him to his grave – aye, and beyond it. Jacob Patterson, I'm sorry for you. You have chosen the poorer part, and you are a poor man in spite of your thousands."

Ernest and his mother lived up on the hill, at the end of the straggling village street. The house was a small, old-fashioned one, painted white, set in the middle of a small but beautiful lawn. George Duncan, during the last rather help-less years of his life, had devoted himself to the cultivation of flowers, shrubs, and trees and, as a result, his lawn was the prettiest in Conway. Ernest worked hard in his spare moments to keep it looking as well as in his father's lifetime, for he loved his little home dearly, and was proud of its beauty.

He ran gaily into the sitting-room.

"Tea ready, lady mother? I'm hungry as a wolf. Good news gives one an appetite. Mr. White has raised my salary a couple of dollars per week. We must celebrate the event somehow this evening. What do you say to a sail on the river and an ice cream at Taylor's afterwards? When a little woman can't out-live her schoolgirl hankering for ice cream – why, Mother, what's the matter? Mother, dear!"

Mrs. Duncan had been standing before the window with her back to the room when Ernest entered. When she turned he saw that she had been crying.

"Oh, Ernest," she said brokenly, "Jacob Patterson has just been here – and he says – he says –"

"What has that old miser been saying to trouble you?" demanded Ernest angrily, taking her hands in his.

"He says he holds your father's promissory note for nine hundred dollars, overdue for several years," answered Mrs. Duncan. "Yes – and he showed me the note, Ernest."

"Father's promissory note for nine hundred!" exclaimed Ernest in bewilderment. "But Father paid that note to James Patterson five years ago, Mother – just before his accident. Didn't you tell me he did?"

"Yes, he did," said Mrs. Duncan, "but –"

"Then where is it?" interrupted Ernest. "Father would keep the receipted note, of course. We must look among his papers."

"You won't find it there, Ernest. We – we don't know where the note is. It – it was lost."

"Lost! That is unfortunate. But you say that Jacob Patterson showed you a promissory note of Father's still in existence? How can that be? It can't possibly be the note he paid. And there couldn't have been another note we knew nothing of?"

"I understand how this note came to be in Jacob Patterson's possession," said Mrs. Duncan more firmly, "but he laughed in my face when I told him. I must tell you the whole story, Ernest. But sit down and get your tea first."

"I haven't any appetite for tea now, Mother," said Ernest soberly. "Let me hear the whole truth about the matter."

"Seven years ago your father gave his note to old James Patterson, Jacob's brother," said Mrs. Duncan. "It was for nine hundred dollars. Two years afterwards the note fell due and he paid James Patterson the full amount with interest. I remember the day well. I have only too good reason to. He went up to the Patterson place in the afternoon with the money. It was a very hot day. James Patterson receipted the note and gave it to your father. Your father always remembered that much; he was also sure that he had the note with him when he left the house. He then went over to see Paul Sinclair. A thunderstorm came up while he was on the road. Then, as you know, Ernest, just as he turned in at Paul Sinclair's gate the lightning flash struck and stunned him. It was weeks before he came to himself at all. He never did come completely to himself again. When, weeks afterwards, I thought of the note and asked him about it, we could not find it; and, search as we did, we never found it. Your father could never remember what he did with it when he left James Patterson's. Neither Mr. Sinclair nor his wife could recollect seeing anything of it at the time of the accident. James Patterson had left for California the very morning after, and he never came back. We did not worry much about the loss of the note then; it did not seem of much moment, and your father was not in a condition to be troubled about the matter."

"But, Mother, this note that Jacob Patterson holds – I don't understand about this."

"I'm coming to that. I remember distinctly that on the

evening when your father came home after signing the note he said that James Patterson drew up a note and he signed it, but just as he did so the old man's pet cat, which was sitting on the table, upset an ink bottle and the ink ran all over the table and stained one end of the note. Old James Patterson was the fussiest man who ever lived, and a stickler for neatness. 'Tut, tut,' he said, 'this won't do. Here, I'll draw up another note and tear this blotted one up.' He did so and your father signed it. He always supposed James Patterson destroyed the first one, and certainly he must have intended to, for there never was an honester man. But he must have neglected to do so for, Ernest, it was that blotted note Jacob Patterson showed me today. He said he found it among his brother's papers. I suppose it has been in the desk up at the Patterson place ever since James went to California. He died last winter and Jacob is his sole heir. Ernest, that note with the compound interest on it for seven years amounts to over eleven hundred dollars. How can we pay it?"

"I'm afraid that this is a very serious business, Mother," said Ernest, rising and pacing the floor with agitated strides. "We shall have to pay the note if we cannot find the other – and even if we could, perhaps. Your story of the drawing up of the second note would not be worth anything as evidence in a court of law – and we have nothing to hope from Jacob Patterson's clemency. No doubt he believes that he really holds Father's unpaid note. He is not a dishonest man; in fact, he rather prides himself on having made all his money honestly. He will exact every penny of the debt. The first thing to do is to have another thorough search for the lost note – although I am afraid that it is a forlorn hope."

A forlorn hope it proved to be. The note did not turn up. Old Jacob Patterson proved obdurate. He laughed to scorn the tale of the blotted note and, indeed, Ernest sadly admitted to himself that it was not a story anybody would be in a hurry to believe.

"There's nothing for it but to sell our house and pay the debt, Mother," he said at last. Ernest had grown old in the days that had followed Jacob Patterson's demand. His boyish face was pale and haggard. "Jacob Patterson will take the case into the law courts if we don't settle at once. Mr. White offered to lend me the money on a mortgage on the place, but I could never pay the interest out of my salary when we have nothing else to live on. I would only get further and further behind. I'm not afraid of hard work, but I dare not borrow money with so little prospect of ever being able to repay it. We must sell the place and rent that little four-roomed cottage of Mr. Percy's down by the river to live in. Oh, Mother, it half kills me to think of your being turned out of your home like this!"

It was a bitter thing for Mrs. Duncan also, but for Ernest's sake she concealed her feelings and affected cheerfulness. The house and lot were sold, Mr. White being the purchaser thereof; and Ernest and his mother removed to the little riverside cottage with such of their household belongings as had not also to be sold to make up the required sum. Even then, Ernest had to borrow two hundred dollars from Mr. White, and he foresaw that the repayal of this sum would cost him much self-denial and privation. It would be necessary to cut their modest expenses down severely. For himself Ernest did not mind, but it hurt him keenly that his mother should lack the little luxuries and comforts to which she had been accustomed. He saw too, in spite of her efforts to hide it, that leaving her old home was a terrible blow to her. Altogether, Ernest felt bitter and disheartened; his step lacked spring and his face its smile. He did his work with dogged faithfulness, but he no longer found pleasure in it. He knew that his mother secretly pined after her lost home where she had gone as a bride, and the knowledge rendered him very unhappy.

PAUL SINCLAIR, his father's friend and cousin, died that winter, leaving two small children. His wife had died the previous year. When his business affairs came to be settled they were found to be sadly involved. There were debts on all sides, and it was soon only too evident that nothing was left for the little boys. They were homeless and penniless.

"What will become of them, poor little fellows?" said Mrs. Duncan pityingly. "We are their only relatives, Ernest. We must give them a home at least."

"Mother, how can we!" exclaimed Ernest. "We are so poor. It's as much as we can do to get along now, and there is that two hundred to pay Mr. White. I'm sorry for Danny and Frank, but I don't see how we can possibly do anything for them."

Mrs. Duncan sighed.

"I know it isn't right to ask you to add to your burden," she said wistfully.

"It is of *you* I am thinking, Mother," said Ernest tenderly. "I can't have your burden added to. You deny yourself too much and work too hard now. What would it be if you took the care of those children upon yourself?"

"Don't think of me, Ernest," said Mrs. Duncan eagerly. "I wouldn't mind. I'd be glad to do anything I could for them, poor little souls. Their father was your father's best friend, and I feel as if it were our duty to do all we can for them. They're such little fellows. Who knows how they would be treated if they were taken by strangers? And they'd most likely be separated, and that would be a shame. But I leave it for you to decide, Ernest. It is your right, for the heaviest part will fall on you."

Ernest did not decide at once. For a week he thought the matter over, weighing pros and cons carefully. To take the two Sinclair boys meant a double portion of toil and self-denial. Had he not enough to bear now? But, on the other side, was it not his duty, nay, his privilege, to help the children if he could? In the end he said to his mother:

"We'll take the little fellows, Mother. I'll do the best I can for them. We'll manage a corner and a crust for them."

So Danny and Frank Sinclair came to the little cottage. Frank was eight and Danny six, and they were small and lively and mischievous. They worshipped Mrs. Duncan, and thought Ernest the finest fellow in the world. When his birthday came around in March, the two little chaps put their heads together in a grave consultation as to what they could give him.

"You know he gave us presents on our birthdays," said Frank. "So we must give him something."

"I'll div him my pottet-knife," said Danny, taking the somewhat battered and loose-jointed affair from his pocket, and gazing at it affectionately.

"I'll give him one of Papa's books," said Frank. "That pretty one with the red covers and the gold letters."

A few of Mr. Sinclair's books had been saved for the boys, and were stored in a little box in their room. The book Frank referred to was an old *History of the Turks*, and its gay cover was probably the best of it, since its contents were of no particular merit.

On Ernest's birthday both boys gave him their offerings after breakfast.

"Here's a pottet-knife for you," said Danny graciously. "It's a bully pottet-knife. It'll cut real well if you hold it dust the wight way. I'll show you."

"And here's a book for you," said Frank. "It's a real pretty book, and I guess it's pretty interesting reading too. It's all about the Turks."

Ernest accepted both gifts gravely, and after the children had gone out he and his mother had a hearty laugh.

"The dear, kind-hearted little lads!" said Mrs. Duncan. "It must have been a real sacrifice on Danny's part to give you his beloved 'pottet-knife.' I was afraid you were going to refuse it at first, and that would have hurt his little feelings terribly. I don't think the *History of the Turks* will keep you up burning the midnight oil. I remember that book of old – I could never forget that gorgeous cover. Mr. Sinclair lent it to your father once, and he said it was absolute trash. Why, Ernest, what's the matter?"

Ernest had been turning the book's leaves over carelessly. Suddenly he sprang to his feet with an exclamation, his face turning white as marble.

"Mother!" he gasped, holding out a yellowed slip of paper. "Look! It's the lost promissory note."

Mother and son looked at each other for a moment. Then Mrs. Duncan began to laugh and cry together.

"Your father took that book with him when he went to pay the note," she said. "He intended to return it to Mr. Sinclair. I remember seeing the gleam of the red binding in his hand as he went out of the gate. He must have slipped the note into it and I suppose the book has never been opened since. Oh, Ernest – do you think – will Jacob Patterson –"

"I don't know, Mother. I must see Mr. White about this. Don't be too sanguine. This doesn't prove that the note Jacob Patterson found wasn't a genuine note also, you know – that is, I don't think it would serve as proof in law. We'll have to leave it to his sense of justice. If he refuses to refund the money I'm afraid we can't compel him to do so."

But Jacob Patterson did not any longer refuse belief to Mrs. Patterson's story of the blotted note. He was a harsh, miserly man, but he prided himself on his strict honesty; he had been fairly well acquainted with his brother's business transactions, and knew that George Duncan had given only one promissory note.

"I'll admit, ma'am, since the receipted note has turned up, that your story about the blotted one must be true," he said surlily. "I'll pay your money back. Nobody can ever say Jacob

Patterson cheated. I took what I believed to be my due. Since I'm convinced it wasn't I'll hand every penny over. Though, mind you, you couldn't make me do it by law. It's my honesty, ma'am, it's my honesty."

Since Jacob Patterson was so well satisfied with the fibre of his honesty, neither Mrs. Duncan nor Ernest was disposed to quarrel with it. Mr. White readily agreed to sell the old Duncan place back to them, and by spring they were settled again in their beloved little home. Danny and Frank were with them, of course.

"We can't be too good to them, Mother," said Ernest. "We really owe all our happiness to them."

"Yes; but, Ernest, if you had not consented to take the homeless little lads in their time of need this wouldn't have come about."

"I've been well rewarded, Mother," said Ernest quietly, "but, even if nothing of the sort had happened, I would be glad that I did the best I could for Frank and Danny. I'm ashamed to think that I was unwilling to do it at first. If it hadn't been for what you said, I wouldn't have. So it is your unselfishness we have to thank for it all, Mother dear."

Anna's Love Letters

RE you going to answer Gilbert's letter tonight, Anna?" asked Alma Williams, standing in the pantry doorway, tall, fair, and grey-eyed, with the sunset light coming down over the dark firs, through the window behind her, and making a primrose nimbus around her shapely head.

Anna, dark, vivid, and slender, was perched on the edge of the table, idly swinging her slippered foot at the cat's head. She smiled wickedly at Alma before replying.

"I am not going to answer it tonight or any other night," she said, twisting her full, red lips in a way that Alma had learned to dread. Mischief was ripening in Anna's brain when that twist was out.

"What do you mean?" asked Alma anxiously.

"Just what I say, dear," responded Anna, with deceptive meekness. "Poor Gilbert is gone, and I don't intend to bother my head about him any longer. He was amusing while he lasted, but of what use is a beau two thousand miles away, Alma?"

Alma was patient – outwardly. It was never of any avail to show impatience with Anna.

"Anna, you are talking foolishly. Of course you are going to answer his letter. You are as good as engaged to him. Wasn't that practically understood when he left?"

"No, no, dear," and Anna shook her sleek black head with the air of explaining matters to an obtuse child. "*I* was the only one who understood. Gil *mis*understood. He thought that I would really wait for him until he should have made enough money to come home and pay off the mortgage. I let him think so, because I hated to hurt his little feelings. But now it's off with the old love and on with a new one for me."

"Anna, you cannot be in earnest!" exclaimed Alma.

But she was afraid that Anna was in earnest. Anna had a

wretched habit of being in earnest when she said flippant things.

"You don't mean that you are not going to write to Gilbert at all – after all you promised?"

Anna placed her elbows daintily on the top of the rocking chair, dropped her pointed chin in her hands, and looked at Alma with black demure eyes.

"I – do – mean – just – that," she said slowly. "I never mean to marry Gilbert Murray. This is final, Alma, and you need not scold or coax, because it would be a waste of breath. Gilbert is safely out of the way, and now I am going to have a good time with a few other delightful men creatures in Exeter."

Anna nodded decisively, flashed a smile at Alma, picked up her cat, and went out. At the door she turned and looked back, with the big black cat snuggled under her chin.

"If you think Gilbert will feel very badly over his letter not being answered, you might answer it yourself, Alma," she said teasingly. "There it is" – she took the letter from the pocket of her ruffled apron and threw it on a chair. "You may read it if you want to; it isn't really a love letter. I told Gilbert he wasn't to write silly letters. Come, pussy, I'm going to get ready for prayer meeting. We've got a nice, new, young, good-looking minister in Exeter, pussy, and that makes prayer meeting *very* interesting."

Anna shut the door, her departing laugh rippling mockingly through the dusk. Alma picked up Gilbert Murray's letter and went to her room. She wanted to cry, since she could not shake Anna. Even if she could have shook her, it would only have made her more perverse. Anna was in earnest; Alma knew that, even while she hoped and believed that it was but the earnestness of a freak that would pass in time. Anna had had one like it a year ago, when she had cast Gilbert off for three months, driving him distracted by flirting with Charlie Moore. Then she had suddenly repented and taken him back. Alma thought that this whim would run its course likewise and leave a repentant Anna. But meanwhile everything might be spoiled. Gilbert might not prove forgiving a second time.

Alma would have given much if she could only have induced Anna to answer Gilbert's letter, but coaxing Anna to do anything was a very sure and effective way of preventing her from doing it.

ALMA AND ANNA had lived alone at the old Williams homestead ever since their mother's death four years before. Exeter matrons thought this hardly proper, since Alma, in spite of her grave ways, was only twenty-four. The farm was rented, so that Alma's only responsibilities were the post office which she kept, and that harum-scarum beauty of an Anna.

The Murray homestead adjoined theirs. Gilbert Murray had grown up with Alma; they had been friends ever since she could remember. Alma loved Gilbert with a love which she herself believed to be purely sisterly, and which nobody else doubted could be, since she had been at pains to make a match – Exeter matrons' phrasing – between Gil and Anna, and was manifestly delighted when Gilbert obligingly fell in love with the latter.

There was a small mortgage on the Murray place which Mr. Murray senior had not been able to pay off. Gilbert determined to get rid of it, and his thoughts turned to the west. His father was an active, hale old man, quite capable of managing the farm in Gilbert's absence. Alexander MacNair had gone to the west two years previously and got work on a new railroad. He wrote to Gilbert to come too, promising him plenty of work and good pay. Gilbert went, but before going he had asked Anna to marry him.

It was the first proposal Anna had ever had, and she managed it quite cleverly, from her standpoint. She told Gilbert that he must wait until he came home again before settling that; meanwhile, they would be *very* good friends – emphasized with a blush – and that he might write to her. She kissed him goodbye, and Gilbert, honest fellow, was quite satisfied. When an Exeter girl had allowed so much to be inferred, it was understood to be equivalent to an engagement. Gilbert had never discerned that Anna was not like the other Exeter girls, but was a law unto herself.

Alma sat down by her window and looked out over the lane where the slim wild cherry trees were bronzing under the autumn frosts. Her lips were very firmly set. Something must be done. But what?

Alma's heart was set on this marriage for two reasons. Firstly, if Anna married Gilbert she would be near her all her life. She could not bear the thought that some day Anna might leave her and go far away to live. In the second and largest place, she desired the marriage because Gilbert did. She had always been desirous, even in the old, childish play-days, that Gilbert should get just exactly what he wanted. She had always taken a keen, strange delight in furthering his wishes. Anna's falseness would surely break his heart, and Alma winced at the thought of his pain.

There was one thing she could do. Anna's tormenting suggestion had fallen on fertile soil. Alma balanced pros and cons, admitting the risk. But she would have taken a tenfold larger risk in the hope of holding secure Anna's place in Gilbert's affections until Anna herself should come to her senses.

When it grew quite dark and Anna had gone lilting down the lane on her way to prayer meeting, Alma lighted her lamp, read Gilbert's letter – and answered it. Her handwriting was much like Anna's. She signed the letter "A. Williams," and there was nothing in it that might not have been written by her to Gilbert; but she knew that Gilbert would believe Anna had written it, and she intended him so to believe. Alma never did a thing halfway when she did it at all. At first she wrote rather constrainedly but, reflecting that in any case Anna would have written a merely friendly letter, she allowed her thoughts to run freely, and the resulting epistle was an excellent one of its kind. Alma had the gift of expression and more brains than Exeter people had ever imagined she possessed. When Gilbert read that letter a fortnight later he was surprised to find that Anna was so clever. He had always, with a secret regret, thought her much inferior to Alma in this respect, but that delightful letter, witty, wise, fanciful, was the letter of a clever woman.

When a year had passed Alma was still writing to Gilbert the letters signed "A. Williams." She had ceased to fear being found out, and she took a strange pleasure in the correspondence for its own sake. At first she had been quakingly afraid of discovery. When she smuggled the letters addressed in Gilbert's handwriting to Miss Anna Williams out of the letter packet and hid them from Anna's eyes, she felt as guilty as if she were breaking all the laws of the land at once. To be sure, she knew that she would have to confess to Anna some day, when the latter repented and began to wish she had written to Gilbert, but that was a very different thing from premature disclosure.

But Anna had as yet given no sign of such repentance, although Alma looked for it anxiously. Anna was having the time of her life. She was the acknowledged beauty of five settlements, and she went forward on her career of conquest quite undisturbed by the jealousies and heart-burnings she provoked on every side.

One moonlight night she went for a sleigh-drive with Charlie Moore of East Exeter – and returned to tell Alma that they were married!

"I knew you would make a fuss, Alma, because you don't

like Charlie, so we just took matters into our own hands. It was so much more romantic, too. I'd always said I'd never be married in any of your dull, commonplace ways. You might as well forgive me and be nice right off, Alma, because you'd have to do it anyway, in time. Well, you do look surprised!"

ALMA ACCEPTED the situation with an apathy that amazed Anna. The truth was that Alma was stunned by a thought that had come to her even while Anna was speaking.

"Gilbert will find out about the letters now, and despise me."

Nothing else, not even the fact that Anna had married shiftless Charlie Moore, seemed worth while considering beside this. The fear and shame of it haunted her like a nightmare; she shrank every morning from the thought of all the mail that was coming that day, fearing that there would be an angry, puzzled letter from Gilbert. He must certainly soon hear of Anna's marriage; he would see it in the home paper; other correspondents in Exeter would write him of it. Alma grew sick at heart thinking of the complications in front of her.

When Gilbert's letter came she left it for a whole day before she could summon courage to open it. But it was a harmless epistle after all; he had not yet heard of Anna's marriage. Alma had at first no thought of answering it, yet her fingers ached to do so. Now that Anna was gone, her loneliness was unbearable. She realized how much Gilbert's letters had meant to her, even when written to another woman. She could bear her life well enough, she thought, if she only had his letters to look forward to.

No more letters came from Gilbert for six weeks. Then came one, alarmed at Anna's silence, anxiously asking the reason for it. Gilbert had heard no word of the marriage. He was working in a remote district where newspapers seldom penetrated. He had no other correspondent in Exeter now except his mother, and she, not knowing that he supposed himself engaged to Anna, had forgotten to mention it.

Alma answered that letter. She told herself recklessly that she would keep on writing to him until he found out. She would lose his friendship anyhow, when that occurred, but meanwhile she would have the letters a little longer. She could not learn to live without them until she had to.

The correspondence slipped back into its old groove. The harassed look which Alma's face had worn, and which Exeter people had attributed to worry over Anna, disappeared. She did not even feel lonely, and reproached herself for lack of proper feeling in missing Anna so little. Besides, to her horror and dismay, she detected in herself a strange undercurrent of relief at the thought that Gilbert could never marry Anna now! She could not understand it. Had not that marriage been her dearest wish for years? Why then should she feel this strange gladness at the impossibility of its fulfilment? Altogether, Alma feared that her condition of mind and morals must be sadly askew. Perhaps, she thought mournfully, this perversion of proper feeling was her punishment for the deception she had practised. She had deliberately done evil that good might come, and now the very imaginations of her heart were stained by that evil. Alma cried herself to sleep many a night in her repentance, but she kept on writing to Gilbert, for all that.

The winter passed, and the spring and summer waned, and Alma's outward life flowed as smoothly as the currents of the seasons, broken only by vivid eruptions from Anna, who came over often from East Exeter, glorying in her young matronhood, "to cheer Alma up." Alma, so said Exeter people, was becoming unsociable and old maidish. She lost her liking for company, and seldom went anywhere among her neighbours. Her once frequent visits across the yard to chat with old Mrs. Murray became few and far between. She could not bear to hear the old lady talking about Gilbert, and she was afraid that some day she would be told that he was coming home. Gilbert's home-coming was the nightmare dread that darkened poor Alma's whole horizon.

ONE OCTOBER DAY, two years after Gilbert's departure, Alma, standing at her window in the reflected glow of a red maple outside, looked down the lane and saw him striding up it! She had had no warning of his coming. His last letter, dated three weeks back, had not hinted at it. Yet there he was – and with him Alma's Nemesis.

She was very calm. Now that the worst had come, she felt quite strong to meet it. She would tell Gilbert the truth, and he would go away in anger and never forgive her, but she deserved it. As she went downstairs, the only thing that really worried her was the thought of the pain Gilbert would suffer when she told him of Anna's faithlessness. She had seen his face as he passed under her window, and it was the face of a blithe man who had not heard any evil tidings. It was left to her to tell him; surely, she thought apathetically, that was punishment enough for what she had done.

With her hand on the doorknob, she paused to wonder what she should say when he asked her why she had not told him of Anna's marriage when it occurred – why she had still continued the deception when it had no longer an end to serve. Well, she would tell him the truth – that it was because she could not bear the thought of giving up writing to him. It was a humiliating thing to confess, but that did not matter – nothing mattered now. She opened the door.

Gilbert was standing on the big round door-stone under the red maple – a tall, handsome young fellow with a bronzed face and laughing eyes. His exile had improved him. Alma found time and ability to reflect that she had never known Gilbert was so fine-looking.

He put his arm around her and kissed her cheek in his frank delight at seeing her again. Alma coldly asked him in. Her face was still as pale as when she came downstairs, but a curious little spot of fiery red blossomed out where Gilbert's lips had touched it.

Gilbert followed her into the sitting-room and looked about eagerly.

"When did you come home?" she said slowly. "I did not know you were expected."

"Got homesick, and just came! I wanted to surprise you all," he answered, laughing. "I arrived only a few minutes ago. Just took time to hug my mother, and here I am. Where's Anna?"

The pent-up retribution of two years descended on Alma's head in the last question of Gilbert's. But she did not flinch. She stood straight before him, tall and fair and pale, with the red maple light streaming in through the open door behind her, staining her light house-dress and mellowing the golden sheen of her hair. Gilbert reflected that Alma Williams was really a very handsome girl. These two years had improved her. What splendid big grey eyes she had! He had always wished that Anna's eyes had not been quite so black.

"Anna is not here," said Alma. "She is married."

"Married!"

Gilbert sat down suddenly on a chair and looked at Alma in bewilderment.

"She has been married for a year," said Alma steadily. "She married Charlie Moore of East Exeter, and has been living there ever since."

"Then," said Gilbert, laying hold of the one solid fact that loomed out of the mist of his confused understanding, "why did she keep on writing letters to me after she was married?"

"She never wrote to you at all. It was I that wrote the letters."

Gilbert looked at Alma doubtfully. Was she crazy? There

was something odd about her, now that he noticed, as she stood rigidly there, with that queer red spot on her face, a strange fire in her eyes, and that weird reflection from the maple enveloping her like an immaterial flame.

"I don't understand," he said helplessly.

Still standing there, Alma told the whole story, giving full explanations, but no excuses. She told it clearly and simply, for she had often pictured this scene to herself and thought out what she must say. Her memory worked automatically, and her tongue obeyed it promptly. To herself she seemed like a machine, talking mechanically, while her soul stood on one side and listened.

When she had finished there was a silence lasting perhaps ten seconds. To Alma it seemed like hours. Would Gilbert overwhelm her with angry reproaches, or would he simply rise up and leave her in unutterable contempt? It was the most tragic moment of her life, and her whole personality was strung up to meet it and withstand it.

"Well, they were good letters, anyhow," said Gilbert finally; "interesting letters," he added, as if by way of a meditative afterthought.

It was so anti-climactic that Alma broke into an hysterical giggle, cut short by a sob. She dropped into a chair by the table and flung her hands over her face, laughing and sobbing softly to herself. Gilbert rose and walked to the door, where he stood with his back to her until she regained her self-control. Then he turned and looked down at her quizzically.

Alma's hands lay limply in her lap, and her eyes were cast down, with tears glistening on the long fair lashes. She felt his gaze on her.

"Can you ever forgive me, Gilbert?" she said humbly.

"I don't know that there is much to forgive," he answered. "I have some explanations to make too and, since we're at it, we might as well get them all over and have done with them. Two years ago I did honestly think I was in love with Anna –

at least when I was round where she was. She had a taking way with her. But, somehow, even then, when I wasn't with her she seemed to kind of grow dim and not count for so awful much after all. I used to wish she was more like you – quieter, you know, and not so sparkling. When I parted from her that last night before I went west, I did feel very bad, and she seemed very dear to me, but it was six weeks from that before her – your – letter came, and in that time she seemed to have faded out of my thoughts. Honestly, I wasn't thinking much about her at all. Then came the letter – and it was a splendid one, too. I had never thought that Anna could write a letter like that, and I was as pleased as Punch about it. The letters kept coming, and I kept on looking for them more and more all the time. I fell in love all over again – with the writer of those letters. I thought it was Anna, but since you wrote the letters, it must have been with you, Alma. I thought it was because she was growing more womanly that she could write such letters. That was why I came home. I wanted to get acquainted all over again, before she grew beyond me altogether – I wanted to find the real Anna the letters showed me. I – I – didn't expect this. But I don't care if Anna is married, so long as the girl who wrote those letters isn't. It's you I love, Alma."

He bent down and put his arm about her, laying his cheek against hers. The little red spot where his kiss had fallen was now quite drowned out in the colour that rushed over her face.

"If you'll marry me, Alma, I'll forgive you," he said.

A little smile escaped from the duress of Alma's lips and twitched her dimples.

"I'm willing to do anything that will win your forgiveness, Gilbert," she said meekly.

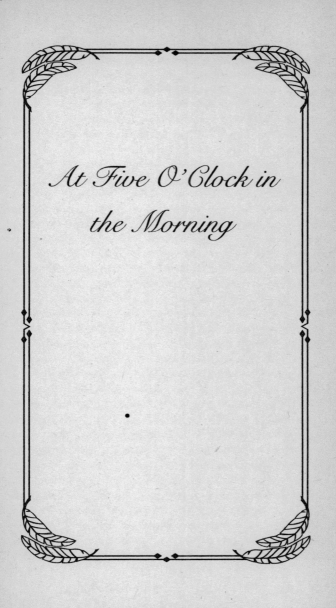

At Five O'Clock in
the Morning

ATE, in the guise of Mrs. Emory dropping a milk-can on the platform under his open window, awakened Murray that morning. Had not Mrs. Emory dropped that can, he would have slumbered peacefully until his usual hour for rising – a late one, be it admitted, for of all the boarders at Sweetbriar Cottage Murray was the most irregular in his habits.

"When a young man," Mrs. Emory was wont to remark sagely and a trifle severely, "prowls about that pond half of the night, a-chasing of things what he calls 'moonlight effecks,' it ain't to be wondered at that he's sleepy in the morning. And it ain't the convenientest thing, nuther and noways, to keep the breakfast table set till the farm folks are thinking of dinner. But them artist men are not like other people, say what you will, and allowance has to be made for them. And I must say that I likes him real well and approves of him every other way."

If Murray had slept late that morning – well, he shudders yet over that "if." But aforesaid Fate saw to it that he woke when the hour of destiny and the milk-can struck, and having awakened he found he could not go to sleep again. It suddenly occurred to him that he had never seen a sunrise on the pond. Doubtless it would be very lovely down there in those dewy meadows at such a primitive hour; he decided to get up and see what the world looked like in the young daylight.

He scowled at a letter lying on his dressing table and thrust it into his pocket that it might be out of sight. He had written it the night before and the writing of it was going to cost him several things – a prospective million among others. So it is hardly to be wondered at if the sight of it did not reconcile him to the joys of early rising.

"Dear life and heart!" exclaimed Mrs. Emory, pausing in the act of scalding a milk-can when Murray emerged from a side door. "What on earth is the matter, Mr. Murray? You ain't sick now, surely? I told you them pond fogs was p'isen after night! If you've gone and got –"

"Nothing is the matter, dear lady," interrupted Murray, "and I haven't gone and got anything except an acute attack of early rising which is not in the least likely to become chronic. But at what hour of the night do you get up, you wonderful woman? Or rather do you ever go to bed at all? Here is the sun only beginning to rise and – positively yes, you have all your cows milked."

Mrs. Emory purred with delight.

"Folks as has fourteen cows to milk has to rise betimes," she answered with proud humility. "Laws, I don't complain – I've lots of help with the milking. How Mrs. Palmer manages, I really cannot comperhend – or rather, how she has managed. I suppose she'll be all right now since her niece came last night. I saw her posting to the pond pasture not ten minutes ago. She'll have to milk all them seven cows herself. But dear life and heart! Here I be palavering away and not a bite of breakfast ready for you!"

"I don't want any breakfast until the regular time for it," assured Murray. "I'm going down to the pond to see the sun rise."

"Now don't you go and get caught in the ma'sh," anxiously called Mrs. Emory, as she never failed to do when she saw him starting for the pond. Nobody ever had got caught in the marsh, but Mrs. Emory lived in a chronic state of fear lest someone should.

"And if you once got stuck in that black mud you'd be sucked right down and never seen or heard tell of again till the day of judgment, like Adam Palmer's cow," she was wont to warn her boarders.

Murray sought his favourite spot for pond dreaming – a bloomy corner of the pasture that ran down into the blue water, with a clump of leafy maples on the left. He was very glad he had risen early. A miracle was being worked before his very eyes. The world was in a flush and tremor of maiden loveliness, instinct with all the marvellous fleeting charm of girlhood and spring and young morning. Overhead the sky was a vast high-sprung arch of unstained crystal. Down over the sand dunes, where the pond ran out into the sea, was a great arc of primrose smitten through with auroral crimson-ings. Beneath it the pond waters shimmered with a hundred fairy hues, but just before him they were clear as a flawless mirror. The fields around him glistened with dews, and a little wandering wind, blowing lightly from some bourne in the hills, strayed down over the slopes, bringing with it an unimaginable odour and freshness, and fluttered over the pond, leaving a little path of dancing silver ripples across the mirror-glory of the water. Birds were singing in the beech woods over on Orchard Knob Farm, answering to each other from shore to shore, until the very air was tremulous with the elfin music of this wonderful midsummer dawn.

"I will get up at sunrise every morning of my life here-after," exclaimed Murray rapturously, not meaning a syllable of it, but devoutly believing he did.

Just as the fiery disc of the sun peered over the sand dunes Murray heard music that was not of the birds. It was a girl's voice singing beyond the maples to his left – a clear sweet voice, blithely trilling out the old-fashioned song, "Five O'Clock in the Morning."

"Mrs. Palmer's niece!"

Murray sprang to his feet and tiptoed cautiously through the maples. He had heard so much from Mrs. Palmer about her niece that he felt reasonably well acquainted with her. Moreover, Mrs. Palmer had assured him that Mollie was a very pretty girl. Now a pretty girl milking cows at sunrise in the meadows sounded well.

Mrs. Palmer had not over-rated her niece's beauty. Murray said so to himself with a little whistle of amazement as he leaned unseen on the pasture fence and looked at the girl who was milking a placid Jersey less than ten yards away from him. Murray's artistic instinct responded to the whole scene with a thrill of satisfaction.

He could see only her profile, but that was perfect, and the colouring of the oval cheek and the beautiful curve of the chin were something to adore. Her hair, ruffled into lovable little ringlets by the morning wind, was coiled in glistening chestnut masses high on her bare head, and her arms, bare to the elbow, were as white as marble. Presently she began to sing again, and this time Murray joined in. She half rose from her milking stool and cast a startled glance at the maples. Then she dropped back again and began to milk determinedly, but Murray could have sworn that he saw a demure smile hovering about her lips. That, and the revelation of her full face, decided him. He sprang over the fence and sauntered across the intervening space of lush clover blossoms.

"Good morning," he said coolly. He had forgotten her other name, and it did not matter; at five o'clock in the morning people who met in dewy clover fields might disregard the conventionalities. "Isn't it rather a large contract for you to be milking seven cows all alone? May I help you?"

Mollie looked up at him over her shoulder. She had glorious grey eyes. Her face was serene and undisturbed. "Can you milk?" she asked.

"Unlikely as it may seem, I can," said Murray. "I have never confessed it to Mrs. Emory, because I was afraid she would inveigle me into milking her fourteen cows. But I don't mind helping you. I learned to milk when I was a shaver on my vacations at a grandfatherly farm. May I have that extra pail?"

Murray captured a milking stool and rounded up another Jersey. Before sitting down he seemed struck with an idea.

"My name is Arnold Murray. I board at Sweetbriar Cottage, next farm to Orchard Knob. That makes us near neighbours."

"I suppose it does," said Mollie.

Murray mentally decided that her voice was the sweetest he had ever heard. He was glad he had arranged his cow at such an angle that he could study her profile. It was amazing that Mrs. Palmer's niece should have such a profile. It looked as if centuries of fine breeding were responsible for it.

"What a morning!" he said enthusiastically. "It harks back to the days when earth was young. They must have had just such mornings as this in Eden."

"Do you always get up so early?" asked Mollie practically.

"Always," said Murray without a blush. Then – "But no, that is a fib, and I cannot tell fibs to you. The truth is your tribute. I never get up early. It was fate that roused me and brought me here this morning. The morning is a miracle – and you. I might suppose you were born of the sunrise, if Mrs. Palmer hadn't told me all about you."

"What did she tell you about me?" asked Mollie, changing cows. Murray discovered that she was tall and that the big blue print apron shrouded a singularly graceful figure.

"She said you were the best-looking girl in Bruce county. I have seen very few of the girls in Bruce county, but I know she is right."

"That compliment is not nearly so pretty as the sunrise one," said Mollie reflectively. "Mrs. Palmer has told me things about you," she added.

"Curiosity knows no gender," hinted Murray.

"She said you were good-looking and lazy and different from other people."

"All compliments," said Murray in a gratified tone. "Lazy?"

"Certainly. Laziness is a virtue in these strenuous days. I was not born with it, but I have painstakingly acquired it, and I am proud of my success. I have time to enjoy life."

"I think that I like you," said Mollie.

"You have the merit of being able to enter into a situation," he assured her.

When the last Jersey was milked they carried the pails down to the spring where the creamers were sunk and strained the milk into them. Murray washed the pails and Mollie wiped them and set them in a gleaming row on the shelf under a big maple.

"Thank you," she said.

"You are not going yet," said Murray resolutely. "The time I saved you in milking three cows belongs to me. We will spend it in a walk along the pond shore. I will show you a path I have discovered under the beeches. It is just wide enough for two. Come."

He took her hand and drew her through the copse into a green lane, where the ferns grew thickly on either side and the pond waters plashed dreamily below them. He kept her hand in his as they went down the path, and she did not try to withdraw it. About them was the great, pure silence of the morning, faintly threaded with caressing sounds – croon of birds, gurgle of waters, sough of wind. The spirit of youth and love hovered over them and they spoke no word.

When they finally came out on a little green nook swimming in early sunshine and arched over by maples, with the wide shimmer of the pond before it and the gold dust of blossoms over the grass, the girl drew a long breath of delight.

"It is a morning left over from Eden, isn't it?" said Murray.

"Yes," said Mollie softly.

Murray bent toward her. "You are Eve," he said. "You are the only woman in the world – for me. Adam must have told Eve just what he thought about her the first time he saw her. There were no conventionalities in Eden – and people could not have taken long to make up their minds. We are in Eden just now. One can say what he thinks in Eden without being ridiculous. You are divinely fair, Eve. Your eyes are stars of the morning – your cheek has the flush it stole from the sunrise – your lips are redder than the roses of paradise. And I love you, Eve."

Mollie lowered her eyes and the long fringe of her lashes lay in a burnished semi-circle on her cheek.

"I think," she said slowly, "that it must have been very delightful in Eden. But we are not really there, you know – we are only playing that we are. And it is time for me to go back. I must get the breakfast – that sounds too prosaic for paradise."

Murray bent still closer.

"Before we remember that we are only playing at paradise, will you kiss me, dear Eve?"

"You are very audacious," said Mollie coldly.

"We are in Eden yet," he urged. "That makes all the difference."

"Well," said Mollie. And Murray kissed her.

They had passed back over the fern path and were in the pasture before either spoke again. Then Murray said, "We have left Eden behind – but we can always return there when we will. And although we were only playing at paradise, I was not playing at love. I meant all I said, Mollie."

"Have you meant it often?" asked Mollie significantly.

"I never meant it – or even played at it – before," he answered. "I did – at one time – contemplate the possibility of playing at it. But that was long ago – as long ago as last night. I am glad to the core of my soul that I decided against it before I met you, dear Eve. I have the letter of decision in my coat pocket this moment. I mean to mail it this afternoon."

"'Curiosity knows no gender,'" quoted Mollie.

"Then, to satisfy your curiosity, I must bore you with some personal history. My parents died when I was a little chap, and my uncle brought me up. He has been immensely good to me, but he is a bit of a tyrant. Recently he picked out a wife for me – the daughter of an old sweetheart of his. I have never even seen her. But she has arrived in town on a visit to some relatives there. Uncle Dick wrote to me to return home at once and pay my court to the lady. I protested. He wrote again – a letter, short and the reverse of sweet. If I refused to do my best to win Miss Mannering he would disown me – never speak to me again – cut me off with a quarter. Uncle always means what he says – that is one of our family traits, you understand. I spent some miserable, undecided days. It was not the threat of disinheritance that worried me, although when you have been brought up to regard yourself as a prospective millionaire it is rather difficult to adjust your vision to a pauper focus. But it was the thought of alienating Uncle Dick. I love the dear, determined old chap like a father. But last night my guardian angel was with me and I decided to remain my own man. So I wrote to Uncle Dick, respectfully but firmly declining to become a candidate for Miss Mannering's hand."

"But you have never seen her," said Mollie. "She may be – almost – charming."

"'If she be not fair to me, what care I how fair she be?'" quoted Murray. "As you say, she may be – almost charming; but she is not Eve. She is merely one of a million other women, as far as I am concerned. Don't let's talk of her. Let us talk only of ourselves – there is nothing else that is half so interesting."

"And will your uncle really cast you off?" asked Mollie.

"Not a doubt of it."

"What will you do?"

"Work, dear Eve. My carefully acquired laziness must be thrown to the winds and I shall work. That is the rule outside of Eden. Don't worry. I've painted pictures that have actually been sold. I'll make a living for us somehow."

"Us?"

"Of course. You are engaged to me."

"I am not," said Mollie indignantly.

"Mollie! Mollie! After that kiss! Fie, fie!"

"You are very absurd," said Mollie. "But your absurdity

has been amusing. I have – yes, positively – I have enjoyed your Eden comedy. But now you must not come any further with me. My aunt might not approve. Here is my path to Orchard Knob farmhouse. There, I presume, is yours to Sweetbriar Cottage. Good morning."

"I am coming over to see you this afternoon," said Murray coolly. "But you needn't be afraid. I will not tell tales out of Eden. I will be a hypocrite and pretend to Mrs. Palmer that we have never met before. But you and I will know and remember. Now, you may go. I reserve to myself the privilege of standing here and watching you out of sight."

THAT AFTERNOON Murray strolled over to Orchard Knob, going into the kitchen without knocking as was the habit in that free and easy world. Mrs. Palmer was lying on the lounge with a pungent handkerchief bound about her head, but keeping a vigilant eye on a very pretty, very plump brown-eyed girl who was stirring a kettleful of cherry preserve on the range.

"Good afternoon, Mrs. Palmer," said Murray, wondering where Mollie was. "I'm sorry to see that you look something like an invalid."

"I've a raging, ramping headache," said Mrs. Palmer solemnly. "I had it all night and I'm good for nothing. Mollie, you'd better take them cherries off. Mr. Murray, this is my niece, Mollie Booth."

"What?" said Murray explosively.

"Miss Mollie Booth," repeated Mrs. Palmer in a louder tone.

Murray regained outward self-control and bowed to the blushing Mollie.

"And what about Eve?" he thought helplessly. "Who – what was she? Did I dream her? Was she a phantom of delight? No, no, phantoms don't milk cows. She was flesh and blood. No chilly nymph exhaling from the mists of the marsh could have given a kiss like that."

"Mollie has come to stay the rest of the summer with me," said Mrs. Palmer. "I hope to goodness my tribulations with hired girls is over at last. They have made a wreck of me."

Murray rapidly reflected. This development, he decided, released him from his promise to tell no tales. "I met a young lady down in the pond pasture this morning," he said deliberately. "I talked with her for a few minutes. I supposed her to be your niece. Who was she?"

"Oh, that was Miss Mannering," said Mrs. Palmer.

"What?" said Murray again.

"Mannering – Dora Mannering," said Mrs. Palmer loudly, wondering if Mr. Murray were losing his hearing. "She came here last night just to see me. I haven't seen her since she was a child of twelve. I used to be her nurse before I was married. I was that proud to think she thought it worth her while to look me up. And, mind you, this morning, when she found me crippled with headache and not able to do a hand's turn, that girl, Mr. Murray, went and milked seven cows" – "only four," murmured Murray, but Mrs. Palmer did not hear him – "for me. Couldn't prevent her. She said she had learned to milk for fun one summer when she was in the country, and she did it. And then she got breakfast for the men – Mollie didn't come till the ten o'clock train. Miss Mannering is as capable as if she had been riz on a farm."

"Where is she now?" demanded Murray.

"Oh, she's gone."

"What?"

"Gone," shouted Mrs. Palmer, "gone. She left on the train Mollie come on. Gracious me, has the man gone crazy? He hasn't seemed like himself at all this afternoon."

Murray had bolted madly out of the house and was striding down the lane.

Blind fool – unspeakable idiot that he had been! To take her for Mrs. Palmer's niece – that peerless creature with the calm acceptance of any situation, which marked the woman

of the world, with the fine appreciation and quickness of rep-
artee that spoke of generations of culture – to imagine that
she could be Mollie Booth! He had been blind, besottedly
blind. And now he had lost her! She would never forgive him;
she had gone without a word or sign.

As he reached the last curve of the lane where it looped
about the apple trees, a plump figure came flying down the
orchard slope.

"Mr. Murray, Mr. Murray," Mollie Booth called breath-
lessly. "Will you please come here just a minute?"

Murray crossed over to the paling rather grumpily. He did
not want to talk with Mollie Booth just then. Confound it,
what did the girl want? Why was she looking so mysterious?

Mollie produced a little square grey envelope from some
feminine hiding place and handed it over the paling.

"She give me this at the station – Miss Mannering did,"
she gasped, "and asked me to give it to you without letting
Aunt Emily Jane see. I couldn't get a chanst when you was
in, but as soon as you went I slipped out by the porch door
and followed you. You went so fast I near died trying to head
you off."

"You dear little soul," said Murray, suddenly radiant. "It is
too bad you have had to put yourself so out of breath on my
account. But I am immensely obliged to you. The next time
your young man wants a trusty private messenger just refer
him to me."

"Git away with you," giggled Mollie. "I must hurry back
'fore Aunt Emily Jane gits wind I'm gone. I hope there's good
news in your girl's letter. My, but didn't you look flat when
Aunt said she'd went!"

Murray beamed at her idiotically. When she had vanished
among the trees he opened his letter.

"Dear Mr. Murray," it ran, "your unblushing audacity
of the morning deserves some punishment. I hereby

punish you by prompt departure from Orchard Knob. Yet I do not dislike audacity, at some times, in some places, in some people. It is only from a sense of duty that I punish it in this case. And it was really pleasant in Eden. If you do not mail that letter, and if you still persist in your very absurd interpretation of the meaning of Eve's kiss, we may meet again in town. Until then I remain,

"Very sincerely yours,

"Dora Lynne Mannering."

Murray kissed the grey letter and put it tenderly away in his pocket. Then he took his letter to his uncle and tore it into tiny fragments. Finally he looked at his watch.

"If I hurry, I can catch the afternoon train to town," he said.

The Letters

UST before the letter was brought to me that evening I was watching the red November sunset from the library window. It was a stormy, unrestful sunset, gleaming angrily through the dark fir boughs that were now and again tossed suddenly and distressfully in a fitful gust of wind. Below, in the garden, it was quite dark, and I could only see dimly the dead leaves that were whirling and dancing uncannily over the roseless paths. The poor dead leaves – yet not quite dead! There was still enough unquiet life left in them to make them restless and forlorn. They hearkened yet to every call of the wind, who cared for them no longer but only played freakishly with them and broke their rest. I felt sorry for the leaves as I watched them in that dull, weird twilight, and angry – in a petulant fashion that almost made me laugh – with the wind that would not leave them in peace. Why should they – and I – be vexed with these transient breaths of desire for a life that had passed us by?

I was in the grip of a bitter loneliness that evening – so bitter and so insistent that I felt I could not face the future at all, even with such poor fragments of courage as I had gathered about me after Father's death, hoping that they would, at least, suffice for my endurance, if not for my content. But now they fell away from me at sight of the emptiness of life.

The emptiness! Ah, it was from that I shrank. I could have faced pain and anxiety and heartbreak undauntedly, but I could not face that terrible, yawning, barren emptiness. I put my hands over my eyes to shut it out, but it pressed in upon my consciousness insistently, and would not be ignored longer.

The moment when a woman realizes that she has nothing to live for – neither love nor purpose nor duty – holds for her the bitterness of death. She is a brave woman indeed who can look upon such a prospect unquailingly, and I was not brave. I was weak and timid. Had not Father often laughed mockingly at me because of it?

It was three weeks since Father had died – my proud, handsome, unrelenting old father, whom I had loved so intensely and who had never loved me. I had always accepted this fact unresentfully and unquestioningly, but it had steeped my whole life in its tincture of bitterness. Father had never forgiven me for two things. I had cost my mother's life and I was not a son to perpetuate the old name and carry on the family feud with the Frasers.

I was a very lonely child, with no playmates or companions of any sort, and my girlhood was lonelier still. The only passion in my life was my love for my father. I would have done and suffered anything to win his affection in return. But all I ever did win was an amused tolerance – and I was grateful for that – almost content. It was much to have something to love and be permitted to love it.

If I had been a beautiful and spirited girl I think Father might have loved me, but I was neither. At first I did not think or care about my lack of beauty; then one day I was alone in the beech wood; I was trying to disentangle my skirt which had caught on some thorny underbrush. A young man came around the curve of the path and, seeing my predicament, bent with murmured apology to help me. He had to kneel to do it, and I saw a ray of sunshine falling through the beeches above us strike like a lance of light athwart the thick brown hair that pushed out from under his cap. Before I thought I put out my hand and touched it softly, then I blushed crimson with shame over what I had done. But he did not know – he never knew.

When he had released my dress he rose and our eyes met for a moment as I timidly thanked him. I saw that he was good to look upon – tall and straight, with broad, stalwart shoulders and a dark, clean-cut face. He had a firm, sensitive mouth and kindly, pleasant, dark blue eyes. I never quite forgot the look in those eyes. It made my heart beat strangely, but it was only for a moment, and the next he had lifted his cap and passed on.

As I went homeward I wondered who he might be. He must be a stranger, I thought – probably a visitor in some of our few neighbouring families. I wondered too if I should meet him again, and found the thought very pleasant.

I knew few men and they were all old, like Father, or at least elderly. They were the only people who ever came to our house, and they either teased me or overlooked me. None of them was at all like this young man I had met in the beech wood, nor ever could have been, I thought.

When I reached home I stopped before the big mirror that hung in the hall and did what I had never done before in my life – looked at myself very scrutinizingly and wondered if I had any beauty. I could only sorrowfully conclude that I had not – I was so slight and pale, and the thick black hair and dark eyes that might have been pretty in another woman seemed only to accentuate the lack of spirit and regularity in my features. I was still standing there, gazing wistfully at my mirrored face with a strange sinking of spirit, when Father came through the hall, his riding whip in his hand. Seeing me, he laughed.

"Don't waste your time gazing into mirrors, Isobel," he said carelessly. "That might have been excusable in former ladies of Shirley whose beauty might pardon and even adorn vanity, but with you it is only absurd. The needle and the cookbook are all that you need concern yourself with."

I was accustomed to such speeches from him, but they had never hurt me so cruelly before. At that moment I would have given all the world only to be beautiful.

The next Sunday I looked across the church, and in the Fraser pew I saw the young man I had met in the wood. He was looking at me with his arms folded over his breast and on his brow a little frown that seemed somehow indicative of pain and surprise. I felt a miserable sense of disappointment. If he were the Frasers' guest I could not expect to meet him again. Father hated the Frasers; all the Shirleys hated them; it was an old feud, bitter and lasting, that had been as much our inheritance for generations as land and money. The only thing Father had ever taken pains to teach me was detestation of the Frasers and all their works. I accepted this as I accepted all the other traditions of my race. I thought it did not matter much. The Frasers were not likely to come my way, and hatred was a good satisfying passion in the lack of all else. I think I rather took a pride in hating them as became my blood.

I did not look at the Fraser pew again, but outside, under the elms, we met him, standing in the dappling light and shadow. He looked very handsome and a little sad. I could not help glancing back over my shoulder as Father and I walked to the gate, and I saw him looking after us with that little frown which again made me think something had hurt him. I liked better the smile he had worn in the beech wood, but I had an odd liking for the frown too, and I think I had a foolish longing to go back to him, put up my fingers and smooth it away.

"So Alan Fraser has come home," said my father.

"Alan Fraser?" I repeated, with a strange, horrible feeling of coldness and chill coming over me like a shadow on a bright day. Alan Fraser, the son of old Malcolm Fraser of Glenellyn! The son of our enemy! He had been living since childhood with his dead mother's people, so much I knew. And this was he! Something stung and smarted in my eyes. I think the sting and smart might have turned to tears if Father had not been looking down at me.

"Yes. Didn't you see him in his father's pew? But I forgot. You are too demure to be looking at the young men in preaching – or out of it, Isobel. You are a model young woman. Odd that the men never like the model young women! Curse old Malcolm Fraser! What right has he to have a son like that when I have nothing but a puling girl? Remember, Isobel, that if you ever meet that young man you are not to speak to or look at him, or even intimate that you are aware of his existence. He is your enemy and the enemy of your race. You will show him that you realize this."

Of course that ended it all – though just what there had been to end would have been hard to say. Not long afterwards I met Alan Fraser again, when I was out for a canter on my mare. He was strolling through the beech wood with a couple of big collies, and he stopped short as I drew near. I had to do it – Father had decreed – my Shirley pride demanded – that I should do it. I looked him unseeingly in the face, struck my mare a blow with my whip, and dashed past him. I even felt angry, I think, that a Fraser should have the power to make me feel so badly in doing my duty.

After that I had forgotten. There was nothing to make me remember, for I never met Alan Fraser again. The years slipped by, one by one, so like each other in their colourlessness that I forgot to take account of them. I only knew that I grew older and that it did not matter since there was nobody to care. One day they brought Father in, white-lipped and groaning. His mare had thrown him, and he was never to walk again, although he lived for five years. Those five years had been the happiest of my life. For the first time I was necessary to someone – there was something for me to do which nobody else could do so well. I was Father's nurse and companion, and I found my pleasure in tending him and amusing him, soothing his hours of pain and brightening his hours of ease. People said I "did my duty" toward him. I had never liked that word "duty," since the day I had ridden past Alan Fraser in the beech wood. I could not connect it with what I did for Father. It was my delight because I loved him. I did not mind the moods and the irritable outbursts that drove others from him.

But now he was dead, and I sat in the sullen dusk, wishing that I need not go on with life either. The loneliness of the big echoing house weighed on my spirit. I was solitary, without companionship. I looked out on the outside world where the only sign of human habitation visible to my eyes was the light twinkling out from the library window of Glenellyn on the dark fir hill two miles away. By that light I knew Alan Fraser must have returned from his long sojourn abroad, for it only shone when he was at Glenellyn. He still lived there, something of a hermit, people said; he had never married, and he cared nothing for society. His companions were books and dogs and horses; he was given to scientific researches and wrote much for the reviews; he travelled a great deal. So much I knew in a vague way. I even saw him occasionally in church, and never thought the years had changed him much, save that his face was sadder and sterner than of old and his hair had become iron-grey. People said that he had inherited and cherished the old hatred of the Shirleys – that he was very bitter against us. I believed it. He had the face of a good hater – or lover – a man who could play with no emotion but must take it in all earnestness and intensity.

When it was quite dark the housekeeper brought in the lights and handed me a letter which, she said, a man had just brought up from the village post office. I looked at it curiously before I opened it, wondering from whom it was. It was post-marked from a city several miles away, and the firm, decided, rather peculiar handwriting was strange to me. I had no correspondents. After Father's death I had received a few perfunctory notes of condolence from distant relatives and family friends. They had hurt me cruelly, for they seemed to exhale a subtle spirit of congratulation on my being released from a long and unpleasant martyrdom of attendance on an invalid, that quite overrode the decorous phrases of conventional sympathy in which they were expressed. I hated those letters for their implied injustice. I was not thankful for my "release." I missed Father miserably and longed passionately for the very tasks and vigils that had evoked their pity.

This letter did not seem like one of those. I opened it and took out some stiff, blackly written sheets. They were undated and, turning to the last, I saw that they were unsigned. With a not unpleasant tingling of interest I sat down by my desk to read. The letter began abruptly:

You will not know by whom this is written. Do not seek to know – now or ever. It is only from behind the veil of your ignorance of my identity that I can ever write to you fully and freely as I wish to write – can say what I wish to say in words denied to a formal and conventional expression of sympathy. Dear lady, let me say to you thus what is in my heart.

I know what your sorrow is, and I think I know what your loneliness must be – the sorrow of a broken tie, the loneliness of a life thrown emptily back on itself. I know how you loved your father – how you must have loved him if those eyes and brow and mouth speak truth; for they tell of a nature divinely rich and deep, giving of its wealth and tenderness ungrudgingly to those who are so happy as to be the objects of its affection. To such a nature bereavement must bring a depth and an agony of grief unknown to shallower souls.

I know what your father's helplessness and need of you meant to you. I know that now life must seem to you a broken and embittered thing and, knowing this, I venture to send this greeting across the gulf of strangerhood between us, telling you that my understanding sympathy is fully and freely yours, and bidding you take heart for the future, which now, it may be, looks so heartless and hopeless to you.

Believe me, dear lady, it will be neither. Courage will come to you with the kind days. You will find noble tasks to do, beautiful and gracious duties waiting along your path. The pain and suffering of the world never dies, and while it lives there will be work for such as you to do, and in the doing of it you will find comfort and strength and the highest joy of living. I believe in you. I believe you will make of your life a beautiful and worthy thing. I give you Godspeed for the years to come. Out of my own loneliness I, an unknown friend, who has never clasped your hand, send this message to you. I understand – I have always understood – and I say to you: "Be of good cheer."

To say that this strange letter was a mystery to me seems an inadequate way of stating the matter. I was completely bewildered, nor could I even guess who the writer might be, think and ponder as I might.

The letter itself implied that the writer was a stranger. The handwriting was evidently that of a man, and I knew no man who could or would have sent such a letter to me.

The very mystery stung me to interest. As for the letter itself, it brought me an uplift of hope and inspiration such as I would not have believed possible an hour earlier. It rang so truly and sincerely, and the mere thought that somewhere I had a friend who cared enough to write it, even in such odd fashion, was so sweet that I was half ashamed of the difference it made in my outlook. Sitting there, I took courage and made a compact with myself that I would justify the writer's faith in me – that I would take up my life as something to be worthily lived for all good, to the disregard of my own selfish sorrow and shrinking. I would seek for something to do – for interests which would bind me to my fellow-creatures – for tasks which would lessen the pains and perils of humankind. An hour before, this would not have seemed to me possible; now it seemed the right and natural thing to do.

A week later another letter came. I welcomed it with an eagerness which I feared was almost childish. It was a much longer letter than the first and was written in quite a different strain. There was no apology for or explanation of the motive for writing. It was as if the letter were merely one of a permitted and established correspondence between old friends. It began with a witty, sparkling review of a new book the writer had just read, and passed from this to crisp comments on the great events, political, scientific, artistic, of the day. The whole letter was pungent, interesting, delightful – an impersonal essay on a dozen vital topics of life and thought. Only at the end was a personal note struck.

"Are you interested in these things?" ran the last paragraph. "In what is being done and suffered and attained in the great busy world? I think you must be – for I have seen you and read what is written in your face. I believe you care for these things as I do – that your being thrills to the 'still, sad music of humanity' – that the songs of the poets I love find an echo in your spirit and the aspirations of all struggling souls a sympathy in your heart. Believing this, I have written freely to you, taking a keen pleasure in thus revealing my thoughts and visions to one who will understand. For I too am friendless, in the sense of one standing alone, shut out from the sweet, intimate communion of feeling and opinion that may be held with the heart's friends. Shall you have read this as a friend, I wonder – a candid, uncritical, understanding friend? Let me hope it, dear lady."

I was expecting the third letter when it came – but not until it did come did I realize what my disappointment would have been if it had not. After that every week brought me a letter; soon those letters were the greatest interest in my life. I had given up all attempts to solve the mystery of their coming and was content to enjoy them for themselves alone. From week to week I looked forward to them with an eagerness that I would hardly confess, even to myself.

And such letters as they were, growing longer and fuller and freer as time went on – such wise, witty, brilliant, pungent letters, stimulating all my torpid life into tingling zest! I had begun to look abroad in my small world for worthy work and found plenty to do. My unknown friend evidently kept track of my expanding efforts, for he commented and criticized, encouraged and advised freely. There was a humour in his letters that I liked; it leavened them with its sanity and reacted on me most wholesomely, counteracting many of the morbid tendencies and influences of my life. I found myself striving to live up to the writer's ideal of philosophy and ambition, as pictured, often unconsciously, in his letters.

They were an intellectual stimulant as well. To understand them fully I found it necessary to acquaint myself thoroughly with the literature and art, the science and the politics they touched upon. After every letter there was something new for me to hunt out and learn and assimilate, until my old narrow mental attitude had so broadened and deepened, sweeping out into circles of thought I had never known or imagined, that I hardly knew myself.

They had been coming for a year before I began to reply to them. I had often wished to do so – there were so many things I wanted to say and discuss, but it seemed foolish to write letters that could not be sent. One day a letter came that kindled my imagination and stirred my heart and soul so deeply that they insistently demanded answering expression. I sat down at my desk and wrote a full reply to it. Safe in the belief that the mysterious friend to whom it was written would never see it, I wrote with a perfect freedom and a total lack of self-consciousness that I could never have attained otherwise. The writing of that letter gave me a pleasure second only to that which the reading of his brought. For the first time I discovered the delight of revealing my thought unhindered by the conventions. Also, I understood better why the writer of those letters had written them. Doubtless he had enjoyed doing so and was not impelled thereto simply by a purely philanthropic wish to help me.

When my letter was finished I sealed it up and locked it away in my desk with a smile at my middle-aged folly. What, I wondered, would all my sedate, serious friends, my associates of mission and hospital committees think if they knew. Well, everybody has, or should have, a pet nonsense in her life. I did not think mine was any sillier than some others I knew, and to myself I admitted that it was very sweet. I knew if those letters ceased to come all savour would go out of my life.

After that I wrote a reply to every letter I received and kept them all locked up together. It was delightful. I wrote out all my doings and perplexities and hopes and plans and wishes – yes, and my dreams. The secret romance of it all made me look on existence with joyous, contented eyes.

Gradually a change crept over the letters I received. Without ever affording the slightest clue to the identity of their writer they grew more intimate and personal. A subtle, caressing note of tenderness breathed from them and thrilled my heart curiously. I felt as if I were being drawn into the writer's life, admitted into the most sacred recesses of his thoughts and feelings. Yet it was all done so subtly, so delicately, that I was unconscious of the change until I discovered it in reading over the older letters and comparing them with the later ones.

Finally a letter came – my first love letter, and surely never was a love letter received under stranger circumstances. It began abruptly as all the letters had begun, plunging into the middle of the writer's strain of thought without any preface. The first words drove the blood to my heart and then sent it flying hotly all over my face.

I love you. I must say it at last. Have you not guessed it before? It has trembled on my pen in every line I have written to you – yet I have never dared to shape it into words before. I know not how I dare now. I only know that I must. What a delight to write it out and know that you will read it. Tonight the mood is on me to tell it to you recklessly and lavishly, never pausing to stint or weigh words. Sweetheart, I love you – love you – love you – dear true, faithful woman soul, I love you with all the heart of a man.

Ever since I first saw you I have loved you. I can never come to tell you so in spoken words; I can only love you from afar and tell my love under the guise of impersonal friendship. It matters not to you, but it matters more than all else in life to me. I am glad that I love you, dear – glad, glad, glad.

There was much more, for it was a long letter. When I had read it I buried my burning face in my hands, trembling with happiness. This strange confession of love meant so much to me; my heart leaped forth to meet it with answering love. What mattered it that we could never meet – that I could not even guess who my lover was? Somewhere in the world was a love that was mine alone and mine wholly and mine forever. What mattered his name or his station, or the mysterious barrier between us? Spirit leaped to spirit unhindered over the fettering bounds of matter and time. I loved and was beloved. Nothing else mattered.

I wrote my answer to his letter. I wrote it fearlessly and unstintedly. Perhaps I could not have written so freely if the letter were to have been read by him; as it was, I poured out the riches of my love as fully as he had done. I kept nothing back, and across the gulf between us I vowed a faithful and enduring love in response to his.

The next day I went to town on business with my lawyers. Neither of the members of the firm was in when I called, but I was an old client, and one of the clerks showed me into the private office to wait. As I sat down my eyes fell on a folded letter lying on the table beside me. With a shock of surprise I recognized the writing. I could not be mistaken – I should have recognized it anywhere.

The letter was lying by its envelope, so folded that only the middle third of the page was visible. An irresistible impulse swept over me. Before I could reflect that I had no business to touch the letter, that perhaps it was unfair to my unknown friend to seek to discover his identity when he wished to hide it, I had turned the letter over and seen the signature.

I laid it down again and stood up, dizzy, breathless, unseeing. Like a woman in a dream I walked through the outer office and into the street. I must have walked on for blocks before I became conscious of my surroundings. The name I had seen signed to that letter was Alan Fraser!

No doubt the reader has long ago guessed it – has wondered why I had not. The fact remains that I had not. Out of the whole world Alan Fraser was the last man whom I should have suspected to be the writer of those letters – Alan Fraser, my hereditary enemy, who, I had been told, cherished the old feud so faithfully and bitterly, and hated our very name.

And yet I now wondered at my long blindness. No one else could have written those letters – no one but him. I read them over one by one when I reached home and, now that I possessed the key, he revealed himself in every line, expression, thought. And he loved me!

I thought of the old feud and hatred; I thought of my pride and traditions. They seemed like the dust and ashes of outworn things – things to be smiled at and cast aside. I took out all the letters I had written – all except the last one – sealed them up in a parcel and directed it to Alan Fraser. Then, summoning my groom, I bade him ride to Glenellyn with it. His look of amazement almost made me laugh, but after he was gone I felt dizzy and frightened at my own daring.

When the autumn darkness came down I went to my room and dressed as the woman dresses who awaits the one man of all the world. I hardly knew what I hoped or expected, but I was all athrill with a nameless, inexplicable happiness. I admit I looked very eagerly into the mirror when I was done, and I thought that the result was not unpleasing. Beauty had never been mine, but a faint reflection of it came over me in the tremulous flush and excitement of the moment. Then the maid came up to tell me that Alan Fraser was in the library.

I went down with my cold hands tightly clasped behind me. He was standing by the library table, a tall, broad-shouldered man, with the light striking upward on his dark, sensitive face and iron-grey hair. When he saw me he came quickly forward.

"So you know – and you are not angry – your letters told me so much. I have loved you since that day in the beech wood, Isobel – Isobel."

His eyes were kindling into mine. He held my hands in a close, impetuous clasp. His voice was infinitely caressing as he pronounced my name. I had never heard it since Father died – I had never heard it at all so musically and tenderly uttered. My ancestors might have turned in their graves just then – but it mattered not. Living love had driven out dead hatred.

"Isobel," he went on, "there was *one* letter unanswered – the last."

I went to my desk, took out the last letter I had written and gave it to him in silence. While he read it I stood in a shadowy corner and watched him, wondering if life could always be as sweet as this. When he had finished he turned to me and held out his arms. I went to them as a bird to her nest, and with his lips against mine the old feud was blotted out forever.

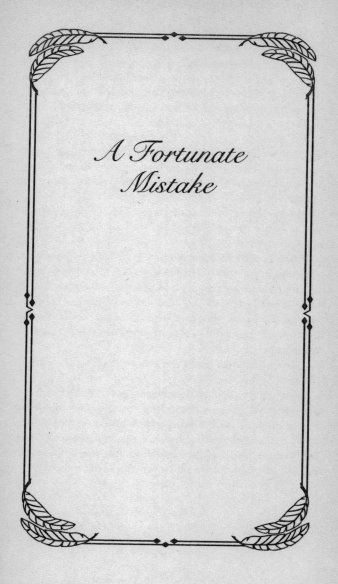

A Fortunate
Mistake

H, dear! oh, dear!" fretted Nan Wallace, twisting herself about uneasily on the sofa in her pretty room. "I never thought before that the days could be so long as they are now."

"Poor you!" said her sister Maude sympathetically. Maude was moving briskly about the room, putting it into the beautiful order that Mother insisted on. It was Nan's week to care for their room, but Nan had sprained her ankle three days ago and could do nothing but lie on the sofa ever since. And very tired of it, too, was wide-awake, active Nan.

"And the picnic this afternoon, too!" she sighed. "I've looked forward to it all summer. And it's a perfect day – and I've got to stay here and nurse this foot."

Nan looked vindictively at the bandaged member, while Maude leaned out of the window to pull a pink climbing rose. As she did so she nodded to someone in the village street below.

"Who is passing?" asked Nan.

"Florrie Hamilton."

"Is she going to the picnic?" asked Nan indifferently.

"No. She wasn't asked. Of course, I don't suppose she expected to be. She knows she isn't in our set. She must feel horribly out of place at school. A lot of the girls say it is ridiculous of her father to send her to Miss Braxton's private school – a factory overseer's daughter."

"She ought to have been asked to the picnic all the same," said Nan shortly. "She is in our class if she isn't in our set. Of course I don't suppose she would have enjoyed herself – or even gone at all, for that matter. She certainly doesn't push herself in among us. One would think she hadn't a tongue in her head."

"She is the best student in the class," admitted Maude, arranging her roses in a vase and putting them on the table at Nan's elbow. "But Patty Morrison and Wilhelmina Patterson had the most to say about the invitations, and they wouldn't have her. There, Nannie dear, aren't those lovely? I'll leave them here to be company for you."

"I'm going to have more company than that," said Nan, thumping her pillow energetically. "I'm not going to mope here alone all the afternoon, with you off having a jolly time at the picnic. Write a little note for me to Florrie Hastings, will you? I'll do as much for you when you sprain your foot."

"What shall I put in it?" said Maude, rummaging out her portfolio obligingly.

"Oh, just ask her if she will come down and cheer a poor invalid up this afternoon. She'll come, I know. And she is such good company. Get Dickie to run right out and mail it."

"I do wonder if Florrie Hamilton will feel hurt over not being asked to the picnic," speculated Maude absently as she slipped her note into an envelope and addressed it.

Florrie Hamilton herself could best have answered that question as she walked along the street in the fresh morning sunshine. She did feel hurt – much more keenly than she would acknowledge even to herself. It was not that she cared about the picnic itself: as Nan Wallace had said, she would not have been likely to enjoy herself if she had gone among a crowd of girls many of whom looked down on her and ignored her. But to be left out when every other girl in the school was invited! Florrie's lip quivered as she thought of it.

"I'll get Father to let me to go to the public school after vacation," she murmured. "I hate going to Miss Braxton's."

Florrie was a newcomer in Winboro. Her father had recently come to take a position in the largest factory of the small town. For this reason Florrie was slighted at school by some of the ruder girls and severely left alone by most of the others. Some, it is true, tried at the start to be friends, but Florrie, too keenly sensitive to the atmosphere around her to respond, was believed to be decidedly dull and mopy. She retreated further and further into herself and was almost as solitary at Miss Braxton's as if she had been on a desert island.

"They don't like me because I am plainly dressed and because my father is not a wealthy man," thought Florrie bitterly. And there was enough truth in this in regard to many of Miss Braxton's girls to make a very uncomfortable state of affairs.

"Here's a letter for you, Flo," said her brother Jack at noon. "Got it at the office on my way home. Who is your swell correspondent?"

Florrie opened the dainty, perfumed note and read it with a face that, puzzled at first, suddenly grew radiant.

"Listen, Jack," she said excitedly.

"Dear Florrie:

"Nan is confined to house, room, and sofa with a sprained foot. As she will be all alone this afternoon, won't you come down and spend it with her? She very much wants you to come – she is so lonesome and thinks you will be just the one to cheer her up.

"Yours cordially,
"Maude Wallace."

"Are you going?" asked Jack.

"Yes – I don't know – I'll think about it," said Florrie absently. Then she hurried upstairs to her room.

"Shall I go?" she thought. "Yes, I will. I dare say Nan has asked me just out of pity because I was not invited to the picnic. But even so it was sweet of her. I've always thought I would like those Wallace girls if I could get really acquainted with them. They've always been nice to me, too – I don't know why I am always so tongue-tied and stupid with them. But I'll go anyway."

That afternoon Mrs. Wallace came into Nan's room.

"Nan, dear, Florrie Hamilton is downstairs asking for you."

"Florrie – Hamilton?"

"Yes. She said something about a note you sent her this morning. Shall I ask her to come up?"

"Yes, of course," said Nan lamely. When her mother had gone out she fell back on her pillows and thought rapidly.

"Florrie Hamilton! Maude must have addressed that note to her by mistake. But she mustn't know it was a mistake – mustn't suspect it. Oh, dear! What shall I ever find to talk to her about? She is so quiet and shy."

Further reflections were cut short by Florrie's entrance. Nan held out her hand with a chummy smile.

"It's good of you to give your afternoon up to visiting a cranky invalid," she said heartily. "You don't know how lonesome I've been since Maude went away. Take off your hat and pick out the nicest chair you can find, and let's be comfy."

Somehow, Nan's frank greeting did away with Florrie's embarrassment and made her feel at home. She sat down in Maude's rocker, then, glancing over to a vase filled with roses, her eyes kindled with pleasure. Seeing this, Nan said, "Aren't they lovely? We Wallaces are very fond of our climbing roses. Our great-grandmother brought the roots out from England with her sixty years ago, and they grow nowhere else in this country."

"I know," said Florrie, with a smile. "I recognized them as soon as I came into the room. They are the same kind of roses as those which grow about Grandmother Hamilton's house in England. I used to love them so."

"In England! Were you ever in England?"

"Oh, yes," laughed Florrie. "And I've been in pretty nearly every other country upon earth – every one that a ship could get to, at least." .

"Why, Florrie Hamilton! Are you in earnest?"

"Indeed, yes. Perhaps you don't know that our 'now-mother,' as Jack says sometimes, is Father's second wife. My own mother died when I was a baby, and my aunt, who had no children of her own, took me to bring up. Her husband was a sea-captain, and she always went on his sea-voyages with him. So I went too. I almost grew up on shipboard. We had delightful times. I never went to school. Auntie had been a teacher before her marriage, and she taught me. Two years ago, when I was fourteen, Father married again, and then he wanted me to go home to him and Jack and our new mother. So I did, although at first I was very sorry to leave Auntie and the dear old ship and all our lovely wanderings."

"Oh, tell me all about them," demanded Nan. "Why, Florrie Hamilton, to think you've never said a word about your wonderful experiences! I love to hear about foreign countries from people who have really been there. Please just talk – and I'll listen and ask questions."

Florrie did talk. I'm not sure whether she or Nan was the more surprised to find that she could talk so well and describe her travels so brightly and humorously. The afternoon passed quickly, and when Florrie went away at dusk, after a dainty tea served up in Nan's room, it was with a cordial invitation to come again soon.

"I've enjoyed your visit so much," said Nan sincerely. "I'm going down to see you as soon as I can walk. But don't wait for that. Let us be good, chummy friends without any ceremony."

When Florrie, with a light heart and a happy smile, had gone, came Maude, sunburned and glowing from her picnic.

"Such a nice time as we had!" she exclaimed. "Wasn't I sorry to think of you cooped up here! Did Florrie come?"

"One Florrie did. Maude, you addressed that note to Florrie Hamilton today instead of Florrie Hastings."

"Nan, surely not! I'm sure –"

"Yes, you did. And she came here. Was I not taken aback at first, Maude!"

"I was thinking about her when I addressed it, and I must have put her name down by mistake. I'm so sorry –"

"You needn't be. I haven't been entertained so charmingly for a long while. Why, Maude, she has travelled almost everywhere – and is so bright and witty when she thaws out. She didn't seem like the same girl at all. She is just perfectly lovely!"

"Well, I'm glad you had such a nice time together. Do you know, some of the girls were very much vexed because she wasn't asked to the picnic. They said that it was sheer rudeness not to ask her, and that it reflected on us all, even if Patty and Wilhelmina were responsible for it. I'm afraid we girls at Miss Braxton's have been getting snobbish, and some of us are beginning to find it out and be ashamed of it."

"Just wait until school opens," said Nan – vaguely enough, it would seem. But Maude understood.

However, they did not have to wait until school opened. Long before that time Winboro girlhood discovered that the Wallace girls were taking Florrie Hamilton into their lives. If the Wallace girls liked her, there must be something in the girl more than was at first thought – thus more than one of Miss Braxton's girls reasoned. And gradually the other girls found, as Nan had found, that Florrie was full of fun and an all-round good companion when drawn out of her diffidence. When Miss Braxton's school reopened Florrie was the class favourite. Between her and Nan Wallace a beautiful and helpful friendship had been formed which was to grow and deepen through their whole lives.

"And all because Maude in a fit of abstraction wrote 'Hamilton' for 'Hastings,'" said Nan to herself one day. But that is something Florrie Hamilton will never know.

The Growing Up of

Cornelia

ANUARY First.

Aunt Jemima gave me this diary for a Christmas present. It's just the sort of gift a person named Jemima would be likely to make.

I can't imagine why Aunt Jemima thought I should like a diary. Probably she didn't think about it at all. I suppose it happened to be the first thing she saw when she started out to do her Christmas duty by me, and so she bought it. I'm sure I'm the last girl in the world to keep a diary. I'm not a bit sentimental and I never have time for soul outpourings. It's jollier to be out skating or snowshoeing or just tramping around. And besides, nothing ever happens to me worth writing in a diary.

Still, since Aunt Jemima gave it to me, I'm going to get the good out of it. I don't believe in wasting even a diary. Father . . . it would be easier to write "Dad," but Dad sounds disrespectful in a diary . . . says I have a streak of old Grandmother Marshall's economical nature in me. So I'm going to write in this book whenever I have anything that might, by any stretch of imagination, be supposed worth while.

Jen and Alice and Sue would have plenty to write about, I dare say. They certainly seem to have jolly times . . . and as for the men . . . but there! People say men are interesting. They may be. But I shall never get well enough acquainted with any of them to find out.

Mother says it is high time I gave up my tomboy ways and came "out" too, because I am eighteen. I coaxed off this winter. It wasn't very hard, because no mother with three older unmarried girls on her hands would be very anxious to bring out a fourth. The girls took my part and advised Mother to let me be a child as long as possible. Mother yielded for this time, but said I must be brought out next winter or people would talk. Oh, I hate the thought of it! People might talk about my not being brought out, but they will talk far more about the blunders I shall make.

The doleful fact is, I'm too wretchedly shy and awkward to live. It fills my soul with terror to think of donning long dresses and putting my hair up and going into society. I can't talk and men frighten me to death. I fall over things as it is, and what will it be with long dresses? As far back as I can remember it has been my one aim and object in life to escape company. Oh, if only one need never grow up! If I could only go back four years and stay there!

Mother laments over it muchly. She says she doesn't know what she has done to have such a shy, unpresentable daughter. *I* know. She married Grandmother Marshall's son, and Grandmother Marshall was as shy as she was economical. Mother triumphed over heredity with Jen and Sue and Alice, but it came off best with me. The other girls are noted for their grace and tact. But I'm the black sheep and always will be. It wouldn't worry me so much if they'd leave me alone and stop nagging me. "Oh, for a lodge in some vast wilderness," where there were no men, no parties, no dinners . . . just quantities of dogs and horses and skating ponds and woods! I need never put on long dresses then, but just be a jolly little girl forever.

However, I've got one beautiful year before me yet, and I mean to make the most of it.

January Tenth.
It is rather good to have a diary to pour out your woes in when you feel awfully bad and have no one to sympathize with you. I've been used to shutting them all up in my soul and then they sometimes fermented and made trouble.

We had a lot of people here to dinner tonight, and that made me miserable to begin with. I had to dress up in a stiff white dress *with a sash*, and Jen tied two big white fly-away bows on my hair that kept rasping my neck and tickling my ears in a most exasperating way. Then an old lady whom I detest tried to make me talk before everybody, and all I could do was to turn as red as a beet and stammer: "Yes, ma'am," "no, ma'am." It made Mother furious, because it is so old-fashioned to say "ma'am." Our old nurse taught me to say it when I was small, and though it has been pretty well governessed out of me since then, it's sure to pop up when I get confused and nervous.

Sue . . . may it be accounted unto her for righteousness . . . contrived that I should go out to dinner with old Mr. Grant, because she knew he goes to dinners for the sake of eating and never talks or wants anybody else to. But when we were crossing the hall I stepped on Mrs. Burnett's train and something tore. Mrs. Burnett gave me a furious look and glowered all through dinner. The meal was completely spoiled for me and I could find no comfort, even in the Nesselrode pudding, which is my favourite dessert.

It was just when the pudding came on that I got the most unkindest cut of all. Mrs. Allardyce remarked that Sidney Elliot was coming home to Stillwater.

Everybody exclaimed and questioned and seemed delighted. I saw Mother give one quick, involuntary look at Jen, and then gaze steadfastly at Mr. Grant to atone for it. Jen is twenty-six, and Stillwater is next door to our place!

As for me, I was so vexed that I might as well have been eating chips for all the good that Nesselrode pudding was to me. If Sidney Elliot were coming home everything would be spoiled. There would be no more ramblings in the Stillwater woods, no more delightful skating on the Stillwater lake. Stillwater has been the only place in the world where I could find the full joy of solitude, and now this, too, was to be taken from me. We had no woods, no lake. I hated Sidney Elliot.

It is ten years since Sidney Elliot closed Stillwater and went abroad. He has stayed abroad ever since and nobody has missed him, I'm sure. I remember him dimly as a tall dark man who used to lounge about alone in his garden and was always reading books. Sometimes he came into our garden and teased us children. He is said to be a cynic and to detest society. If this latter item be a fact I almost feel a grim pity for him. He may detest it, but he will be dragged into it. Rich bachelors are few and far between in Riverton, and the mammas will hunt him down.

I feel like crying. If Sidney Elliot comes home I shall be debarred from Stillwater. I have roamed its demesnes for ten beautiful years, and I'm sure I love them a hundredfold better than he does, or can. It is flagrantly unfair. Oh, I hate him!

January Twentieth.

No, I don't. I believe I like him. Yet it's almost unbelievable. I've always thought men so detestable.

I'm tingling all over with the surprise and pleasure of a little unexpected adventure. For the first time I have something really worth writing in a diary . . . and I'm glad I have a diary to write it in. Blessings on Aunt Jemima! May her shadow never grow less.

This evening I started out for a last long lingering ramble in my beloved Stillwater woods. The last, I thought, because I knew Sidney Elliot was expected home next week, and after that I'd have to be cooped up on our lawn. I dressed myself comfortably for climbing fences and skimming over snowy wastes. That is, I put on the shortest old tweed skirt I have and a red jacket with sleeves three years behind the fashion, but jolly pockets to put your hands in, and a still redder tam. Thus accoutred, I sallied forth.

It was such a lovely evening that I couldn't help enjoying myself in spite of my sorrows. The sun was low and creamy, and the snow was so white and the shadows so slender and blue. All through the lovely Stillwater woods was a fine frosty stillness. It was splendid to skim down those long wonderful avenues of crusted snow, with the mossy grey boles on either hand, and overhead the lacing, leafless boughs. I just drank in the air and the beauty until my very soul was thrilling, and I went on and on and on until I was most delightfully lost. That is, I didn't know just where I was, but the woods weren't so big but that I'd be sure to come out safely somewhere; and, oh, it was so glorious to be there all alone and never a creature to worry me.

At last I turned into a long aisle that seemed to lead right out into the very heart of a deep-red overflowing winter sunset. At its end I found a fence, and I climbed up on that fence and sat there, so comfortably, with my back against a big beech and my feet dangling.

Then I saw him!

I knew it was Sidney Elliot in a moment. He was just as tall and just as black-eyed; he was still given to lounging evidently, for he was leaning against the fence a panel away from me and looking at me with an amused smile. After my first mad impulse to rush away and bury myself in the wilderness that smile put me at ease. If he had looked grave or polite I would have been as miserably shy as I've always been in a man's presence. But it was the smile of a grandfather for a child, and I just grinned cheerfully back at him.

He ploughed along through the thick drift that was soft and spongy by the fence and came close up to me.

"You must be little Cornelia," he said with another aged smile. "Or rather, you *were* little Cornelia. I suppose you are big Cornelia now and want to be treated like a young lady?"

"Indeed, I don't," I protested. "I'm not grown up and I don't want to be. You are Mr. Elliot, I suppose. Nobody expected you till next week. What made you come so soon?"

"A whim of mine," he said. "I'm full of whims and crotchets. Old bachelors always are. But why did you ask that question in a tone which seemed to imply that you resented my coming so soon, Miss Cornelia?"

"Oh, don't tack the Miss on," I implored. "Call me

Cornelia . . . or better still, Nic, as Dad does. I *do* resent your coming so soon. I resent your coming at all. And, oh, it is such a satisfaction to tell you so."

He smiled with his eyes . . . a deep, black, velvety smile. But he shook his head sorrowfully.

"I must be getting very old," he said. "It's a sign of age when a person finds himself unwelcome and superfluous."

"Your age has nothing to do with it," I retorted. "It is because Stillwater is the only place I have to run wild in . . . and running wild is all I'm fit for. It's so lovely and roomy I can lose myself in it. I shall die or go mad if I'm cooped up on our little pocket handkerchief of a lawn."

"But why should you be?" he inquired gravely.

I reflected . . . and was surprised.

"After all, I don't know . . . now . . . why I should be," I admitted. "I thought you wouldn't want me prowling about your domains. Besides, I was afraid I'd meet you . . . and I don't like meeting men. I hate to have them around . . . I'm so shy and awkward."

"Do you find me very dreadful?" he asked.

I reflected again . . . and was again surprised.

"No, I don't. I don't mind you a bit . . . any more than if you were Dad."

"Then you mustn't consider yourself an exile from Stillwater. The woods are yours to roam in at will, and if you want to roam them alone you may, and if you'd like a companion once in a while command me. Let's be good friends, little lass. Shake hands on it."

I slipped down from the fence and shook hands with him. I did like him very much . . . he was so nice and unaffected and brotherly . . . just as if I'd known him all my life. We walked down the long white avenue, where everything was growing dusky, and I had told him all my troubles before we got to the end of it. He was so sympathetic and agreed with me that it was a pity people had to grow up. He promised to come over tomorrow and look at Don's leg. Don is one of my dogs, and he has got a bad leg. I've been doctoring it myself, but it doesn't get any better. Sidney thinks he can cure it. He says I must call him Sidney if I want him to call me Nic.

When we got to the lake, there it lay all gleaming and smooth as glass . . . the most tempting thing.

"What a glorious possible slide," he said. "Let us have it, little lass."

He took my hand and we ran down the slope and went skimming over the ice. It *was* glorious. The house came in sight as we reached the other side. It was big and dark and silent.

"So the old place is still standing," said Sidney, looking up at it. In the dusk I thought his face had a tender, reverent look instead of the rather mocking expression it had worn all along.

"Haven't you been there yet?" I asked quickly.

"No. I'm stopping at the hotel over in Croyden. The house will need some fixing up before it's fit to live in. I just came down tonight to look at it and took a short cut through the woods. I'm glad I did. It was worth while to see you come tramping down that long white avenue when you thought yourself alone with the silence. I thought I had never seen a child so full of the pure joy of existence. Hold fast to that, little lass, as long as you can. You'll never find anything to take its place after it goes. You jolly little child!"

"I'm eighteen," I said suddenly. I don't know what made me say it.

He laughed and pulled his coat collar up around his ears.

"Never," he mocked. "You're about twelve . . . stay twelve, and always wear red caps and jackets, you vivid thing. Good night."

He was off across the lake, and I came home. Yes, I do like him, even if he is a man.

February Twentieth.
I've found out what diaries are for . . . to work off blue moods in, moods that come on without any reason whatever and therefore can't be confided to any fellow creature. You scribble away for a while . . . and then it's all gone . . . and your soul feels clear as crystal once more.

I always go to Sidney now in a blue mood that has a real cause. He can cheer me up in five minutes. But in such a one as this, which is quite unaccountable, there's nothing for it but a diary.

Sidney has been living at Stillwater for a month. It seems as if he must have lived there always.

He came to our place the next day after I met him in the woods. Everybody made a fuss over him, but he shook them off with an ease I envied and whisked me out to see Don's leg. He has fixed it up so that it is as good as new now, and the dogs like him almost better than they like me.

We have had splendid times since then. We are just the jolliest chums and we tramp about everywhere together and go skating and snowshoeing and riding. We read a lot of books together too, and Sidney always explains everything I don't understand. I'm not a bit shy and I can always find plenty to say to him. He isn't at all like any other man I know.

Everybody likes him, but the women seem to be a little afraid of him. They say he is so terribly cynical and satirical. He goes into society a good bit, although he says it bores him. He says he only goes because it would bore him worse to stay home alone.

There's only one thing about Sidney that I hardly like. I think he rather overdoes it in the matter of treating me as if I were a little girl. Of course, I don't want him to look upon me as grown up. But there is a medium in all things, and he really needn't talk as if he thought I was a child of ten and had no earthly interest in anything but sports and dogs. These *are* the best things . . . I suppose . . . but I understand lots of other things too, only I can't convince Sidney that I do. I know he is laughing at me when I try to show him I'm not so childish as he thinks me. He's indulgent and whimsical, just as he would be with a little girl who was making believe to be grown up. Perhaps next winter, when I put on long dresses and come out, he'll stop regarding me as a child. But next winter is so horribly far off.

The day we were fussing with Don's leg I told Sidney that Mother said I'd have to be grown up next winter and how I hated it, and I made him promise that when the time came he would use all his influence to beg me off for another year. He said he would, because it was a shame to worry children about society. But somehow I've concluded not to bother making a fuss. I have to come out some time, and I might as well take the plunge and get it over.

Mrs. Burnett was here this evening fixing up some arrangements for a charity bazaar she and Jen are interested in, and she talked most of the time about Sidney . . . for Jen's benefit, I suppose, although Jen and Sid don't get on at all. They fight every time they meet, so I don't see why Mrs. Burnett should think things.

"I wonder what he'll do when Mrs. Rennie comes to the Glasgows' next month," said Mrs. Burnett.

"Why should he do anything?" asked Jen.

"Oh, well, you know there was something between them . . . an understanding if not an engagement . . . before she married Rennie. They met abroad . . . my sister told me all about it . . . and Mr. Elliot was quite infatuated with her. She was a very handsome and fascinating girl. Then she threw him over and married old Jacob Rennie . . . for his millions, of course, for he certainly had nothing else to recommend him. Amy says Mr. Elliot was never the same man again. But Jacob died obligingly two years ago and Mrs. Rennie is free now; so I dare say they'll make it up. No doubt that is why she is coming to Riverton. Well, it would be a very suitable match."

I'm so glad I never liked Mrs. Burnett.

I wonder if it is true that Sidney did care for that horrid woman . . . of course she is horrid! Didn't she marry an old man for his money? . . . and cares for her still. It is no business of mine, of course, and it doesn't matter to me at all. But I rather hope he doesn't . . . because it would spoil everything if he got married. He wouldn't have time to be chums with me then.

I don't know why I feel so dull tonight. Writing in this diary doesn't seem to have helped me as much as I thought it would, either. I dare say it's the weather. It must be the weather. It is a wet, windy night and the rain is thudding against the window. I hate rainy nights.

I wonder if Mrs. Rennie is really as handsome as Mrs. Burnett says. I wonder how old she is. I wonder if she ever cared for Sidney . . . no, she didn't. No woman who cared for Sidney could ever have thrown him over for an old moneybag. I wonder if I shall like her. No, I won't. I'm sure I shan't like her.

My head is aching and I'm going to bed.

March Tenth.

Mrs. Rennie was here to dinner tonight. My head was aching again, and Mother said I needn't go down to dinner if I'd rather not; but a dozen headaches could not have kept me back, or a dozen men either, even supposing I'd have to talk to them all. I wanted to see Mrs. Rennie. Nothing has been talked of in Riverton for the last fortnight but Mrs. Rennie. I've heard of her beauty and charm and costumes until I'm sick of the subject. Today I spoke to Sidney about her. Before I thought I said right out, "Mrs. Rennie is to dine with us tonight."

"Yes?" he said in a quiet voice.

"I'm dying to see her," I went on recklessly. "I've heard so much about her. They say she's so beautiful and fascinating. *Is* she? *You* ought to know."

Sidney swung the sled around and put it in position for another coast.

"Yes, I know her," he admitted tranquilly. "She is a very handsome woman, and I suppose most people would consider her fascinating. Come, Nic, get on the sled. We have just time for one more coast, and then you must go in."

"You were once a good friend . . . a very good friend . . . of Mrs. Rennie's, weren't you, Sid?" I said.

A little mocking gleam crept into his eyes, and I instantly realized that he was looking upon me as a rather impertinent child.

"You've been listening to gossip, Nic," he said. "It's a bad habit, child. Don't let it grow on you. Come."

I went, feeling crushed and furious and ashamed.

I knew her at once when I went down to the drawing-room. There were three other strange women there, but I knew she was the only one who could be Mrs. Rennie. I felt such a horrible queer sinking feeling at my heart when I saw her. Oh, she was beautiful . . . I had never seen anyone so beautiful. And Sidney was standing beside her, talking to her, with a smile on his face, but none in his eyes . . . I noticed *that* at a glance.

She was so tall and slender and willowy. Her dress was wonderful, and her bare throat and shoulders were like pearls. Her hair was pale, pale gold, and her eyes long-lashed and sweet, and her mouth like a scarlet blossom against her creamy face. I thought of how I must look beside her . . . an awkward little girl in a short skirt with my hair in a braid and too many hands and feet, and I would have given anything then to be tall and grown-up and graceful.

I watched her all the evening and the queer feeling in me somewhere grew worse and worse. I couldn't eat anything. Sidney took Mrs. Rennie in; they sat opposite to me and talked all the time.

I was so glad when the dinner was over and everybody

gone. The first thing I did when I escaped to my room was to go to the glass and look myself over just as critically and carefully as if I were somebody else. I saw a great rope of dark brown hair . . . a brown skin with red cheeks . . . a big red mouth . . . a pair of grey eyes. That was all. And when I thought of that shimmering witch woman with her white skin and shining hair I wanted to put out the light and cry in the dark. Only I've never cried since I was a child and broke my last doll, and I've got so out of the habit that I don't know how to go about it.

April Fifth.

Aunt Jemima would not think I was getting the good out of my diary. A whole month and not a word! But there was nothing to write, and I've felt too miserable to write if there had been. I don't know what is the matter with me. I'm just cross and horrid to everyone, even to poor Sidney.

Mrs. Rennie has been queening it in Riverton society for the past month. People rave over her and I admire her horribly, although I don't like her. Mrs. Burnett says that a match between her and Sidney Elliot is a foregone conclusion.

It's plain to be seen that Mrs. Rennie loves Sidney. Even I can see that, and I don't know much about such things. But it puzzles me to know how Sidney regards her. I have never thought he showed any sign of really caring for her. But then, he isn't the kind that would.

"Nic, I wonder if you will ever grow up," he said to me today, laughing, when he caught me racing over the lawn with the dogs.

"I'm grown up now," I said crossly. "Why, I'm eighteen and a half and I'm two inches taller than any of the other girls."

Sidney laughed, as if he were heartily amused at something.

"You're a blessed baby," he said, "and the dearest, truest, jolliest little chum ever a fellow had. I don't know what I'd do without you, Nic. You keep me sane and wholesome. I'm a tenfold better man for knowing you, little girl."

I was rather pleased. It was nice to think I was some good to Sidney.

"Are you going to the Trents' dinner tonight?" I asked.

"Yes," he said briefly.

"Mrs. Rennie will be there," I said.

Sidney nodded.

"Do you think her so very handsome, Sidney?" I said. I had never mentioned Mrs. Rennie to him since the day we were coasting, and I didn't mean to now. The question just asked itself.

"Yes, very; but not as handsome as you will be ten years from now, Nic," said Sidney lightly.

"Do you think I'm handsome, Sidney?" I cried.

"You will be when you're grown up," he answered, looking at me critically.

"Will you be going to Mrs. Greaves' reception after the dinner?" I asked.

"Yes, I suppose so," said Sidney absently. I could see he wasn't thinking of me at all. I wondered if he were thinking of Mrs. Rennie.

April Sixth.

Oh, something so wonderful has happened. I can hardly believe it. There are moments when I quake with the fear that it is all a dream. I wonder if I can really be the same Cornelia Marshall I was yesterday. No, I'm *not* the same . . . and the difference is so blessed.

Oh, I'm so happy! My heart bubbles over with happiness and song. It's so wonderful and lovely to be a woman and know it and know that other people know it.

You dear diary, you were made for this moment . . . I shall write all about it in you and so fulfil your destiny. And then I shall put you away and never write anything more in you, because I shall not need you . . . I shall have Sidney.

Last night I was all alone in the house . . . and I was so lonely and miserable. I put my chin on my hands and I thought . . . and thought . . . and thought. I imagined Sidney at the Greaves', talking to Mrs. Rennie with that velvety smile in his eyes. I could see her, graceful and white, in her trailing, clinging gown, with diamonds about her smooth neck and in her hair. I suddenly wondered what I would look like in evening dress with my hair up. I wondered if Sidney would like me in it.

All at once I got up and rushed to Sue's room. I lighted the gas, rummaged, and went to work. I piled my hair on top of my head, pinned it there, and thrust a long silver dagger through it to hold a couple of pale white roses she had left on her table. Then I put on her last winter's party dress. It was such a pretty pale yellow thing, with touches of black lace, and it didn't matter about its being a little old-fashioned, since it fitted me like a glove. Finally I stepped back and looked at myself.

I saw a woman in that glass . . . a tall, straight creature with crimson cheeks and glowing eyes . . . and the thought in my mind was so insistent that it said itself aloud: "Oh, I wish Sidney could see me now!"

At that very moment the maid knocked at the door to tell me that Mr. Elliot was downstairs asking for me. I did not hesitate a second. With my heart beating wildly I trailed downstairs to Sidney.

He was standing by the fireplace when I went in, and looked very tired. When he heard me he turned his head and our eyes met.

All at once a terrible thing happened . . . at least, I thought it a terrible thing then. *I knew why I had wanted Sidney to realize that I was no longer a child.* It was because I loved him! I knew it the moment I saw that strange, new expression leap into his eyes.

"Cornelia," he said in a stunned sort of voice. "Why . . . Nic . . . why, little girl . . . you're a woman! How blind I've been! And now I've lost my little chum."

"Oh, no, no," I said wildly. I was so miserable and confused I didn't know what I said. "Never, Sidney. I'd rather be a little girl and have you for a friend . . . I'll always be a little girl! It's all this hateful dress. I'll go and take it off . . . I'll . . ."

And then I just put my hands up to my burning face and the tears that would never come before came in a flood.

All at once I felt Sidney's arms about me and felt my head drawn to his shoulder.

"Don't cry, dearest," I heard him say softly. "You can never be a little girl to me again . . . my eyes are opened . . . but I didn't want you to be. I want you to be my big girl . . . mine, all mine, forever."

What happened after that isn't to be written in a diary. I won't even write down the things he said about how I looked, because it would seem so terribly vain, but I can't help thinking of them, for I am so happy.

*Aunt Susanna's
Birthday Celebration*

GOOD afternoon, Nora May. I'm real glad to see you. I've been watching you coming down the hill and hoping you'd turn in at our gate. Going to visit with me this afternoon? That's good. I'm feeling so happy and delighted and I've been hankering for someone to tell it all to.

Tell you about it? Well, I guess I might as well. It ain't any breach of confidence.

You didn't know Anne Douglas? She taught school here three years ago, afore your folks moved over from Talcott. She belonged up Montrose way and she was only eighteen when she came here to teach. She boarded with us and her and me were the greatest chums. She was just a sweet girl.

She was the prettiest teacher we ever had, and that's saying a good deal, for Springdale has always been noted for getting good-looking schoolmarms, just as Miller's Road is noted for its humly ones.

Anne had *yards* of brown wavy hair and big, dark blue eyes. Her face was kind o' pale, but when she smiled you would have to smile too, if you'd been chief mourner at your own funeral. She was a well-spring of joy in the house, and we all loved her.

Gilbert Martin began to drive her the very first week she was here. Gilbert is my sister Julia's son, and a fine young fellow he is. It ain't good manners to brag of your own relations, but I'm always forgetting and doing it. Gil was a great pet of mine. He was so bright and nice-mannered everybody liked him. Him and Anne were a fine-looking couple, Nora May. Not but what they had their shortcomings. Anne's nose was a mite too long and Gil had a crooked mouth. Besides, they was both pretty proud and sperrited and high-strung.

But they thought an awful lot of each other. It made me feel young again to see 'em. Anne wasn't a mossel vain, but nights she expected Gil she'd prink for hours afore her glass, fixing her hair this way and that, and trying on all her good clothes to see which become her most. I used to love her for it. And I used to love to see the way Gil's face would light up when she came into a room or place where he was. Amanda Perkins, she says to me once, "Anne Douglas and Gil Martin are most terrible struck on each other." And she said it in a tone that indicated that it was a dreadful disgraceful and unbecoming state of affairs. Amanda had a disappointment once and it soured her. I immediately responded, "Yes, they are most terrible struck on each other," and I said it in a tone that indicated I thought it a most beautiful and lovely thing that they should be so.

And so it was. You're rather too young to be thinking of such things, Nora May, but you'll remember my words when the time comes.

Another nephew of mine, James Ebenezer Lawson – he calls himself James E. back there in town, and I don't blame him, for I never could stand Ebenezer for a name myself; but that's neither here nor there. Well, he said their love was idyllic. I ain't very sure what that means. I looked it up in the dictionary after James Ebenezer left – I wouldn't display my ignorance afore him – but I can't say that I was much the wiser for it. Anyway, it meant something real nice; I was sure of that by the way James Ebenezer spoke and the wistful look in his eyes. James Ebenezer isn't married; he was to have been, and she died a month afore the wedding day. He was never the same man again.

Well, to get back to Gilbert and Anne. When Anne's school year ended in June she resigned and went home to get ready to be married. The wedding was to be in September, and I promised Anne faithful I'd go over to Montrose in August for two weeks and help her to get her quilts ready. Anne thought that nobody could quilt like me. I was as tickled as a girl at the thought of visiting with Anne for two weeks, but I never went; things happened before August.

I don't know rightly how the trouble began. Other folks – jealous folks – made mischief. Anne was thirty miles away and Gilbert couldn't see her every day to keep matters clear and fair. Besides, as I've said, they were both proud and high-sperrited. The upshot of it was they had a terrible quarrel and the engagement was broken.

When two people don't care overly much for each other, Nora May, a quarrel never amounts to much between them, and it's soon made up. But when they love each other better than life it cuts so deep and hurts so much that nine times out of ten they won't ever forgive each other. The more you love anybody, Nora May, the more he can hurt you. To be sure, you're too young to be thinking of such things.

It all came like a thunderclap on Gil's friends here at Greendale, because we hadn't ever suspected things were going wrong. The first thing we knew was that Anne had gone up west to teach school again at St. Mary's, eighty miles away, and Gilbert, he went out to Manitoba on a harvest excursion and stayed there. It just about broke his parents' hearts. He was their only child and they just worshipped him.

Gil and Anne both wrote to me off and on, but never a word, not so much as a name, did they say of each other. I'd 'a' writ and asked 'em the rights of the fuss if I could, in hopes of patching it up, but I can't write now – my hand is too shaky – and mebbe it was just as well, for meddling is terribly risky work in a love trouble, Nora May. Ninety-nine times out of a hundred the last state of a meddler and them she meddles with is worse than the first.

So I just set tight and said nothing, while everybody else in the clan was talking Anne and Gil sixty words to the minute.

Well, last birthday morning I was feeling terrible disper-rited. I had made up my mind that my birthday was always to be a good thing for other people, and there didn't seem one blessed thing I could do to make anybody glad. Emma Matilda and George and the children were all well and happy and wanted for nothing that I could give them. I begun to be afraid I'd lived long enough, Nora May. When a woman gets to the point where she can't give a gift of joy to anyone, there ain't much use in her living. I felt real old and worn out and useless.

I was sitting here under these very trees – they was just budding out in leaf then, as young and cheerful as if they wasn't a hundred years old. And I sighed right out loud and said, "Oh, Grandpa Holland, it's time I was put away up on the hill there with you." And with that the gate banged and there was Nancy Jane Whitmore's boy, Sam, with two letters for me.

One was from Anne up at St. Mary's and the other was from Gil out in Manitoba.

I read Anne's first. She just struck right into things in the first paragraph. She said her year at St. Mary's was nearly up, and when it was she meant to quit teaching and go away to New York and learn to be a trained nurse. She said she was just broken-hearted about Gilbert, and would always love him to the day of her death. But she knew he didn't care anything more about her after the way he had acted, and there was nothing left for her in life but to do something for other people, and so on and so on, for twelve mortal pages. Anne is a fine writer, and I just cried like a babe over that letter, it was so touching, although I was enjoying myself hugely all the time, I was so delighted to find out that Anne loved Gilbert still. I was getting skeered she didn't, her letters all winter had been so kind of jokey and frivolous, all about the good times she was having, and the parties she went to, and the new dresses she got. New dresses! When I read that letter of Anne's, I knew that all the purple and fine linen in the world was just like so much sackcloth and ashes to her as long as Gilbert was sulking out on a prairie farm.

Well, I wiped my eyes and polished up my specs, but I might have spared myself the trouble, for in five minutes,

Nora May, there was I sobbing again over Gilbert's letter. By the most curious coincidence he had opened his heart to me too. Being a man, he wasn't so discursive as Anne; he said his say in four pages, but I could read the heartache between the lines. He wrote that he was going to Klondike and would start in a month's time. He was sick of living now that he'd lost Anne. He said he loved her better than his life and always would, and could never forget her, but he knew she didn't care anything about him now after the way she'd acted, and he wanted to get as far away from her and the torturing thought of her as he could. So he was going to Klondike – going to Klondike, Nora May, when his mother was writing to him to come home every week and Anne was breaking her heart for him at St. Mary's.

Well, I folded up them letters and, says I, "Grandpa Holland, I guess my birthday celebration is here ready to hand." I thought real hard. I couldn't write myself to explain to those two people that they each thought the world of each other still – my hands are too stiff; and I couldn't get anyone else to write because I couldn't let out what they'd told me in confidence. So I did a mean, dishonourable thing, Nora May. I sent Anne's letter to Gilbert and Gilbert's to Anne. I asked Emma Matilda to address them, and Emma Matilda did it and asked no questions. I brought her up that way.

Then I settled down to wait. In less than a month Gilbert's mother had a letter from him saying that he was coming home to settle down and marry Anne. He arrived home yesterday and last night Anne came to Springdale on her way home from St. Mary's. They came to see me this morning and said things to me I ain't going to repeat because they would sound fearful vain. They were so happy that they made me feel as if it was a good thing to have lived eighty years in a world where folks could be so happy. They said their new joy was my birthday gift to them. The wedding is to be in September and I'm going to Montrose in August to help Anne with her quilts. I don't think anything will happen to prevent this time – no quarrelling, anyhow. Those two young creatures have learned their lesson. You'd better take it to heart too, Nora May. It's less trouble to learn it at second hand. Don't you ever quarrel with your real beau – it don't matter about the sham ones, of course. Don't take offence at trifles or listen to what other people tell you about him – outsiders, that is, that want to make mischief. What you think about him is of more importance than what they do. To be sure, you're too young yet to be thinking of such things at all. But just mind what old Aunt Susanna told you when your time comes.

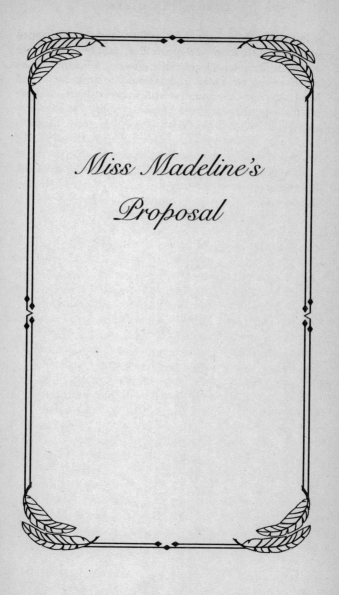

Miss Madeline's
Proposal

AUNTIE, I have something to tell you," said Lina, with a blush that made her look more than ever like one of the climbing roses that nodded about the windows of the "old Churchill place," as it was always called in Lower Wentworth.

Miss Madeline, sitting in the low rocker by the parlour window, seemed like the presiding genius of the place. Everything about her matched her sweet old-fashionedness, from the crown of her soft brown hair, dressed in the style of her long ago girlhood, to the toes of her daintily slippered feet. Outside of the old Churchill place, in the busy streets of the up-to-date little town, Miss Madeline might have seemed out of harmony with her surroundings. But here, in this dim room, faintly scented with whiffs from the rose garden outside, she was like a note in some sweet, perfect melody of old time.

Lina, sitting on a little stool at Miss Madeline's feet with her curly head in her aunt's lap, was as pretty as Miss Madeline herself had once been. She was also very happy, and her happiness seemed to envelop her as in an atmosphere and lend her a new radiance and charm. Miss Madeline loved her pretty niece very dearly and patted the curly head tenderly with her slender white hands.

"What is it, my dear?"

"I'm – I'm engaged," whispered Lina, hiding her face in Miss Madeline's flowered muslin lap.

"Engaged!" Miss Madeline's tone was one of surprise and awe. She blushed as she said the word as deeply as Lina had done. Then she went on, with a little quiver of excitement in her voice, "To whom, my dear?"

"Oh, you don't know him, Auntie, but I hope you will soon. His name is Ralph Wylde. Isn't it pretty? I met him last winter, and we became very good friends. But we had a quarrel before I came down here and, oh, I have been so unhappy over it. Three weeks ago he wrote me and begged my pardon – so nice of him, because I was really all to blame, you know. And he said he loved me and – all that, you know."

"No, I don't know," said Miss Madeline gently. "But – but – I can imagine."

"Oh, I was so happy. I wrote back and I had this letter from him today. He is coming down tomorrow. You'll be glad to see him, won't you, Auntie?"

"Oh, yes, my dear, and I am glad for your sake – very glad. You are sure you love him?"

"Yes, indeed," said Lina, with a little laugh, as if wondering how anyone could doubt it.

Presently, Miss Madeline said in a shy voice, "Lina, did – did you ever receive a proposal of marriage from anybody besides Mr. Wylde?"

Lina laughed roguishly. "Why, yes, Auntie, ever so many. A dozen, at least."

"Oh, my dear!" cried Miss Madeline in a slightly shocked tone.

"But I did, really. Sometimes it was horrid and sometimes it was funny. It all depended on the man. Dear me, how red and uncomfortable most of them looked – all but the fifth. He was so cool and businesslike that he almost surprised me into accepting him."

"And – and what did you feel like, Lina?"

"Oh, frightened, mostly – but I always wanted to laugh too. You must know how it is yourself, Auntie. What did you feel like when somebody proposed to you?"

Miss Madeline flushed from chin to brow.

"Oh, Lina," she faltered as if she were confessing something very disgraceful, yet to which she was impelled by her strict truthfulness, "I – I – never had a proposal in my life – not one."

Lina opened her big brown eyes in amazement. "Why, Aunt Madeline! And you so pretty! What was the reason?"

"I've often wondered," said Miss Madeline faintly. "I *was* pretty, as you say – it's so long ago I can say that now. And I had many gentlemen friends. But nobody ever wanted to marry me. I sometimes wish that – that I could have had just one proposal. Not that I wanted to marry, you know, I do not mean that, but just so that it wouldn't have seemed that I was different from anybody else. It is very foolish of me to wish it, I know, and even wicked – for if I had not cared for the person it would have made him very unhappy. But then, he would have forgotten and I would have remembered. It would always have been something to be a little proud of."

"Yes," said Lina absently; her thoughts had gone back to Ralph.

That evening a letter was left at the front door of the old Churchill place. It was addressed in a scholarly hand to Miss Madeline Churchill, and Amelia Kent took it in. Amelia had been Miss Madeline's "help" for years and had grown grey in her service. In Amelia's loyal eyes Miss Madeline was still young and beautiful; she never doubted that the letter was for her mistress. Nobody else there was ever addressed as "Miss Madeline."

Miss Madeline was sitting by the window of her own room watching the sunset through the elms and reading her evening portion of Thomas à Kempis. She never liked to be disturbed when so employed but she read her letter after Amelia had gone out.

When she came to a certain paragraph, she turned very pale and Thomas à Kempis fell to the floor unheeded. When she had finished the letter she laid it on her lap, clasped her hands, and said, "Oh, oh, oh," in a faint, tremulous voice. Her cheeks were very pink and her eyes very bright. She did not even pick up Thomas à Kempis but went to the door and called Lina.

"What is it, Auntie?" asked Lina curiously, noticing the signs of unusual excitement about Miss Madeline.

Miss Madeline held out her letter with a trembling hand.

"Lina, dear, this is a letter from the Rev. Cecil Thorne. It – it is – a proposal of marriage. I feel terribly upset. How very strange that it should come so soon after our talk this morning! I want you to read it! Perhaps I ought not to show it to anyone – but I would like you to see it."

Lina took the letter and read it through. It was unmistakably a proposal of marriage and was, moreover, a very charming epistle of its kind, albeit a little stiff and old-fashioned.

"How funny!" said Lina when she came to the end.

"Funny!" exclaimed Miss Madeline, with a trace of indignation in her gentle voice.

"Oh, I didn't mean that the letter was funny," Lina hastened to explain, "only that, as you said, it is odd to think of it coming so soon after our talk."

But this was a little fib on Lina's part. She *had* thought that the letter or, rather, the fact that it had been written to Miss Madeline, funny. The Rev. Cecil Thorne was Miss Madeline's pastor. He was a handsome, scholarly man of middle age, and Lina had seen a good deal of him during her summer in Lower Wentworth. She had taught the infant class in Sunday School and sometimes she had thought that the minister was in love with her. But she must have been mistaken, she reflected; it must have been her aunt after all, and the Rev. Cecil Thorne's shyly displayed interest in her must have been purely professional.

"What a goose I was to be afraid he was in love with me!" she thought. Aloud she said, "He says he will call tomorrow evening to receive your answer."

"And, oh, what can I say to him?" murmured Miss Madeline in dismay. She wished she had a little of Lina's experience.

"You are going to – you will accept him, won't you?" asked Lina curiously.

"Oh, my dear, no!" cried Miss Madeline almost vehemently. "I couldn't think of such a thing. I am very sorry; do you think he will feel badly?"

"Judging from his letter I feel sure he will," said Lina decidedly.

Miss Madeline sighed. "Oh, dear me! It is very unpleasant. But of course I must refuse him. What a beautiful letter he writes, too. I feel very much disturbed by this."

Miss Madeline picked up Thomas à Kempis, smoothed him out repentantly, and placed the letter between his leaves.

WHEN THE REV. Cecil Thorne called at the old Churchill place next evening at sunset and asked for Miss Madeline Churchill, Amelia showed him into the parlour and went to call her mistress. Mr. Thorne sat down by the window that looked out on the lawn. His heart gave a bound as he caught a glimpse of an airy white muslin among the trees and a ripple of distant laughter. The next minute Lina appeared, strolling down the secluded path that curved about the birches. A young man was walking beside her with his arm around her. They crossed the green square before the house and disappeared in the rose garden.

Mr. Thorne leaned back in his chair and put his hand over his eyes. He felt that he had received his answer, and it was a very bitter moment for him. He had hardly dared hope that this bright, beautiful child could care for him, yet the realization came home to him none the less keenly. When Miss Madeline, paling and flushing by turns, came shyly in he had recovered his self-control sufficiently to be able to say "good evening" in a calm voice.

Miss Madeline sat down opposite to him. At that moment she was devoutly thankful that she had never had any other proposal to refuse. It was a dreadful ordeal. If he would only help her out! But he did not speak and every moment of silence made it worse.

"I – received your letter, Mr. Thorne," she faltered at last, looking distressfully down at the floor.

"My letter!" Mr. Thorne turned towards her. In her agitation Miss Madeline did not notice the surprise in his face and tone.

"Yes," she said, gaining a little courage since the ice was broken. "It – it – was a very great surprise to me. I never thought you – you cared for me as – as you said. And I am very sorry because – because I cannot return your affection. And so, of course, I cannot marry you."

Mr. Thorne put his hand over his eyes again. He understood now that there had been some mistake and that Miss Madeline had received the letter he had written to her niece. Well, it did not matter – the appearance of the young man in the garden had settled that. Would he tell Miss Madeline of her mistake? No, it would only humiliate her and it made no difference, since she had refused him.

"I suppose it is of no use to ask you to reconsider your decision?" he said.

"Oh, no," cried Miss Madeline almost aghast. She was afraid he might ask it after all. "Not in the least use. I am sorry – so very sorry – but I could not answer differently. We – I hope – this will make no difference in our friendly relations, Mr. Thorne?"

"Not at all," said Mr. Thorne gravely. "We will try to forget that it has happened."

He bowed sadly and went out. Miss Madeline watched him guiltily as he walked across the lawn. He looked heartbroken. How dreadful it had been! And Lina had refused twelve men! How could she have lived through it?

"Perhaps one gets accustomed to doing it," reflected Miss Madeline. "But I am sure I never could."

"Did Mr. Thorne feel very badly?" whispered Lina that night.

"I'm afraid he did," confessed Miss Madeline sorrowfully. "He looked so pale and sad, Lina, that my heart ached for him. I am very thankful that I have never had any other proposals to decline. It is a very unpleasant experience. But," she added, with a little tinge of satisfaction in her sweet voice, "I am glad I had one. It – it has made me feel more like other people, you know, dear."

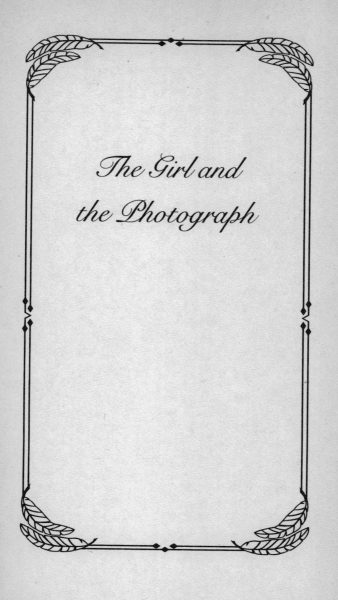

The Girl and
the Photograph

HEN I heard that Peter Austin was in Vancouver I hunted him up. I had met Peter ten years before when I had gone east to visit my father's people, and had spent a few weeks with an uncle in Croyden. The Austins lived across the street from Uncle Tom, and Peter and I had struck up a friendship, although he was a hobbledehoy of awkward sixteen and I, at twenty-two, was older and wiser and more dignified than I've ever been since or ever expect to be again. Peter was a jolly little round freckled chap. He was all right when no girls were around; when they were he retired within himself like a misanthropic oyster, and was about as interesting. This was the one point upon which we always disagreed. Peter couldn't endure girls; I was devoted to them by the wholesale. The Croyden girls were pretty and vivacious. I had a score of flirtations during my brief sojourn among them.

But when I went away the face I carried in my memory was not that of any girl with whom I had walked and driven and played the game of hearts.

It was ten years ago, but I had never been quite able to forget that girl's face. Yet I had seen it but once and then only for a moment. I had gone for a solitary ramble in the woods over the river and, in a lonely little valley dim with pines, where I thought myself alone, I had come suddenly upon her, standing ankle-deep in fern on the bank of a brook, the late evening sunshine falling yellowly on her uncovered dark hair. She was very young – no more than sixteen; yet the face and eyes were already those of a woman. Such a face! Beautiful? Yes, but I thought of that afterward, when I was alone. With that face before my eyes I thought only of its purity and sweetness, of the lovely soul and rich mind looking out of the great, greyish-blue eyes which, in the dimness of the pine shadows, looked almost black. There was something in the face of that child-woman I had never seen before and was destined never to see again in any other face. Careless boy though I was, it stirred me to the deeps. I felt that she must have been waiting forever in that pine valley for me and that, in finding her, I had found all of good that life could offer me.

I would have spoken to her, but before I could shape my greeting into words that should not seem rude or presumptuous, she had turned and gone, stepping lightly across the brook and vanishing in the maple copse beyond. For no more than ten seconds had I gazed into her face, and the soul of her, the real woman behind the fair outwardness, had looked back into my eyes; but I had never been able to forget it.

When I returned home I questioned my cousins diplomatically as to who she might be. I felt strangely reluctant to do so – it seemed in some way sacrilege; yet only by so doing could I hope to discover her. They could tell me nothing; nor did I meet her again during the remainder of my stay in Croyden, although I never went anywhere without looking for her, and haunted the pine valley daily in the hope of seeing her again. My disappointment was so bitter that I laughed at myself.

I thought I was a fool to feel thus about a girl I had met for a moment in a chance ramble – a mere child at that, with her hair still hanging in its long glossy schoolgirl braid. But when I remembered her eyes, my wisdom forgave me.

Well, that was ten years ago; in those ten years the memory had, I must confess, grown dimmer. In our busy western life a man had not much time for sentimental recollections. Yet I had never been able to care for another woman. I wanted to; I wanted to marry and settle down. I had come to the time of life when a man wearies of drifting and begins to hanker for a calm anchorage in some snug haven of his own. But, somehow, I shirked the matter. It seemed rather easier to let things slide.

At this stage Peter came west. He was something in a bank, and was as round and jolly as ever; but he had evidently changed his attitude towards girls, for his rooms were full of their photos. They were stuck around everywhere and they were all pretty. Either Peter had excellent taste, or the Croyden photographers knew how to flatter. But there was one on the mantel which attracted my attention especially. If the photo were to be trusted the girl was quite the prettiest I had ever seen.

"Peter, what pretty girl's picture is this on your mantel?" I called out to Peter, who was in his bedroom, donning evening dress for some function.

"That's my cousin, Marian Lindsay," he answered. "She *is* rather nice-looking, isn't she. Lives in Croyden now – used to live up the river at Chiselhurst. Didn't you ever chance across her when you were in Croyden?"

"No," I said. "If I had I wouldn't have forgotten her face."

"Well, she'd be only a kid then, of course. She's twenty-six now. Marian is a mighty nice girl, but she's bound to be an old maid. She's got notions – ideals, she calls 'em. All the Croyden fellows have been in love with her at one time or another but they might as well have made up to a statue. Marian really hasn't a spark of feeling or sentiment in her. Her looks are the best part of her, although she's confoundedly clever."

Peter spoke rather squiffily. I suspected that he had been one of the smitten swains himself. I looked at the photo for a few minutes longer, admiring it more every minute and, when I heard Peter coming out, I did an unjustifiable thing – I took that photo and put it in my pocket.

I expected Peter would make a fuss when he missed it, but that very night the house in which he lived was burned to the ground. Peter escaped with the most important of his goods and chattels, but all the counterfeit presentments of his dear divinities went up in smoke. If he ever thought particularly of Marian Lindsay's photograph he must have supposed that it shared the fate of the others.

As for me, I propped my ill-gotten treasure up on my mantel and worshipped it for a fortnight. At the end of that time I went boldly to Peter and told him I wanted him to introduce me by letter to his dear cousin and ask her to agree to a friendly correspondence with me.

Oddly enough, I did not do this without some reluctance, in spite of the fact that I was as much in love with Marian Lindsay as it was possible to be through the medium of a picture. I thought of the girl I had seen in the pine wood and felt an inward shrinking from a step that might divide me from her forever. But I rated myself for this nonsense. It was in the highest degree unlikely that I should ever meet the girl of the pines again. If she were still living she was probably some other man's wife. I would think no more about it.

Peter whistled when he heard what I had to say.

"Of course I'll do it, old man," he said obligingly. "But I warn you I don't think it will be much use. Marian isn't the sort of girl to open up a correspondence in such a fashion. However, I'll do the best I can for you."

"Do. Tell her I'm a respectable fellow with no violent bad habits and all that. I'm in earnest, Peter. I want to make that girl's acquaintance, and this seems the only way at present. I can't get off just now for a trip east. Explain all this, and use your cousinly influence in my behalf if you possess any."

Peter grinned.

"It's not the most graceful job in the world you are putting on me, Curtis," he said. "I don't mind owning up now that I was pretty far gone on Marian myself two years ago. It's all over now, but it was bad while it lasted. Perhaps Marian will consider your request more favourably if I put it in the light of a favour to myself. She must feel that she owes me something for wrecking my life."

Peter grinned again and looked at the one photo he had contrived to rescue from the fire. It was a pretty, snub-nosed little girl. She would never have consoled me for the loss of Marian Lindsay, but every man to his taste.

In due time Peter sought me out to give me his cousin's answer.

"Congratulations, Curtis. You've out-Caesared Caesar. You've conquered without even going and seeing. Marian agrees to a friendly correspondence with you. I am amazed, I admit – even though I did paint you up as a sort of Sir Galahad and Lancelot combined. I'm not used to seeing proud Marian do stunts like that, and it rather takes my breath."

I wrote to Marian Lindsay after one farewell dream of the girl under the pines. When Marian's letters began to come regularly I forgot the other one altogether.

Such letters – such witty, sparkling, clever, womanly, delightful letters! They completed the conquest her picture had begun. Before we had corresponded six months I was besottedly in love with this woman whom I had never seen. Finally, I wrote and told her so, and I asked her to be my wife.

A fortnight later her answer came. She said frankly that she believed she had learned to care for me during our correspondence, but that she thought we should meet in person before coming to any definite understanding. Could I not arrange to visit Croyden in the summer? Until then we would better continue on our present footing.

I agreed to this, but I considered myself practically engaged, with the personal meeting merely to be regarded as a sop to the Cerberus of conventionality. I permitted myself to use a decidedly lover-like tone in my letters henceforth, and I hailed it as a favourable omen that I was not rebuked for this, although Marian's own letters still retained their pleasant, simple friendliness.

Peter had at first tormented me mercilessly about the affair, but when he saw I did not like his chaff he stopped it. Peter was always a good fellow. He realized that I regarded the matter seriously, and he saw me off when I left for the east with a grin tempered by honest sympathy and understanding.

"Good luck to you," he said. "If you win Marian Lindsay you'll win a pearl among women. I haven't been able to grasp her taking to you in this fashion, though. It's so unlike Marian. But, since she undoubtedly has, you are a lucky man."

I arrived in Croyden at dusk and went to Uncle Tom's. There I found them busy with preparations for a party to be given that night in honour of a girl friend who was visiting my cousin Edna. I was secretly annoyed, for I wanted to hasten at once to Marian. But I couldn't decently get away, and on second thoughts I was consoled by the reflection that she would probably come to the party. I knew she belonged to the same social set as Uncle Tom's girls. I should, however, have preferred our meeting to have been under different circumstances.

From my stand behind the palms in a corner I eagerly scanned the guests as they arrived. Suddenly my heart gave a bound. Marian Lindsay had just come in.

I recognized her at once from her photograph. It had not flattered her in the least; indeed, it had not done her justice, for her exquisite colouring of hair and complexion were quite lost in it. She was, moreover, gowned with a taste and smartness eminently admirable in the future Mrs. Eric Curtis. I felt a thrill of proprietary pride as I stepped out from behind the palms. She was talking to Aunt Grace, but her eyes fell on me. I expected a little start of recognition, for I had sent her an excellent photograph of myself; but her gaze was one of blankest unconsciousness.

I felt something like disappointment at her non-recognition, but I consoled myself by the reflection that people often fail to recognize other people whom they have seen only in photographs, no matter how good the likeness may be. I waylaid Edna, who was passing at that time, and said, "Edna, I want you to introduce me to the girl who is talking to your mother."

Edna laughed.

"So you have succumbed at first sight to our Croyden beauty? Of course I'll introduce you, but I warn you beforehand that she is the most incorrigible flirt in Croyden or out of it. So take care."

It jarred on me to hear Marian called a flirt. It seemed so out of keeping with her letters and the womanly delicacy and fineness revealed in them. But I reflected that women sometimes find it hard to forgive another woman who absorbs more than her share of lovers, and generally take their revenge by dubbing her a flirt, whether she deserves the name or not.

We had crossed the room during this reflection. Marian turned and stood before us, smiling at Edna, but evincing no recognition whatever of myself. It is a piquant experience to find yourself awaiting an introduction to a girl to whom you are virtually engaged.

"Dorothy dear," said Edna, "this is my cousin, Mr. Curtis, from Vancouver. Eric, this is Miss Armstrong."

I suppose I bowed. Habit carries us mechanically through many impossible situations. I don't know what I looked like or what I said, if I said anything. I don't suppose I betrayed my dire confusion, for Edna went off unconcernedly without another glance at me.

Dorothy Armstrong! Gracious powers – who – where – why? If this girl was Dorothy Armstrong who was Marian Lindsay? To whom was I engaged? There was some awful mistake somewhere, for it could not be possible that there were two girls in Croyden who looked exactly like the photograph reposing in my valise at that very moment. I stammered like a schoolboy.

"I – oh – I – your face seems familiar to me, Miss Armstrong. I – I – think I must have seen your photograph somewhere."

"Probably in Peter Austin's collection," smiled Miss

Armstrong. "He had one of mine before he was burned out. How is he?"

"Peter? Oh, he's well," I replied vaguely. I was thinking a hundred words to the second, but my thoughts arrived nowhere. I was staring at Miss Armstrong like a man bewitched. She must have thought me a veritable booby. "Oh, by the way – can you tell me – do you know a Miss Lindsay in Croyden?"

Miss Armstrong looked surprised and a little bored. Evidently she was not used to having newly introduced young men inquiring about another girl.

"Marian Lindsay? Oh, yes."

"Is she here tonight?" I said.

"No, Marian is not going to parties just now, owing to the recent death of her aunt, who lived with them."

"Does she – oh – does she look like you at all?" I inquired idiotically.

Amusement glimmered out over Miss Armstrong's boredom. She probably concluded that I was some harmless lunatic.

"Like me? Not at all. There couldn't be two people more dissimilar. Marian is quite dark. I am fair. And our features are altogether unlike. Why, good evening, Jack. Yes, I believe I did promise you this dance."

She bowed to me and skimmed away with Jack. I saw Aunt Grace bearing down upon me and fled incontinently. In my own room I flung myself on a chair and tried to think the matter out. Where did the mistake come in? How had it happened? I shut my eyes and conjured up the vision of Peter's room that day. I remembered vaguely that, when I had picked up Dorothy Armstrong's picture, I had noticed another photograph that had fallen face downward beside it. That must have been Marian Lindsay's, and Peter had thought I meant it.

And now what a position I was in! I was conscious of bitter disappointment. I had fallen in love with Dorothy

Armstrong's photograph. As far as external semblance goes it was she whom I loved. I was practically engaged to another woman – a woman who, in spite of our correspondence, seemed to me now, in the shock of this discovery, a stranger. It was useless to tell myself that it was the mind and soul revealed in those letters that I loved, and that that mind and soul were Marian Lindsay's. It was useless to remember that Peter had said she was pretty. Exteriorly, she was a stranger to me; hers was not the face which had risen before me for nearly a year as the face of the woman I loved. Was ever unlucky wretch in such a predicament before?

Well, there was only one thing to do. I must stand by my word. Marian Lindsay was the woman I had asked to marry me, whose answer I must shortly go to receive. If that answer were "yes" I must accept the situation and banish all thought of Dorothy Armstrong's pretty face.

Next evening at sunset I went to "Glenwood," the Lindsay place. Doubtless, an eager lover might have gone earlier, but an eager lover I certainly was not. Probably Marian was expecting me and had given orders concerning me, for the maid who came to the door conveyed me to a little room behind the stairs – a room which, as I felt as soon as I entered it, was a woman's pet domain. In its books and pictures and flowers it spoke eloquently of dainty femininity. Somehow, it suited the letters. I did not feel quite so much the stranger as I had felt. Nevertheless, when I heard a light footfall on the stairs, my heart beat painfully. I stood up and turned to the door, but I could not look up. The footsteps came nearer; I knew that a white hand swept aside the *portière* at the entrance; I knew that she had entered the room and was standing before me.

With an effort I raised my eyes and looked at her. She stood, tall and gracious, in a ruby splendour of sunset falling through the window beside her. The light quivered like living radiance over a dark proud head, a white throat, and a face before whose perfect loveliness the memory of Dorothy Armstrong's laughing prettiness faded like a star in the sunrise, nevermore in the fullness of the day to be remembered. Yet it was not of her beauty I thought as I stood spellbound before her. I seemed to see a dim little valley full of whispering pines, and a girl standing under their shadows, looking at me with the same great, greyish-blue eyes which gazed upon me now from Marian Lindsay's face – the same face, matured into gracious womanhood, that I had seen ten years ago and loved – aye, loved – ever since. I took an unsteady step forward.

"Marian?" I said.

WHEN I GOT HOME that night I burned Dorothy Armstrong's photograph. The next day I went to my cousin Tom, who owns the fashionable studio of Croyden and, binding him over to secrecy, bought one of Marian's latest photographs from him. It is the only secret I have ever kept from my wife.

Before we were married Marian told me something.

"I always remembered you as you looked that day under the pines," she said. "I was only a child, but I think I loved you then and ever afterwards. When I dreamed my girl's dream of love your face rose up before me. I had the advantage of you that I knew your name – I had heard of you. When Peter wrote about you I knew who you were. That was why I agreed to correspond with you. I was afraid it was a forward – an unwomanly thing to do. But it seemed my chance for happiness and I took it. I am glad I did."

I did not answer in words, but lovers will know how I did answer.

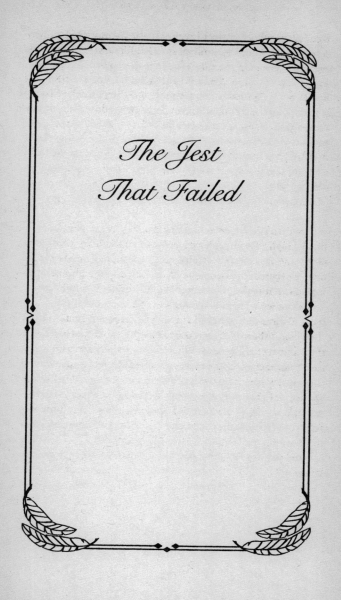

The Jest
That Failed

I THINK it is simply a disgrace to have a person like that in our class," said Edna Hayden in an injured tone.

"And she doesn't seem a bit ashamed of it, either," said Agnes Walters.

"Rather proud of it, I should say," returned her roommate, spitefully. "It seems to me that if I were so poor that I had to 'room' myself and dress as dowdily as she does that I really couldn't look anybody in the face. What must the boys think of her? And if it wasn't for her being in it, our class would be the smartest and dressiest in the college – even those top-lofty senior girls admit that."

"It's a shame," said Agnes, conclusively. "But she needn't expect to associate with our set. I, for one, won't have anything to do with her."

"Nor I. I think it is time she should be taught her place. If we could only manage to inflict some decided snub on her, she might take the hint and give up trying to poke herself in where she doesn't belong. The idea of her consenting to be elected on the freshmen executive! But she seems impervious to snubs."

"Edna, let's play a joke on her. It will serve her right. Let us send an invitation in somebody's name to the senior 'prom.'"

"The very thing! And sign Sidney Hill's name to it. He's the handsomest and richest fellow at Payzant, and belongs to one of the best families in town, and he's awfully fastidious besides. No doubt she will feel immensely flattered and, of course, she'll accept. Just think how silly she'll feel when she finds out he never sent it. Let's write it now, and send it at once. There is no time to lose, for the 'prom' is on Thursday night."

The freshmen co-eds at Payzant College did not like Grace Seeley – that is to say, the majority of them. They were a decidedly snobbish class that year. No one could deny that

Grace was clever, but she was poor, dressed very plainly – "dowdily," the girls said – and "roomed" herself, that phrase meaning that she rented a little unfurnished room and cooked her own meals over an oil stove.

The "senior prom," as it was called, was the annual reception which the senior class gave in the middle of every autumn term. It was the smartest and gayest of all the college functions, and a Payzant co-ed who received an invitation to it counted herself fortunate. The senior girls were included as a matter of course, but a junior, soph, or freshie could not go unless one of the senior boys invited her.

Grace Seeley was studying Greek in her tiny room that afternoon when the invitation was brought to her. It was scrupulously orthodox in appearance and form, and Grace never doubted that it was genuine, although she felt much surprised that Sidney Hill, the leader of his class and the foremost figure in all college sports and societies, should have asked her to go with him to the senior prom.

But she was girlishly pleased at the prospect. She was as fond of a good time as any other girl, and she had secretly wished very much that she could go to the brilliant and much talked about senior prom.

Grace was quite unaware of her own unpopularity among her class co-eds, although she thought it was very hard to get acquainted with them. Without any false pride herself, and of a frank, independent nature, it never occurred to her that the other Payzant freshies could look down on her because she was poor, or resent her presence among them because she dressed plainly.

She straightway wrote a note of acceptance to Sidney Hill, and that young man naturally felt much mystified when he opened and read it in the college library next morning.

"Grace Seeley," he pondered. "That's the jolly girl with the brown eyes that I met at the philomathic the other night. She thanks me for my invitation to the senior prom, and accepts with pleasure. Why, I certainly never invited her or anyone else to go with me to the senior prom. There must be some mistake."

Grace passed him at this moment on her way to the Latin classroom. She bowed and smiled in a friendly fashion, and Sidney Hill felt decidedly uncomfortable. What was he to do? He did not like to think of putting Miss Seeley in a false position because somebody had sent her an invitation in his name.

"I suppose it is some cad who has a spite at me that has done it," he reflected, "but if so I'll spoil his game. I'll take Miss Seeley to the prom as if I had never intended doing anything else. She shan't be humiliated just because there is someone at Payzant who would stoop to that sort of thing."

So he walked up the hall with Grace and expressed his pleasure at her acceptance, and on the evening of the prom he sent her a bouquet of white carnations, whose spicy fragrance reminded her of her own little garden at home. Grace thought it extremely nice of him, and dressed in a flutter of pleasant anticipation.

Her gown was a very simple one of sheer white organdie, and was the only evening dress she had. She knew there would be many smarter dresses at the reception, but the knowledge did not disturb her sensible head in the least.

She fingered the dainty white frills lovingly as she remembered the sunny summer days at home in the little sewing-room, where cherry boughs poked their blossoms in at the window, when her mother and sisters had helped her to make it, with laughing prophesies and speculations as to its first appearance. Into seam and puff and frill many girlish hopes and dreams had been sewn, and they all came back to Grace as she put it on, and helped to surround her with an atmosphere of happiness.

When she was ready she picked up her bouquet and looked herself over in the mirror, from the top of her curly head to the tips of her white shoes, with a little nod of satisfaction. Grace was not exactly pretty, but she had such a bright, happy face and such merry brown eyes and such a friendly smile that she was very pleasant to look upon, and a great many people thought so that night.

Grace had never in all her life before had so good a time as she had at that senior prom. The seniors were quick to discover her unaffected originality and charm, and everywhere she went she was the centre of a merry group. In short, Grace, as much to her own surprise as anyone's, found herself a social success.

Presently Sidney brought his brother up to be introduced, and the latter said:

"Miss Seeley, will you excuse my asking if you have a brother or any relative named Max Seeley?"

Grace nodded. "Oh, yes; my brother Max. He is a doctor out west."

"I was sure of it," said Murray Hill triumphantly. "You resemble him so strongly. Please don't consider me as a stranger a minute longer, for Max and I are like brothers. Indeed, I owe my life to him. Last summer I was out there on a surveying expedition, and I took typhoid in a little out-of-the-way place where good nursing was not to be had for love or money. Your brother attended me and he managed to pull me through. He never left me day or night until I was out of danger, and he worked like a Trojan for me."

"Dear old Max," said Grace, her brown eyes shining with pride and pleasure. "That is so like him. He is such a dear brother and I haven't seen him for four years. To see somebody who knows him so well is next best thing to seeing himself."

"He is an awfully fine fellow," said Mr. Hill heartily, "and I'm delighted to have met the 'little sister' he used to talk so much about. I want you to come over and meet my mother and sister. They have heard me talk so much about Max that they think almost as much of him as I do, and they will be glad to meet his sister."

Mrs. Hill, a handsome, dignified lady who was one of the chaperones of the prom, received Grace warmly, while Beatrice Hill, an extremely pretty, smartly gowned girl, made her feel at home immediately.

"You came with Sid, didn't you?" she whispered. "Sid is so sly – he never tells us whom he is going to take anywhere. But when I saw you come in with him I knew I was going to like you, you looked so jolly. And you're really the sister of that splendid Dr. Seeley who saved Murray's life last summer? And to think you've been at Payzant nearly a whole term and we never knew it!"

"Well, how have you enjoyed our prom, Miss Seeley?" asked Sid, as they walked home together under the arching elms of the college campus.

"Oh, it was splendid," said Grace enthusiastically. "Everybody was so nice. And then to meet someone who could tell me so much about Max! I must write them home all about it before I sleep, just to calm my head a bit. Mother and the girls will be so interested, and I must send Lou and Mab a carnation apiece for their scrapbooks."

"Give me one back, please," said Sid. And Grace, with a little blush, did so.

That night, while Grace was slipping the stems of her carnations and putting them into water, three little bits of conversation were being carried on which it is necessary to report in order to round up this story neatly and properly, as all stories should be rounded up.

In the first place, Beatrice Hill was saying to Sidney, "Oh, Sid, that Miss Seeley you had at the prom is a lovely girl. I don't know when I've met anyone I liked so much. She was so jolly and friendly and she didn't put on learned airs at all, as so many of those Payzant girls do. I asked her all about herself and she told me, and all about her mother and sisters and home and the lovely times they had together, and how hard they worked to send her to college too, and how she taught school in vacations and 'roomed' herself to help along. Isn't it so brave and plucky of her! I know we are going to be great friends."

"I hope so," said Sidney briefly, "because I have an idea that she and I are going to be very good friends too."

And Sidney went upstairs and put away a single white carnation very carefully.

In the second place, Mrs. Hill was saying to her eldest son, "I liked that Miss Seeley very much. She seemed a very sweet girl."

And, finally, Agnes Walters and Edna Hayden were discussing the matter in great mystification in their room.

"I can't understand it at all," said Agnes slowly. "Sid Hill took her to the prom and he must have sent her those carnations too. She could never have afforded them herself. And did you see the fuss his people made over her? I heard Beatrice telling her that she was coming to call on her tomorrow, and Mrs. Hill said she must look upon 'Beechlawn' as her second home while she was at Payzant. If the Hills are going to take her up we'll have to be nice to her."

"I suppose," said Edna conclusively, "the truth of the matter is that Sid Hill meant to ask her anyway. I dare say he asked her long ago, and she would know our invitation was a fraud. So the joke is on ourselves, after all."

But, as you and I know, that, with the exception of the last sentence, was not the truth of the matter at all.

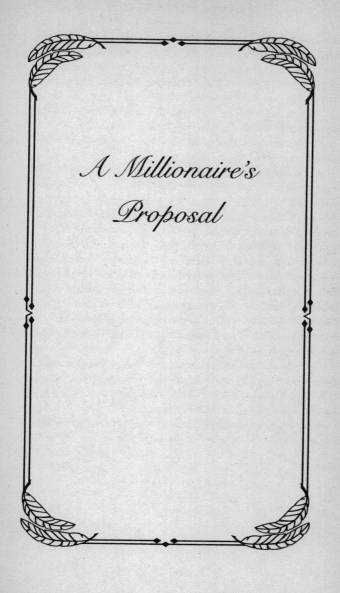

A Millionaire's

Proposal

THRUSH Hill, Oct. 5, 18—.

It is all settled at last, and in another week I shall have left Thrush Hill. I am a little bit sorry and a great bit glad. I am going to Montreal to spend the winter with Alicia.

Alicia – it used to be plain Alice when she lived at Thrush Hill and made her own dresses and trimmed her own hats – is my half-sister. She is eight years older than I am. We are both orphans, and Aunt Elizabeth brought us up here at Thrush Hill, the most delightful old country place in the world, half smothered in big willows and poplars, every one of which I have climbed in the early tomboy days of gingham pinafores and sun-bonnets.

When Alicia was eighteen she married Roger Gresham, a man of forty. The world said that she married him for his money. I dare say she did. Alicia was tired of poverty.

I don't blame her. Very likely I shall do the same thing one of these days, if I get the chance – for I too am tired of poverty.

When Alicia went to Montreal she wanted to take me with her, but I wanted to be outdoors, romping in the hay or running wild in the woods with Jack.

Jack Willoughby – Dr. John H. Willoughby, it reads on his office door – was the son of our nearest neighbour. We were chums always, and when he went away to college I was heartbroken. The vacations were the only joy of my life then.

I don't know just when I began to notice a change in Jack, but when he came home two years ago, a full-fledged M.D. – a great, tall, broad-shouldered fellow, with the sweetest moustache, and lovely thick black hair, just made for poking one's fingers through – I realized it to the full. Jack was grown up. The dear old days of bird-nesting and nutting and coasting and fishing and general delightful goings-on were over forever.

I was sorry at first. I wanted "Jack." "Dr. Willoughby" seemed too distinguished and far away.

I suppose he found a change in me, too. I had put on long skirts and wore my hair up. I had also found out that I had a complexion, and that sunburn was not becoming. I honestly thought I looked pretty, but Jack surveyed me with decided disapprobation.

"What have you done to yourself? You don't look like the same girl. I'd never know you in that rig-out, with all those flippery-trippery curls all over your head. Why don't you comb your hair straight back, and let it hang in a braided tail, like you used to?"

This didn't suit me at all. When I expect a compliment and get something quite different I always get snippy. So I said, with what I intended to be crushing dignity, "that I supposed I wasn't the same girl; I had grown up, and if he didn't like my curls he needn't look at them. For my part, I thought them infinitely preferable to that horrid, conceited-looking moustache he had grown."

"I'll shave it off if it doesn't suit you," said Jack amiably.

Jack is always so provokingly good-humoured. When you've taken pains and put yourself out – even to the extent of fibbing about a moustache – to exasperate a person, there is nothing more annoying than to have him keep perfectly angelic.

But after a while Jack and I adjusted ourselves to the change in each other and became very good friends again. It was quite a different friendship from the old, but it was very pleasant. Yes, it was; I *will* admit that much.

I was provoked at Jack's determination to settle down for life in Valleyfield, a horrible, humdrum, little country village.

"You'll never make your fortune there, Jack," I said spitefully. "You'll just be a poor, struggling country doctor all your life, and you'll be grey at forty."

"I don't expect to make a fortune, Kitty," said Jack quietly.

"Do you think that is the one desirable thing? I shall never be a rich man. But riches are not the only thing that makes life pleasant."

"Well, I think they have a good deal to do with it, anyhow," I retorted. "It's all very well to pretend to despise wealth, but it's generally a case of sour grapes. *I* will own up honestly that I'd *love* to be rich."

It always seems to make Jack blue and grumpy when I talk like that. I suppose that is one reason why he never asked me to settle down in life as a country doctor's wife. Another was, no doubt, that I always nipped his sentimental sproutings religiously in the bud.

Three weeks ago Alicia wrote to me, asking me to spend the winter with her. Her letters always make me just gasp with longing for the life they describe.

Jack's face, when I told him about it, was so woebegone that I felt a stab of remorse, even in the heyday of my delight.

"Do you really mean it, Kitty? Are you going away to leave me?"

"You won't miss me much," I said flippantly – I had a creepy, crawly presentiment that a scene of some kind was threatening – "and I'm awfully tired of Thrush Hill and country life, Jack. I suppose it is horribly ungrateful of me to say so, but it is the truth."

"I shall miss you," he said soberly.

Somehow he had my hands in his. *How* did he ever get them? I was sure I had them safely tucked out of harm's way behind me. "You know, Kitty, that I love you. I am a poor man – perhaps I may never be anything else – and this may seem to you very presumptuous. But I cannot let you go like this. Will you be my wife, dear?"

Wasn't it horribly straightforward and direct? So like Jack! I tried to pull my hands away, but he held them fast. There was nothing to do but answer him. That "no" I had determined to say must be said, but, oh! how woefully it did stick in my throat!

And I honestly believe that by the time I got it out it would have been transformed into a "yes," in spite of me, had it not been for a certain paragraph in Alicia's letter which came providentially to my mind:

> Not to flatter you, Katherine, you are a beauty, my dear – if your photo is to be trusted. If you have not discovered that fact before – how should you, indeed, in a place like Thrush Hill? – you soon will in Montreal. With your face and figure you will make a sensation.
>
> There is to be a nephew of the Sinclairs here this winter. He is an American, immensely wealthy, and will be the catch of the season. A word to the wise, etc. Don't get into any foolish entanglement down there. I have heard some gossip of you and our old playfellow, Jack Willoughby. I hope it is nothing but gossip. You can do better than that, Katherine.

That settled Jack's fate, if there ever had been any doubt.

"Don't talk like that, Jack," I said hurriedly. "It is all nonsense. I think a great deal of you as a friend and – and – all that, you know. But I can never marry you."

"Are you sure, Kitty?" said Jack earnestly. "Don't you care for me at all?"

It was horrid of Jack to ask that question!

"No," I said miserably, "not – not in that way, Jack. Oh, don't ever say anything like this to me again."

He let go of my hands then, white to the lips.

"Oh, don't look like that, Jack," I entreated.

"I can't help it," he said in a low voice. "But I won't bother you again, dear. It was foolish of me to expect – to hope for anything of the sort. You are a thousand times too good for me, I know."

"Oh, indeed I'm not, Jack," I protested. "If you knew how horrid I am, really, you'd be glad and thankful for your escape. Oh, Jack, I wish people never grew up."

Jack smiled sadly.

"Don't feel badly over this, Kitty. It isn't your fault. Good night, dear."

He turned my face up and kissed me squarely on the mouth. He had never kissed me since the summer before he went away to college. Somehow it didn't seem a bit the same as it used to; it was – nicer now.

After he went away I came upstairs and had a good, comfortable howl. Then I buried the whole affair decently. I am not going to think of it any more.

I shall always have the highest esteem for Jack, and I hope he will soon find some nice girl who will make him happy. Mary Carter would jump at him, I know. To be sure, she is as homely as she can be and live. But, then, Jack is always telling me how little he cares for beauty, so I have no doubt she will suit him admirably.

As for myself – well, I am ambitious. I don't suppose my ambition is a very lofty one, but such as it is I mean to hunt it down. Come. Let me put it down in black and white, once for all, and see how it looks:

I mean to marry the rich nephew of the Sinclairs.

There! It is out, and I feel better. How mercenary and awful it looks written out in cold blood like that. I wouldn't have Jack or Aunt Elizabeth – dear, unworldly old soul – see it for the world. But I wouldn't mind Alicia.

Poor dear Jack!

Montreal, Dec. 16, 18—.

This is a nice way to keep a journal. But the days when I could write regularly are gone by. That was when I was at Thrush Hill.

I am having a simply divine time. How in the world did I ever contrive to live at Thrush Hill?

To be sure, I felt badly enough that day in October when I left it. When the train left Valleyfield I just cried like a baby.

Alicia and Roger welcomed me very heartily, and after the first week of homesickness – I shiver yet when I think of it – was over, I settled down to my new life as if I had been born to it.

Alicia has a magnificent home and everything heart could wish for – jewels, carriages, servants, opera boxes, and social position. Roger is a model husband apparently. I must also admit that he is a model brother-in-law.

I could feel Alicia looking me over critically the moment we met. I trembled with suspense, but I was soon relieved.

"Do you know, Katherine, I am glad to see that your photograph didn't flatter you. Photographs so often do. I am positively surprised at the way you have developed, my dear; you used to be such a scrawny little brown thing. By the way, I hope there is nothing between you and Jack Willoughby?"

"No, of course not," I answered hurriedly. I had intended to tell Alicia all about Jack, but when it came to the point I couldn't.

"I am glad of that," said Alicia, with a relieved air. "Of course, I've no doubt Jack is a good fellow enough. He was a nice boy. But he would not be a suitable husband for you, Katherine."

I knew that very well. That was just why I had refused him. But it made me wince to hear Alicia say it. I instantly froze up – Alicia says dignity is becoming to me – and Jack's name has never been mentioned between us since.

I made my bow to society at an "At Home" which Alicia gave for that purpose. She drilled me well beforehand, and I think I acquitted myself decently. Charlie Vankleek, whose verdict makes or mars every debutante in his set, has approved of me. He called me a beauty, and everybody now believes that I am one, and greets me accordingly.

I met Gus Sinclair at Mrs. Brompton's dinner. Alicia declares it was a case of love at first sight. If so, I must confess that it was all on one side.

Mr. Sinclair is undeniably ugly – even Alicia has to admit that – and can't hold a candle to Jack in point of looks, for Jack, poor boy, was handsome, if he were nothing else. But, as Alicia does not fail to remind me, Mr. Sinclair's homeliness is well gilded.

Apart from his appearance, I really liked him very much. He is a gentlemanly little fellow – his head reaches about to my shoulder – cultured and travelled, and can talk splendidly, which Jack never could.

He took me into dinner at Mrs. Brompton's, and was very attentive. You may imagine how many angelic glances I received from the other candidates for his favour.

Since then I have been having the gayest time imaginable. Dances, dinners, luncheons, afternoon teas, "functions" to no end, and all delightful.

Aunt Elizabeth writes to me, but I have never heard a word from Jack. He seems to have forgotten my existence completely. No doubt he has consoled himself with Mary Carter.

Well, that is all for the best, but I must say I did not think Jack could have forgotten me so soon or so absolutely. Of course it does not make the least difference to me.

The Sinclairs and the Bromptons and the Curries are to dine here tonight. I can see myself reflected in the long mirror before me, and I really think my appearance will satisfy even Gus Sinclair's critical eye. I am pale, as usual; I never have any colour. That used to be one of Jack's grievances. He likes pink and white milkmaidish girls. My "magnificent pallor" didn't suit him at all.

But, what is more to the purpose, it suits Gus Sinclair. He admires the statuesque style.

Montreal, Jan. 20, 18—.

Here it is a whole month since my last entry. I am sitting here decked out in "gloss of satin and glimmer of pearls" for Mrs. Currie's dance. These few minutes, after I emerge from the hands of my maid and before the carriage is announced, are almost the only ones I ever have to myself.

I am having a good time still. Somehow, though, it isn't as exciting as it used to be. I'm afraid I'm very changeable. I believe I must be homesick.

I'd love to get a glimpse of dear old Thrush Hill and Aunt Elizabeth, and J— but, no! I will not write that.

Mr. Sinclair has not spoken yet, but there is no doubt that he soon will. Of course, I shall accept him when he does, and I coolly told Alicia so when she just as coolly asked me what I meant to do.

"Certainly, I shall marry him," I said crossly, for the subject always irritates me. "Haven't I been laying myself out all winter to catch him? That is the bold, naked truth, and ugly enough it is. My dearly beloved sister, I mean to accept Mr. Sinclair, without any hesitation, whenever I get the chance."

"I give you credit for more sense than to dream of doing anything else," said Alicia in relieved tones. "Katherine, you are a very lucky girl."

"Because I am going to marry a rich man for his money?" I said coldly.

Sometimes I get snippy with Alicia these days.

"No," said my half-sister in an exasperated way. "Why will you persist in speaking in that way? You are very provoking. It is not likely I would wish to see you throw yourself away on a poor man, and I'm sure you must like Gus."

"Oh, yes, I like him well enough," I said listlessly. "To be sure, I did think once, in my salad days, that liking wasn't quite all in an affair of this kind. I was absurd enough to imagine that love had something to do with it."

"Don't talk so nonsensically," said Alicia sharply. "Love!

Well, of course, you ought to love your husband, and you will. He loves you enough, at all events."

"Alicia," I said earnestly, looking her straight in the face and speaking bluntly enough to have satisfied even Jack's love of straightforwardness, "you married for money and position, so people say. Are you happy?"

For the first time that I remembered, Alicia blushed. She was very angry.

"Yes, I did marry for money," she said sharply, "and I don't regret it. Thank heaven, I never was a fool."

"Don't be vexed, Alicia," I entreated. "I only asked because – well, it is no matter."

Montreal, Jan. 25, 18—.

It is bedtime, but I am too excited and happy and miserable to sleep. Jack has been here – dear old Jack! How glad I was to see him.

His coming was so unexpected. I was sitting alone in my room this afternoon – I believe I was moping – when Bessie brought up his card. I gave it one rapturous look and tore downstairs, passing Alicia in the hall like a whirlwind, and burst into the drawing-room in a most undignified way.

"Jack!" I cried, holding out both hands to him in welcome.

There he was, just the same old Jack, with his splendid big shoulders and his lovely brown eyes. And his necktie was crooked, too; as soon as I could get my hands free I put them up and straightened it out for him. How nice and old-timey that was!

"So you are glad to see me, Kitty?" he said as he squeezed my hands in his big strong paws.

"'Deed and 'deed I am, Jack. I thought you had forgotten me altogether. And I've been so homesick and so – so every-thing," I said incoherently. "And, oh, Jack, I've so many ques-tions to ask I don't know where to begin. Tell me all the Thrush Hill and Valleyfield news, tell me everything that has happened since I left. How many people have you killed off? And, oh, why didn't you come to see me before?"

"I didn't think I should be wanted, Kitty," Jack answered quietly. "You seemed to be so absorbed in your new life that old friends and interests were crowded out."

"So I was at first," I answered penitently. "I was dazzled, you know. The glare was too much for my Thrush Hill brown. But it's different now. How did you happen to come, Jack?"

"I had to come to Montreal on business, and I thought it would be too bad if I went back without coming to see what they had been doing in Vanity Fair to my little playmate."

"Well, what do you think they have been doing?" I asked saucily.

I had on a particularly fetching gown and knew I was looking my best. Jack, however, looked me over with his head on one side.

"Well, I don't know, Kitty," he said slowly. "That is a stunning sort of dress you have on – not so pretty, though, as that old blue muslin you used to wear last summer – and your hair is pretty good. But you look rather disdainful and, after all, I believe I prefer Thrush Hill Kitty."

How like Jack that was. He never thought me really pretty, and he is too honest to pretend he does.

But I didn't care. I just laughed, and we sat down together and had a long, delightful, chummy talk.

Jack told me all the Valleyfield gossip, not forgetting to mention that Mary Carter was going to be married to a minister in June. Jack didn't seem to mind it a bit, so I guess he couldn't have been particularly interested in Mary.

In due time Alicia sailed in. I suppose she had found out from Bessie who my caller was, and felt rather worried over the length of our tête-à-tête.

She greeted Jack very graciously, but with a certain polite condescension of which she is past mistress. I am sure Jack felt it, for, as soon as he decently could, he got up to go. Alicia asked him to remain to dinner.

"We are having a few friends to dine with us, but it is quite an informal affair," she said sweetly.

I felt that Jack glanced at me for the fraction of a second. But I remembered that Gus Sinclair was coming too, and I did not look at him.

Then he declined quietly. He had a business engagement, he said.

I suppose Alicia had noticed that look at me, for she showed her claws.

"Don't forget to call any time you are in Montreal," she said more sweetly than ever. "I am sure Katherine will always be glad to see any of her old friends, although some of her new ones *are* proving very absorbing – one, in especial. Don't blush, Katherine, I am sure Mr. Willoughby won't tell any tales out of school to your old Valleyfield friends."

I was not blushing, and I was furious. It was really too bad of Alicia, although I don't see why I need have cared.

Alicia kept her eye on us both until Jack was fairly gone. Then she remarked in the patronizing tone which I detest:

"Really, Katherine, Jack Willoughby has developed into quite a passable-looking fellow, although he is rather shabby. But I suppose he is poor."

"Yes," I answered curtly, "he is poor, in everything except youth and manhood and goodness and truth! But I suppose those don't count for anything."

Whereupon Alicia lifted her eyebrows and looked me over.

Just at dusk a box arrived with Jack's compliments. It was full of lovely white carnations, and must have cost the extravagant fellow more than he has any business to waste on flowers. I was beast enough to put them on when I went down to listen to another man's love-making.

This evening I sparkled and scintillated with unusual

brilliancy, for Jack's visit and my consequent crossing of swords with Alicia had produced a certain elation of spirits. When Gus Sinclair was leaving he asked if he might see me alone tomorrow afternoon.

I knew what that meant, and a cold shiver went up and down my backbone. But I looked down at him – spick-and-span and glossy – *his* neckties are never crooked – and said, yes, he might come at three o'clock.

Alicia had noticed our aside – when did anything ever escape her? – and when he was gone she asked, significantly, what secret he had been telling me.

"He wants to see me alone tomorrow afternoon. I suppose you know what that means, Alicia?"

"Ah," purred Alicia, "I congratulate you, my dear."

"Aren't your congratulations a little premature?" I asked coldly. "I haven't accepted him yet."

"But you will?"

"Oh, certainly. Isn't it what we've schemed and angled for? I'm very well satisfied."

And so I am. But I wish it hadn't come so soon after Jack's visit, because I feel rather upset yet. Of course I like Gus Sinclair very much, and I am sure I shall be very fond of him.

Well, I must go to bed now and get my beauty sleep. I don't want to be haggard and hollow-eyed at that important interview tomorrow – an interview that will decide my destiny.

Thrush Hill, May 6, 18—.

Well, it did decide it, but not exactly in the way I anticipated. I can look back on the whole affair quite calmly now, but I wouldn't live it over again for all the wealth of Ind.

That day when Gus Sinclair came I was all ready for him. I had put on my very prettiest new gown to do honour to the occasion, and Alicia smilingly assured me I was looking very well.

"And *so* cool and composed. Will you be able to keep that up? Don't you really feel a little nervous, Katherine?"

"Not in the least," I said. "I suppose I ought to be, according to traditions, but I never felt less flustered in my life."

When Bessie brought up Gus Sinclair's card Alicia dropped a pecky little kiss on my cheek, and pushed me toward the door. I went down calmly, although I'll admit that my heart *was* beating wildly. Gus Sinclair was plainly nervous, but I was composed enough for both. You would really have thought that I was in the habit of being proposed to by a millionaire every day.

"I suppose you know what I have come to say," he said, standing before me, as I leaned gracefully back in a big chair, having taken care that the folds of my dress fell just as they should.

And then he proceeded to say it in a rather jumbled-up fashion, but very sincerely.

I remember thinking at the time that he must have composed the speech in his head the night before, and rehearsed it several times, but was forgetting it in spots.

When he ended with the self-same question that Jack had asked me three months before at Thrush Hill he stooped and took my hands.

I looked up at him. His good, homely face was close to mine, and in his eyes was an unmistakable look of love and tenderness.

I opened my mouth to say yes.

And then there came over me in one rush the most awful realization of the sacrilege I was going to commit.

I forgot everything except that I loved Jack Willoughby, and that I could never, never marry anybody in the world except him.

Then I pulled my hands away and burst into hysterical, undignified tears.

"I beg your pardon," said Mr. Sinclair. "I did not mean to startle you. Have I been too abrupt? Surely you must have known – you must have expected –"

"Yes – yes – I knew," I cried miserably, "and I intended right up to this very minute to marry you. I'm so sorry – but I can't – I can't."

"I don't understand," he said in a bewildered tone. "If you expected it, then why – why – don't you care for me?"

"No, that's just it," I sobbed. "I don't love you at all – and I do love somebody else. But he is poor, and I hate poverty. So I refused him, and I meant to marry you just because you are rich."

Such a pained look came over his face. "I did not think this of you," he said in a low tone.

"Oh, I know I have acted shamefully," I said. "You can't think any worse of me than I do of myself. How you must despise me!"

"No," he said, with a grim smile, "if I did it would be easier for me. I might not love you then. Don't distress yourself, Katherine. I do not deny that I feel greatly hurt and disappointed, but I am glad you have been true to yourself at last. Don't cry, dear."

"You're very good," I answered disconsolately, "but all the same the fact remains that I have behaved disgracefully to you, and I know you think so. Oh, Mr. Sinclair, please, please, go away. I feel so miserably ashamed of myself that I cannot look you in the face."

"I am going, dear," he said gently. "I know all this must be very painful to you, but it is not easy for me, either."

"Can you forgive me?" I said wistfully.

"Yes, my dear, completely. Do not let yourself be unhappy over this. Remember that I will always be your friend. Goodbye."

He held out his hand and gave mine an earnest clasp. Then he went away.

I remained in the drawing-room, partly because I wanted to finish out my cry, and partly because, miserable coward that I was, I didn't dare face Alicia. Finally she came in, her face wreathed with anticipatory smiles. But when her eyes fell on my forlorn, crumpled self she fairly jumped.

"Katherine, what is the matter?" she asked sharply. "Didn't Mr. Sinclair –"

"Yes, he did," I said desperately. "And I've refused him. There now, Alicia!"

Then I waited for the storm to burst. It didn't all at once. The shock was too great, and at first quite paralyzed my half-sister.

"Katherine," she gasped, "are you crazy? Have you lost your senses?"

"No, I've just come to them. It's true enough, Alicia. You can scold all you like. I know I deserve it, and I won't flinch. I did really intend to take him, but when it came to the point I couldn't. I didn't love him."

Then, indeed, the storm burst. I never saw Alicia so angry before, and I never got so roundly abused. But even Alicia has her limits, and at last she grew calmer.

"You have behaved disgracefully," she concluded. "I am disgusted with you. You have encouraged Gus Sinclair markedly right along, and now you throw him over like this. I never dreamed that you were capable of such unwomanly behaviour."

"That's a hard word, Alicia," I protested feebly.

She dealt me a withering glance. "It does not begin to be as hard as your shameful conduct merits. To think of losing a fortune like that for the sake of sentimental folly! I didn't think you were such a consummate fool."

"I suppose you absorbed all the sense of our family," I said drearily. "There now, Alicia, do leave me alone. I'm down in the very depths already."

"What do you mean to do now?" said Alicia scornfully.

"Go back to Valleyfield and marry that starving country doctor of yours, I suppose?"

I flared up then; Alicia might abuse me all she liked, but I wasn't going to hear a word against Jack.

"Yes, I will, if he'll have me," I said, and I marched out of the room and upstairs, with my head very high.

Of course I decided to leave Montreal as soon as I could. But I couldn't get away within a week, and it was a very unpleasant one. Alicia treated me with icy indifference, and I knew I should never be reinstated in her good graces.

To my surprise, Roger took my part. "Let the girl alone," he told Alicia. "If she doesn't love Sinclair, she was right in refusing him. I, for one, am glad that she has got enough truth and womanliness in her to keep her from selling herself."

Then he came to the library where I was moping, and laid his hand on my head.

"Little girl," he said earnestly, "no matter what anyone says to you, never marry a man for his money or for any other reason on earth except because you love him."

This comforted me greatly, and I did not cry myself to sleep that night as usual.

At last I got away. I had telegraphed to Jack: "Am coming home Wednesday; meet me at train," and I knew he would be there. How I longed to see him again – dear, old, badly treated Jack.

I got to Valleyfield just at dusk. It was a rainy evening, and everything was slush and fog and gloom. But away up I saw the home light at Thrush Hill, and Jack was waiting for me on the platform.

"Oh, Jack!" I said, clinging to him, regardless of appearances. "Oh, I'm so glad to be back."

"That's right, Kitty. I knew you wouldn't forget us. How well you are looking!"

"I suppose I ought to be looking wretched," I said

penitently. "I've been behaving very badly, Jack. Wait till we get away from the crowd and I'll tell you all about it."

And I did.

I didn't gloss over anything, but just confessed the whole truth. Jack heard me through in silence, and then he kissed me.

"Can you forgive me, Jack, and take me back?" I whispered, cuddling up to him.

And he said – but, on second thought, I will not write down what he said.

We are to be married in June.

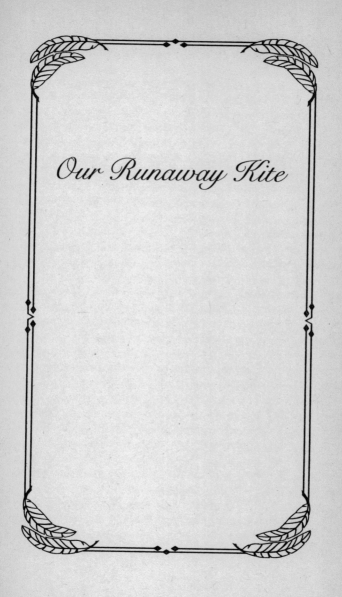

Our Runaway Kite

F course there was nobody for us to play with on the Big Half Moon, but then, as Claude says, you can't have everything. We just had to make the most of each other, and we did.

The Big Half Moon is miles from anywhere, except the Little Half Moon. But nobody lives there, so that doesn't count.

We live on the Big Half Moon. "We" are Father and Claude and I and Aunt Esther and Mimi and Dick. It used to be only Father and Claude and I. It is all on account of the kite that there are more of us. This is what I want to tell you about.

Father is the keeper of the Big Half Moon lighthouse. He has always been the keeper ever since I can remember, although that isn't very long. I am only eleven years old. Claude is twelve.

In winter, when the harbour is frozen over, there isn't any need of a light on the Big Half Moon, and we all move over to the mainland, and Claude and Mimi and Dick and I go to school. But as soon as spring comes, back we sail to our own dear island, so glad that we don't know what to do with ourselves.

The funny part used to be that people always pitied us when the time came for us to return. They said we must be so lonesome over there, with no other children near us, and not even a woman to look after us.

Why, Claude and I were never lonesome. There was always so much to do, and Claude is splendid at making believe. He makes the very best pirate chief I ever saw. Dick is pretty good, but he can never roar out his orders in the blood-curdling tones that Claude can.

Of course Claude and I would have liked to have someone to play with us, because it is hard to run pirate caves and things like that with only two. But we used to quarrel a good deal with the mainland children in winter, so perhaps it was just as well that there were none of them on the Big Half Moon. Claude and I never quarrelled. We used to argue sometimes and get excited, but that was as far as it ever went. When I saw Claude getting too excited I gave in to him. He is a boy, you know, and they have to be humoured; they are not like girls.

As for having a woman to look after us, I thought that just too silly, and so did Claude. What did we need with a woman when we had Father? He could cook all we wanted to eat and make molasses taffy that was just like a dream. He kept our clothes all mended, and everything about the lighthouse was neat as wax. Of course I helped him lots. I like pottering round.

He used to hear our lessons and tell us splendid stories and saw that we always said our prayers. Claude and I wouldn't have done anything to make him feel bad for the world. Father is just lovely.

To be sure, he didn't seem to have any relations except us. This used to puzzle Claude and me. Everybody on the mainland had relations; why hadn't we? Was it because we lived on an island? We thought it would be so jolly to have an uncle and aunt and some cousins. Once we asked Father about it, but he looked so sorrowful all of a sudden that we wished we hadn't. He said it was all his fault. I didn't see how that could be, but I never said anything more about it to Father. Still, I did wish we had some relations.

It is always lovely out here on the Big Half Moon in summer. When it is fine the harbour is blue and calm, with little winds and ripples purring over it, and the mainland shores look like long blue lands where fairies dwell. Away out over the bar, where the big ships go, it is always hazy and pearl-tinted, like the inside of the mussel shells. Claude says he is going to sail out there when he grows up. I would like to too, but Claude says I can't because I'm a girl. It is dreadfully inconvenient to be a girl at times.

When it storms it is grand to see the great waves come crashing up against the Big Half Moon as if they meant to swallow it right down. You can't see the Little Half Moon at all then; it is hidden by the mist and spume.

We had our pirate cave away up among the rocks, where we kept an old pistol with the lock broken, a rusty cutlass, a pair of knee boots, and Claude's jute beard and wig. Down on the shore, around one of the horns of the Half Moon, was the Mermaid's Pool, where we sailed our toy boats and watched for sea kelpies. We never saw any. Dick says there is no such thing as a kelpy. But then Dick has no imagination. It is no argument against a thing that you've never seen it. I have never seen the pyramids, either, but I know that there are pyramids.

Every summer we had some hobby. The last summer before Dick and Mimi came we were crazy about kites. A winter boy on the mainland showed Claude how to make them, and when we went back to the Big Half Moon we made kites galore. Even pirating wasn't such good fun. Claude would go around to the other side of the Big Half Moon and we would play shipwrecked mariners signalling to each other with kites. Oh, it was very exciting.

We had one kite that was a dandy. It was as big as we could make it and covered with lovely red paper; we had pasted gold tinsel stars all over it and written our names out in full on it – Claude Martin Leete and Philippa Brewster Leete, Big Half Moon Lighthouse. That kite had the most magnificent tail, too.

It used to scare the gulls nearly to death when we sent up our kites. They didn't know what to make of them. And the Big Half Moon is such a place for gulls – there are hundreds of them here.

One day there was a grand wind for kite-flying, and Claude and I were having a splendid time. We used our smaller kites for signalling, and when we got tired of that Claude sent me to the house for the big one. I'm sure I don't know how it happened, but when I was coming back over the rocks I tripped and fell, and my elbow went clear through that lovely kite. You would never have believed that one small elbow could make such a big hole. Claude said it was just like a girl to fall and stick her elbow through a kite, but I don't see why it should be any more like a girl than a boy. Do you?

We had to hurry to fix the kite if we wanted to send it up before the wind fell, so we rushed into the lighthouse to get some paper. We knew there was no more red paper, and the looks of the kite were spoiled, anyhow, so we just took the first thing that came handy – an old letter that was lying on the bookcase in the sitting-room. I suppose we shouldn't have taken it, although, as matters turned out, it was the best thing we could have done; but Father was away to the mainland to buy things, and we never thought it could make any difference about an old yellow letter. It was one Father had taken from a drawer in the bookcase which he had cleaned out the night before. We patched the kite up with the letter, a sheet on each side, and dried it by the fire. Then we started out, and up went the kite like a bird. The wind was glorious, and it soared and strained like something alive. All at once – snap! And there was Claude, standing with a bit of cord in his hand, looking as foolish as a flatfish, and our kite sailing along at a fearful rate of speed over to the mainland.

I might have said to Claude, So like a boy! but I didn't. Instead, I sympathized with him, and pointed out that it really didn't matter because I had spoiled it by jabbing my elbow through it. By this time the kite was out of sight, and we never expected to see or hear of it again.

A MONTH LATER a letter came to the Big Half Moon for Father. Jake Wiggins brought it over in his sloop. Father went off by himself to read it, and such a queer-looking face as he had when he came back! His eyes looked as if he had been crying, but that couldn't be, I suppose, because Claude says men never cry. Anyhow, his face was all glad and soft and smiley.

"Do you two young pirates and freebooters want to know what has become of your kite?" he said.

Then he sat down beside us on the rocks at the Mermaid's Pool and told us the whole story, and read his letter to us. It was the most amazing thing.

It seems Father had had relations after all – a brother and a sister in particular. But when he was a young man he quarrelled with his brother, who didn't treat him very well – but he's been dead for years, so I won't say a word against him – and had gone away from home. He never went back, and he never even let them know he was living.

Father says that this was very wrong of him, and I suppose it was, since he says so; but I don't see how Father could do anything wrong.

Anyway, he had a sister Esther whom he loved very much; but he felt bitter against her too, because he thought she took his brother's part too much. So, though a letter of hers, asking him to go back, did reach him, he never answered it, and he never heard anything more. Years afterward he felt sorry and went back, but his brother was dead and his sister had gone away, and he couldn't find out a single thing about her.

So much for that; and now about the kite. The letter Father had just received was from his sister, our Aunt Esther and the mother of Dick and Mimi. She was living at a place hundreds of miles inland. Her husband was dead and, as we found out later, although she did not say a word about it in the letter, she was very poor. One day when Dick and Mimi were out in the woods looking for botany specimens they saw something funny in the top of a tree. Dick climbed up and got it. It was a big red kite with a patch on each side and names written on it. They carried it home to their mother. Dick has since told us that she turned as pale as the dead when she saw our names on it. You see, Philippa was her mother's name and Claude was her father's. And when she read the letter that was pasted over the hole in the kite she knew who we must be, for it was the very letter she had written to her brother so long ago. So she sat right down and wrote again, and this was the letter Jake Wiggins brought to the Big Half Moon. It was a beautiful letter. I loved Aunt Esther before I ever saw her, just from that letter.

Next day Father got Jake to take his place for a few days, and he left Claude and me over on the mainland while he went to see Aunt Esther. When he came back he brought Aunt Esther and Dick and Mimi with him, and they have been here ever since.

You don't know how splendid it is! Aunt Esther is such a dear, and Dick and Mimi are too jolly for words. They love the Big Half Moon as well as Claude and I do, and Dick makes a perfectly elegant shipwrecked mariner.

But the best of it all is that we have relations now!

The Schoolmaster's Letters

A T sunset the schoolmaster went up to his room to write a letter to her. He always wrote to her at the same time – when the red wave of the sunset, flaming over the sea, surged in at the little curtainless window and flowed over the pages he wrote on. The light was rose-red and imperial and spiritual, like his love for her, and seemed almost to dye the words of the letters in its own splendid hues – the letters to her which she never was to see, whose words her eyes never were to read, and whose love and golden fancy and rainbow dreams never were to be so much as known by her. And it was because she never was to see them that he dared to write them, straight out of his full heart, taking the exquisite pleasure of telling her what he never could permit himself to tell her face to face. Every evening he wrote thus to her, and the hour so spent glorified the entire day. The rest of the hours – all the other hours of the commonplace day – he was merely a poor schoolmaster with a long struggle before him, one who might not lift his eyes to gaze on a star. But at this hour he was her equal, meeting her soul to soul, telling out as a man might all his great love for her, and wearing the jewel of it on his brow. What wonder indeed that the precious hour which made him a king, crowned with a mighty and unselfish passion, was above all things sacred to him? And doubly sacred when, as tonight, it followed upon an hour spent with her? Its mingled delight and pain were almost more than he could bear.

He went through the kitchen and the hall and up the narrow staircase with a glory in his eyes that thus were held from seeing his sordid surroundings. Link Houseman, sprawled out on the platform before the kitchen door, saw him pass with that rapt face, and chuckled. Link was ill enough to look at any time, with his sharp, freckled features and foxy eyes. When he chuckled his face was that of an unholy imp.

But the schoolmaster took no heed of him. Neither did he heed the girl whom he met in the hall. Her handsome, sullen face flushed crimson under the sting of his utter disregard, and her black eyes followed him up the stairs with a look that was not good to see.

"Sis," whispered Link piercingly, "come out here! I've got a joke to tell you, something about the master and his girl. You ain't to let on to him you know, though. I found it out last night when he was off to the shore. That old key of Uncle Jim's was just the thing. He's a softy, and no mistake."

UPSTAIRS in his little room, the schoolmaster was writing his letter. The room was as bare and graceless as all the other rooms of the farmhouse where he had boarded during his term of teaching; but it looked out on the sea, and was hung with such priceless tapestry of his iris dreams and visions that it was to him an apartment in a royal palace. From it he gazed afar on bays that were like great cups of sapphire brimming over with ruby wine for gods to drain, on headlands that were like amethyst, on wide sweeps of sea that were blue and far and mysterious; and ever the moan and call of the ocean's heart came up to his heart as of one great, hopeless love and longing crying out to another love and longing, as great and hopeless. And here, in the rose-radiance of the sunset, with the sea-music in the dim air, he wrote his letter to her.

My Lady: How beautiful it is to think that there is nothing to prevent my loving you! There is much – everything – to prevent me from telling you that I love you. But nothing has any right to come between my heart and its own; it is permitted to love you forever and ever and serve and reverence you in secret and silence. For so much, dear, I thank life, even though the price of the permission must always be the secret and the silence.

I have just come from you, my lady. Your voice is still in my ears; your eyes are still looking into mine, gravely yet half smilingly, sweetly yet half provokingly. Oh, how dear and human and girlish and queenly you are – half saint and half very womanly woman! And how I love you with all there is of me to love – heart and soul and brain, every fibre of body and spirit thrilling to the wonder and marvel and miracle of it! You do not know it, my sweet, and you must never know it. You would not even wish to know it, for I am nothing to you but one of many friends, coming into your life briefly and passing out of it, of no more account to you than a sunshiny hour, a bird's song, a bursting bud in your garden. But the hour and the bird and the flower gave you a little delight in their turn, and when you remembered them once before forgetting, that was their reward and blessing. That is all I ask, dear lady, and I ask that only in my own heart. I am content to love you and be forgotten. It is sweeter to love you and be forgotten than it would be to love any other woman and live in her lifelong remembrance: so humble has love made me, sweet, so great is my sense of my own unworthiness.

Yet love must find expression in some fashion, dear, else it is only pain, and hence these letters to you which you will never read. I put all my heart into them; they are the best and highest of me, the buds of a love that can never bloom openly in the sunshine of your life. I weave a chaplet of them, dear, and crown you with it. They will never fade, for such love is eternal.

It is a whole summer since I first met you. I had been waiting for you all my life before and did not know it. But I knew it when you came and brought with you a sense of completion and fulfilment. This has been the precious year of my life, the turning-point to which all things past tended and all things future must look back. Oh, my dear, I thank you for this year! It has been your royal gift to me, and I shall be rich and great forever because of it. Nothing can ever take it from me, nothing can mar it. It were well to have lived a lifetime of loneliness for such a boon – the price would not be too high. I would not give my one perfect summer for a generation of other men's happiness.

There are those in the world who would laugh at me, who would pity me, Una. They would say that the love I have poured out in secret at your feet has been wasted, that I am a poor weak fool to squander all my treasure of affection on a woman who does not care for me and who is as far above me as that great white star that is shining over the sea. Oh, my dear, they do not know, they cannot understand. The love I have given you has not left me poorer. It has enriched my life unspeakably; it has opened my eyes and given me the gift of clear vision for those things that matter; it has been a lamp held before my stumbling feet whereby I have avoided snares and pitfalls of baser passions and unworthy dreams. For all this I thank you, dear, and for all this surely the utmost that I can give of love and reverence and service is not too much.

I could not have helped loving you. But if I could have helped it, knowing with just what measure of pain and joy it would brim my cup, I would have chosen to love you, Una. There are those who strive to forget a hopeless love. To me, the greatest misfortune that life could bring would be that I should forget you. I want to remember you always and love you and long for you. That would be unspeakably better than any happiness that could come to me through forgetting.

Dear lady, good night. The sun has set; there is now but one fiery dimple on the horizon, as if a golden finger had dented it – now it is gone; the mists are coming up over the sea.

A kiss on each of your white hands, dear. Tonight I am too humble to lift my thoughts to your lips.

The schoolmaster folded up his letter and held it against his cheek for a little space while he gazed out on the silver-shining sea with his dark eyes full of dreams. Then he took from his shabby trunk a little inlaid box and unlocked it with a twisted silver key. It was full of letters – his letters to Una. The first had been written months ago, in the early promise of a northern spring. They linked together the golden weeks of the summer. Now, in the purple autumn, the box was full, and the schoolmaster's term was nearly ended.

He took out the letters reverently and looked over them, now and then murmuring below his breath some passages scattered through the written pages. He had laid bare his heart in those letters, writing out what he never could have told her, even if his love had been known and returned, for dead and gone generations of stern and repressed forefathers laid their unyielding fingers of reserve on his lips, and the shyness of dreamy, book-bred youth stemmed the language of eye and tone.

I will love you forever and ever. And even though you know it not, surely such love will hover around you all your life. Like an invisible benediction, not understood but dimly felt, guarding you from ill and keeping far from you all things and thoughts of harm and evil!

Sometimes I let myself dream. And in those dreams you love me, and we go out to meet life together. I have dreamed that you kissed me – dreamed it so reverently that the dream did your womanhood no wrong. I have dreamed that you put your hands in mine and said, "I love you." Oh, the rapture of it!

We may give all we will if we do not ask for a return. There should be no barter in love. If, by reason of the greatness of my love for you, I were to ask your love in return, I should be a base creature. It is only because I am content to love and serve for the sake of loving and serving that I have the right to love you.

I have a memory of a blush of yours – a rose of the years that will bloom forever in my garden of remembrance. Tonight you blushed when I came upon you suddenly among the flowers. You were startled – perhaps I had broken too rudely on some girlish musing; and straightway your round, pale curve of cheek and your white arch of brow were made rosy as with the dawn of a beautiful sunrise. I shall see you forever as you looked at that time. In my mad moments I shall dream, knowing all the while that it is only a dream, that you blushed with delight at my coming. I shall be able to picture forevermore how you would look at one you loved.

Tonight the moon was low in the west. It hung over the sea like a shallop of ruddy gold moored to a star in the harbour of the night. I lingered long and watched it, for I knew that you, too, were watching it from your window that looks on the sea. You told me once that you always watched the moon set. It has been a bond between us ever since.

This morning I rose at dawn and walked on the shore to think of you, because it seemed the most fitting time. It was before sunrise, and the world was virgin. All the east was a shimmer of silver and the morning star floated in it like a dissolving pearl. The sea was a great miracle. I walked up and down by it and said your name over and over again. The hour was sacred to you. It was as pure and unspoiled as your own soul. Una, who will bring into your life the sunrise splendour and colour of love?

Do you know how beautiful you are, Una? Let me tell you, dear. You are tall, yet you have to lift your eyes a little to meet mine. Such dear eyes, Una! They are dark blue, and when you smile they are like wet violets in sunshine. But when you are pensive they are more lovely still – the spirit and enchantment of the sea at twilight passes into them then. Your hair has the gloss and brownness of ripe nuts, and your face is always pale. Your lips have a trick of falling apart in a half-smile when you listen. They told me before I knew you that you were pretty. Pretty! The word is cheap and tawdry. You are beautiful, with the beauty of a pearl or a star or a white flower.

Do you remember our first meeting? It was one evening last spring. You were in your garden. The snow had not all gone, but your hands were full of pale, early flowers. You wore a white shawl over your shoulders and head. Your face was turned upward a little, listening to a robin's call in the leafless trees above you. I thought God had never made anything so lovely and love-deserving. I loved you from that moment, Una.

This is your birthday. The world has been glad of you for twenty years. It is fitting that there have been bird songs and sunshine and blossom today, a great light and fragrance over land and sea. This morning I went far afield to a long, lonely valley lying to the west, girt round about with dim old pines, where feet of men seldom tread, and there I searched until I found some rare flowers meet to offer you. I sent them to you with a little book, an old book. A new book, savouring of the shop and marketplace, however beautiful it might be, would not do for you. So I sent the book that was my mother's. She read it and loved it – the faded rose-leaves she placed in it are there still. At first, dear, I almost feared to send it. Would you miss its meaning? Would you laugh a little at the shabby volume with its pencil marks and its rose-leaves? But I knew you would not; I knew you would understand.

Today I saw you with the child of your sister in your arms. I felt as the old painters must have felt when they painted their Madonnas. You bent over his shining golden head, and on your face was the mother passion and tenderness that is God's finishing touch to the beauty of womanhood. The next moment you were laughing with him – two children playing together. But I had looked upon you in that brief space. Oh, the pain and joy of it!

It is so sweet, dear, to serve you a little, though it be only in opening a door for you to pass through, or handing you a book or a sheet of music! Love wishes to do so much for the beloved! I can do so little for you, but that little is sweet.

This evening I read to you the poem which you had asked me to read. You sat before me with your brown head leaning on your hands and your eyes cast down. I stole dear glances at you between the lines. When I finished I put a red, red rose from your garden between the pages and crushed the book close on it. That poem will always be dear to me, stained with the life-blood of a rose-like hour.

I do not know which is the sweeter, your laughter or your sadness. When you laugh you make me glad, but when you are sad I want to share in your sadness and soothe it. I think I am nearer to you in your sorrowful moods.

Today I met you by accident at the turn of the lane. Nothing told me that you were coming – not even the wind, that should have known. I was sad, and then all at once I saw you, and wondered how I could have been sad. You walked past me with a smile, as if you had tossed me a rose. I stood and watched you out of sight. That meeting was the purple gift the day gave me.

Today I tried to write a poem to you, Una, but I could not find words fine enough, as a lover could find no raiment dainty enough for his bride. The old words other men have used in singing to their loves seemed too worn and common for you. I wanted only new words, crystal clear or coloured only by the iris of the light, not words that have been steeped and stained with all the hues of other men's thoughts. So I burned the verses that were so unworthy of you.

Una, some day you will love. You will watch for him; you will blush at his coming, be sad at his going. Oh, I cannot think of it!

Today I saw you when you did not see me. I was walking on the shore, and as I came around a rock you were sitting on the other side. I drew back a little and looked at you. Your hands were clasped over your knees; your hat had fallen back, and the sea wind was ruffling your hair. Your face was lifted to the sky, your lips were parted, your eyes were full of light. You seemed to be listening to something that made you happy. I crept gently away, that I might not mar your dream. Of what were you thinking, Una?

I must leave you soon. Sometimes I think I cannot bear it. Oh, Una, how selfish it is of me to wish that you might love me! Yet I do wish it, although I have nothing to offer you but a great love and all my willing work of hand and brain. If you loved me, I fear I should be weak enough to do you the wrong of wooing you. I want you so much, dear!

The schoolmaster added the last letter to the others and locked the box. When he unlocked it again, two days later, the letters were gone.

He gazed at the empty box with dilated eyes. At first he could not realize what had happened. The letters could not be gone! He must have made a mistake, have put them in some other place! With trembling fingers he ransacked his trunk. There was no trace of the letters. With a groan he dropped his face in his hands and tried to think.

His letters were gone – those precious letters, held almost too sacred for his own eyes to read after they were written – had been stolen from him! The inmost secrets of his soul had been betrayed. Who had done this hideous thing?

He rose and went downstairs. In the farmyard he found Link tormenting his dog. Link was happy only when he was tormenting something. He never had been afraid of anything in his life before, but now absolute terror took possession of him at sight of the schoolmaster's face. Physical strength and force had no power to frighten the sullen lad, but all the irresistible might of a fine soul roused to frenzy looked out in the young man's blazing eyes, dilated nostrils, and tense white mouth. It cowed the boy, because it was something he could not understand. He only realized that he was in the presence of a force that was not to be trifled with.

"Link, where are my letters?" said the schoolmaster.

"I didn't take 'em, Master!" cried Link, crumpling up visibly in his sheer terror. "I didn't. I never teched 'em! It was Sis. I told her not to – I told her you'd be awful mad, but she wouldn't tend to me. It was Sis took 'em. Ask her, if you don't believe me."

The schoolmaster believed him. Nothing was too horrible to believe just then. "What has she done with them?" he said hoarsely.

"She – she sent 'em to Una Clifford," whimpered Link. "I told her not to. She's mad at you, cause you went to see Una and wouldn't go with her. She thought Una would be mad at you for writing 'em, cause the Cliffords are so proud and think themselves above everybody else. So she sent 'em. I – I told her not to."

The schoolmaster said not another word. He turned his back on the whining boy and went to his room. He felt sick with shame. The indecency of the whole thing revolted him. It was as if his naked heart had been torn from his breast and held up to the jeers of a vulgar world by the merciless hand of a scorned and jealous woman. He felt stunned as if by a physical blow.

After a time his fierce anger and shame died into a calm desperation. The deed was done beyond recall. It only remained for him to go to Una, tell her the truth, and implore her pardon. Then he must go from her sight and presence forever.

IT WAS DUSK when he went to her home. They told him that she was in the garden, and he found her there, standing at the curve of the box walk, among the last late-blooming flowers of the summer.

Have you thought from his letters that she was a wonderful woman of marvellous beauty? Not so. She was a sweet and slender slip of girlhood, with girlhood's own charm and freshness. There were thousands like her in the world – thank God for it! – but only one like her in one man's eyes.

He stood before her mute with shame, his boyish face white and haggard. She had blushed crimson all over her dainty paleness at sight of him, and laid her hand quickly on the breast of her white gown. Her eyes were downcast and her breath came shortly.

He thought her silence the silence of anger and scorn. He wished that he might fling himself in the dust at her feet.

"Una – Miss Clifford – forgive me!" he stammered miserably. "I – I did not send them. I never meant that you should see them. A shameful trick has been played upon me. Forgive me!"

"For what am I to forgive you?" she asked gravely. She did not look up, but her lips parted in the little half-smile he loved. The blush was still on her face.

"For my presumption," he whispered. "I – I could not help loving you, Una. If you have read the letters you know all the rest."

"I have read the letters, every word," she answered, pressing her hand a little more closely to her breast. "Perhaps I should not have done so, for I soon discovered that they were not meant for me to read. I thought at first you had sent them, although the writing of the address on the packet did not look like yours; but even when I knew you did not I could not help reading them all. I do not know who sent them, but I am very grateful to the sender."

"Grateful?" he said wonderingly.

"Yes. I have something to forgive you, but not – not your presumption. It is your blindness, I think – and – and your cruel resolution to go away and never tell me of your – your love for me. If it had not been for the sending of these letters I might never have known. How can I forgive you for that?"

"Una!" he said. He had been very blind, but he was beginning to see. He took a step nearer and took her hands. She threw up her head and gazed, blushingly, steadfastly, into his eyes. From the folds of her gown she drew forth the little packet of letters and kissed it.

"Your dear letters!" she said bravely. "They have given me the right to speak out. I will speak out! I love you, dear! I will be content to wait through long years until you can claim me. I – I have been so happy since your letters came!"

He put his arms around her and drew her head close to his. Their lips met.

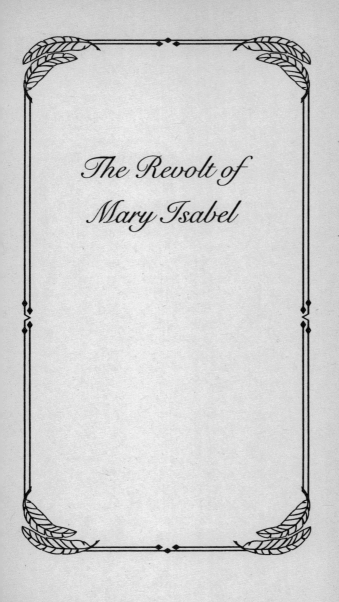

The Revolt of

Mary Isabel

"For a woman of forty, Mary Isabel, you have the least sense of any person I have ever known," said Louisa Irving.

Louisa had said something similar in spirit to Mary Isabel almost every day of her life. Mary Isabel had never resented it, even when it hurt her bitterly. Everybody in Latimer knew that Louisa Irving ruled her meek little sister with a rod of iron and wondered why Mary Isabel never rebelled. It simply never occurred to Mary Isabel to do so; all her life she had given in to Louisa and the thought of refusing obedience to her sister's Mede-and-Persian decrees never crossed her mind. Mary Isabel had only one secret from Louisa and she lived in daily dread that Louisa would discover it. It was a very harmless little secret, but Mary Isabel felt rightly sure that Louisa would not tolerate it for a moment.

They were sitting together in the dim living room of their quaint old cottage down by the shore. The window was open and the sea-breeze blew in, stirring the prim white curtains fitfully, and ruffling the little rings of dark hair on Mary Isabel's forehead – rings which always annoyed Louisa. She thought Mary Isabel ought to brush them straight back, and Mary Isabel did so faithfully a dozen times a day; and in ten minutes they crept down again, kinking defiance to Louisa, who might make Mary Isabel submit to her in all things but had no power over naturally curly hair. Louisa had never had any trouble with her own hair; it was straight and sleek and mouse-coloured – what there was of it.

Mary Isabel's face was flushed and her wood-brown eyes looked grieved and pleading. Mary Isabel was still pretty, and vanity is the last thing to desert a properly constructed woman.

"I can't wear a bonnet yet, Louisa," she protested. "Bonnets have gone out for everybody except really old ladies. I want a hat: one of those pretty, floppy ones with pale blue forget-me-nots."

Then it was that Louisa made the remark quoted above.

"I wore a bonnet before I was forty," she went on ruthlessly, "and so should every decent woman. It is absurd to be thinking so much of dress at your age, Mary Isabel. I don't know what sort of a way you'd bedizen yourself out if I'd let you, I'm sure. It's fortunate you have somebody to keep you from making a fool of yourself. I'm going to town tomorrow and I'll pick you out a suitable black bonnet. You'd look nice starring round in leghorn and forget-me-nots, now, wouldn't you?"

Mary Isabel privately thought she would, but she gave in, of course, although she did hate bitterly that unbought, unescapable bonnet.

"Well, do as you think best, Louisa," she said with a sigh. "I suppose it doesn't matter much. Nobody cares how I look anyhow. But can't I go to town with you? I want to pick out my new silk."

"I'm as good a judge of black silk as you," said Louisa shortly. "It isn't safe to leave the house alone."

"But I don't want a black silk," cried Mary Isabel. "I've worn black so long; both my silk dresses have been black. I want a pretty silver-grey, something like Mrs. Chester Ford's."

"Did anyone ever hear such nonsense?" Louisa wanted to know, in genuine amazement. "Silver-grey silk is the most unserviceable thing in the world. There's nothing like black for wear and real elegance. No, no, Mary Isabel, don't be foolish. You must let me choose for you; you know you never had any judgment. Mother told you so often enough. Now, get your sunbonnet and take a walk to the shore. You look tired. I'll get the tea."

Louisa's tone was kind though firm. She was really good to Mary Isabel as long as Mary Isabel gave her her own way peaceably. But if she had known Mary Isabel's secret she would never have permitted those walks to the shore.

Mary Isabel sighed again, yielded, and went out. Across a green field from the Irving cottage Dr. Donald Hamilton's big house was hooding itself in the shadows of the thick fir grove that enabled the doctor to have a garden. There was no shelter at the cottage, so the Irving "girls" never tried to have a garden. Soon after Dr. Hamilton had come there to live he had sent a bouquet of early daffodils over by his housekeeper. Louisa had taken them gingerly in her extreme fingertips, carried them across the field to the lawn fence, and cast them over it, under the amused grey eyes of portly Dr. Hamilton, who was looking out of his office window. Then Louisa had come back to the porch door and ostentatiously washed her hands.

"I guess that will settle Donald Hamilton," she told the secretly sorry Mary Isabel triumphantly, and it did settle him – at least as far as any farther social advances were concerned.

Dr. Hamilton was an excellent physician and an equally excellent man. Louisa Irving could not have picked a flaw in his history or character. Indeed, against Dr. Hamilton himself she had no grudge, but he was the brother of a man she hated and whose relatives were consequently taboo in Louisa's eyes. Not that the brother was a bad man either; he had simply taken the opposite side to the Irvings in a notable church feud of a dozen years ago, and Louisa had never since held any intercourse with him or his fellow sinners.

Mary Isabel did not look at the Hamilton house. She kept her head resolutely turned away as she went down the shore lane with its wild sweet loneliness of salt-withered grasses and piping sea-winds. Only when she turned the corner of the fir-wood, which shut her out from view of the houses, did she look timidly over the line-fence. Dr. Hamilton was standing there, where the fence ran out to the sandy shingle, smoking his little black pipe, which he took out and put away when

Mary Isabel came around the firs. Men did things like that instinctively in Mary Isabel's company. There was something so delicately virginal about her, in spite of her forty years, that they gave her the reverence they would have paid to a very young, pure girl.

Dr. Hamilton smiled at the little troubled face under the big sunbonnet. Mary Isabel had to wear a sunbonnet. She would never have done it from choice.

"What is the matter?" asked the doctor, in his big, breezy, old-bachelor voice. He had another voice for sick-beds and rooms of bereavement, but this one suited best with the purring of the waves and winds.

"How do you know that anything is the matter?" Mary Isabel parried demurely.

"By your face. Come now, tell me what it is."

"It is really nothing. I have just been foolish, that is all. I wanted a hat with forget-me-nots and a grey silk, and Louisa says I must have black and a bonnet."

The doctor looked indignant but held his peace. He and Mary Isabel had tacitly agreed never to discuss Louisa, because such discussion would not make for harmony. Mary Isabel's conscience would not let the doctor say anything uncomplimentary of Louisa, and the doctor's conscience would not let him say anything complimentary. So they left her out of the question and talked about the sea and the boats and poetry and flowers and similar non-combustible subjects.

THESE CLANDESTINE MEETINGS had been going on for two months, ever since the day they had just happened to meet below the firs. It never occurred to Mary Isabel that the doctor meant anything but friendship; and if it had occurred to the doctor, he did not think there would be much use in saying so. Mary Isabel was too hopelessly under Louisa's thumb. She might keep tryst below the firs occasionally – so long as

Louisa didn't know – but to no farther lengths would she dare go. Besides, the doctor wasn't quite sure that he really wanted anything more. Mary Isabel was a sweet little woman, but Dr. Hamilton had been a bachelor so long that it would be very difficult for him to get out of the habit; so difficult that it was hardly worth while trying when such an obstacle as Louisa Irving's tyranny loomed in the way. So he never tried to make love to Mary Isabel, though he probably would have if he had thought it of any use. This does not sound very romantic, of course, but when a man is fifty, romance, while it may be present in the fruit, is assuredly absent in blossom.

"I suppose you won't be going to the induction of my nephew Thursday week?" said the doctor in the course of the conversation.

"No. Louisa will not permit it. I had hoped," said Mary sabel with a sigh, as she braided some silvery shore-grasses nervously together, "that when old Mr. Moody went away she would go back to the church here. And I think she would if – if –"

"If Jim hadn't come in Mr. Moody's place," finished the doctor with his jolly laugh.

Mary Isabel coloured prettily. "It is not because he is your nephew, doctor. It is because – because –"

"Because he is the nephew of my brother who was on the other side in that ancient church fracas? Bless you, I understand. What a good hater your sister is! Such a tenacity in holding bitterness from one generation to another commands admiration of a certain sort. As for Jim, he's a nice little chap, and he is coming to live with me until the manse is repaired."

"I am sure you will find that pleasant," said Mary Isabel primly.

She wondered if the young minister's advent would make any difference in regard to these shore-meetings; then decided quickly that it would not; then more quickly still that it wouldn't matter if it did.

"He will be company," admitted the doctor, who liked company and found the shore road rather lonesome. "I had a letter from him today saying that he'd come home with me from the induction. By the way, they're tearing down the old post office today. And that reminds me – by Jove, I'd all but forgotten. I promised to go up and see Mollie Marr this evening; Mollie's nerves are on the rampage again. I must rush."

With a wave of his hand the doctor hurried off. Mary Isabel lingered for some time longer, leaning against the fence, looking dreamily out to sea. The doctor was a very pleasant companion. If only Louisa would allow neighbourliness! Mary Isabel felt a faint, impotent resentment. She had never had anything other girls had: friends, dresses, beaus; and it was all Louisa's fault – Louisa who was going to make her wear a bonnet for the rest of her life. The more Mary Isabel thought of that bonnet the more she hated it.

That evening Warren Marr rode down to the shore cottage on horseback and handed Mary Isabel a letter, a strange, scrumpled, soiled, yellow letter. When Mary Isabel saw the handwriting on the envelope she trembled and turned as deadly pale as if she had seen a ghost.

"Here's a letter for you," said Warren, grinning. "It's been a long time on the way – nigh fifteen years. Guess the news'll be rather stale. We found it behind the old partition when we tore it down today."

"It is my brother Tom's writing," said Mary Isabel faintly. She went into the room trembling, holding the letter tightly in her clasped hands. Louisa had gone up to the village on an errand; Mary Isabel almost wished she were home; she hardly felt equal to the task of opening Tom's letter alone. Tom had been dead for ten years and this letter gave her an uncanny sensation, as of a message from the spirit-land.

Fifteen years ago Thomas Irving had gone to California and five years later he had died there. Mary Isabel, who had idolized her brother, almost grieved herself to death at the time.

Finally she opened the letter with ice-cold fingers. It had been written soon after Tom reached California. The first two pages were filled with descriptions of the country and his "job."

On the third Tom began abruptly:

Look here, Mary Isabel, you are not to let Louisa boss you about as she was doing when I was at home. I was going to speak to you about it before I came away, but I forgot. Lou is a fine girl, but she is too domineering, and the more you give in to her the worse it makes her. You're far too easy-going for your own welfare, Mary Isabel, and for your own sake I wish you had more spunk. Don't let Louisa live your life for you; just you live it yourself. Never mind if there is some friction at first; Lou will give in when she finds she has to, and you'll both be the better for it. I want you to be real happy, Mary Isabel, but you won't be if you don't assert your independence. Giving in the way you do is bad for both you and Louisa. It will make her a tyrant and you a poor-spirited creature of no account in the world. Just brace up and stand firm.

When she had read the letter through Mary Isabel took it to her own room and locked it in her bureau drawer. Then she sat by her window, looking out into a sea-sunset, and thought it over. Coming in the strange way it had, the letter seemed a message from the dead, and Mary Isabel had a superstitious conviction that she must obey it. She had always had a great respect for Tom's opinion. He was right – oh, she felt that he was right. What a pity she had not received the letter long ago, before the shackles of habit had become so firmly riveted. But it was not too late yet. She would rebel at last and – how had Tom phrased it – oh, yes, assert her independence. She owed it to Tom. It had been his wish – and he was dead – and she would do her best to fulfil it.

"I shan't get a bonnet," thought Mary Isabel determinedly. "Tom wouldn't have liked me in a bonnet. From this out I'm just going to do exactly as Tom would have liked me to do, no matter how afraid I am of Louisa. And, oh, I am horribly afraid of her."

Mary Isabel was every whit as much afraid the next morning after breakfast but she did not look it, by reason of the flush on her cheeks and the glint in her brown eyes. She had put Tom's letter in the bosom of her dress and she pressed her fingertips on it that the crackle might give her courage.

"Louisa," she said firmly, "I am going to town with you."

"Nonsense," said Louisa shortly.

"You may call it nonsense if you like, but I am going," said Mary Isabel unquailingly. "I have made up my mind on that point, Louisa, and nothing you can say will alter it."

Louisa looked amazed. Never before had Mary Isabel set her decrees at naught.

"Are you crazy, Mary Isabel?" she demanded.

"No, I am not crazy. But I am going to town and I am going to get a silver-grey silk for myself and a new hat. I will not wear a bonnet and you need never mention it to me again, Louisa."

"If you are going to town I shall stay home," said Louisa in a cold, ominous tone that almost made Mary Isabel quake. If it had not been for that reassuring crackle of Tom's letter I fear Mary Isabel would have given in. "This house can't be left alone. If you go, I'll stay."

Louisa honestly thought that would bring the rebel to terms. Mary Isabel had never gone to town alone in her life. Louisa did not believe she would dare to go. But Mary Isabel did not quail. Defiance was not so hard after all, once you had begun.

Mary Isabel went to town and she went alone. She spent the whole delightful day in the shops, unhampered by Louisa's scorn and criticism in her examination of all the pretty things displayed. She selected a hat she felt sure Tom would like – a pretty crumpled grey straw with forget-me-nots and ribbons. Then she bought a grey silk of a lovely silvery shade.

When she got back home she unwrapped her packages and showed her purchases to Louisa. But Louisa neither looked at them nor spoke to Mary Isabel. Mary Isabel tossed her head and went to her own room. Her draught of freedom had stimulated her, and she did not mind Louisa's attitude half as much as she would have expected. She read Tom's letter over again to fortify herself and then she dressed her hair in a fashion she had seen that day in town and pulled out all the little curls on her forehead.

The next day she took the silver-grey silk to the Latimer dressmaker and picked out a fashionable design for it. When the silk dress came home, Louisa, who had thawed out somewhat in the meantime, unbent sufficiently to remark that it fitted very well.

"I am going to wear it to the induction tomorrow," Mary Isabel said, boldly to all appearances, quakingly in reality. She knew that she was throwing down the gauntlet for good and all. If she could assert and maintain her independence in this matter Louisa's power would be broken forever.

TWELVE YEARS before this, the previously mentioned schism had broken out in the Latimer church. The minister had sided with the faction which Louisa Irving opposed. She had promptly ceased going to his church and withdrew all financial support. She paid to the Marwood church, fifteen miles away, and occasionally she hired a team and drove over there to service. But she never entered the Latimer church again nor allowed Mary Isabel to do so. For that matter, Mary Isabel did not wish to go. She had resented the minister's attitude almost as bitterly as Louisa. But when Mr. Moody accepted a call elsewhere Mary Isabel hoped that she and Louisa might return to their old church home. Possibly they might have done so had not the congregation called the young, newly fledged James Anderson. Mary Isabel would not have cared for this, but Louisa sternly said that neither she nor any of hers should ever darken the doors of a church where the nephew of Martin Hamilton preached. Mary Isabel had regretfully acquiesced at the time, but now she had made up her mind to go to church and she meant to begin with the induction service.

Louisa stared at her sister incredulously.

"Have you taken complete leave of your senses, Mary Isabel?"

"No. I've just come to them," retorted Mary Isabel recklessly, gripping a chair-back desperately so that Louisa should not see how she was trembling. "It is all foolishness to keep away from church just because of an old grudge. I'm tired of staying home Sundays or driving fifteen miles to Marwood to hear poor old Mr. Grattan. Everybody says Mr. Anderson is a splendid young man and an excellent preacher, and I'm going to attend his services regularly."

Louisa had taken Mary Isabel's first defiance in icy disdain. Now she lost her temper and raged. The storm of angry words beat on Mary Isabel like hail, but she fronted it staunchly. She seemed to hear Tom's voice saying, "Live your own life, Mary Isabel; don't let Louisa live it for you," and she meant to obey him.

"If you go to that man's induction I'll never forgive you," Louisa concluded.

Mary Isabel said nothing. She just primmed up her lips very determinedly, picked up the silk dress, and carried it to her room.

The next day was fine and warm. Louisa said no word all the morning. She worked fiercely and slammed things around noisily. After dinner Mary Isabel went to her room and came down presently, fine and dainty in her grey silk, with the forget-me-not hat resting on the soft loose waves of her hair. Louisa was blacking the kitchen stove.

She shot one angry glance at Mary Isabel, then gave a short, contemptuous laugh, the laugh of an angry woman who finds herself robbed of all weapons except ridicule.

Mary Isabel flushed and walked with an unfaltering step out of the house and up the lane. She resented Louisa's laughter. She was sure there was nothing so very ridiculous about her appearance. Women far older than she, even in Latimer, wore light dresses and fashionable hats. Really, Louisa was very disagreeable.

"I have put up with her ways too long," thought Mary Isabel, with a quick, unwonted rush of anger. "But I never shall again – no, never, let her be as vexed and scornful as she pleases."

The induction services were interesting, and Mary Isabel enjoyed them. Doctor Hamilton was sitting across from her and once or twice she caught him looking at her admiringly. The doctor noticed the hat and the grey silk and wondered how Mary Isabel had managed to get her own way concerning them. What a pretty woman she was! Really, he had never realized before how very pretty she was. But then he had never seen her except in a sunbonnet or with her hair combed primly back.

But when the service was over Mary Isabel was dismayed to see that the sky had clouded over and looked very much like rain. Everybody hurried home, and Mary Isabel tripped along the shore road filled with anxious thoughts about her dress. That kind of silk always spotted, and her hat would be ruined if it got wet. How foolish she had been not to bring an umbrella!

She reached her own doorstep panting just as the first drop of rain fell.

"Thank goodness," she breathed.

Then she tried to open the door. It would not open.

She could see Louisa sitting by the kitchen window, calmly reading.

"Louisa, open the door quick," she called impatiently.

Louisa never moved a muscle, although Mary Isabel knew she must have heard.

"Louisa, do you hear what I say?" she cried, reaching over and tapping on the pane imperiously. "Open the door at once. It is going to rain – it is raining now. Be quick."

Louisa might as well have been a graven image for all the response she gave. Then did Mary Isabel realize her position. Louisa had locked her out purposely, knowing the rain was coming. Louisa had no intention of letting her in; she meant to keep her out until the dress and hat of her rebellion were spoiled. This was Louisa's revenge.

Mary Isabel turned with a gasp. What should she do? The padlocked doors of hen-house and well-house and wood-house revealed the thoroughness of Louisa's vindictive design. Where should she go? She would go somewhere. She would not have her lovely new dress and hat spoiled!

She caught her ruffled skirts up in her hand and ran across the yard. She climbed the fence into the field and ran across that. Another drop of rain struck her cheek. She never glanced back or she would have seen a horrified face peering from the cottage kitchen window. Louisa had never dreamed that Mary Isabel would seek refuge over at Dr. Hamilton's.

Dr. Hamilton, who had driven home from church with the young minister, saw her coming and ran to open the door for her. Mary Isabel dashed up the verandah steps, breathless, crimson-cheeked, trembling with pent-up indignation and sense of outrage.

"Louisa locked me out, Dr. Hamilton," she cried almost hysterically. "She locked me out on purpose to spoil my dress. I'll never forgive her; I'll never go back to her, never, never, unless she asks me to. I had to come here. I was not going to have my dress ruined to please Louisa."

"Of course not – of course not," said Dr. Hamilton sooth-ingly, drawing her into his big cosy living room. "You did per-fectly right to come here, and you are just in time. There is the rain now in good earnest."

Mary Isabel sank into a chair and looked at Dr. Hamilton with tears in her eyes.

"Wasn't it an unkind, unsisterly thing to do?" she asked piteously. "Oh, I shall never feel the same towards Louisa again. Tom was right – I didn't tell you about Tom's letter but I will by and by. I shall not go back to Louisa after her locking me out. When it stops raining I'll go straight up to my cousin Ella's and stay with her until I arrange my plans. But one thing is certain, I shall not go back to Louisa."

"I wouldn't," said the doctor recklessly. "Now, don't cry and don't worry. Take off your hat – you can go to the spare room across the hall, if you like. Jim has gone upstairs to lie down; he has a bad headache and says he doesn't want any tea. So I was going to get up a bachelor's snack for myself. My housekeeper is away. She heard at church that her mother was ill and went over to Marwood."

When Mary Isabel came back from the spare room, a little calmer but with traces of tears on her pink cheeks, the doctor had as good a tea-table spread as any woman could have had. Mary Isabel thought it was fortunate that the little errand boy, Tommy Brewster, was there, or she certainly would have been dreadfully embarrassed, now that the flame of her anger had blown out. But later on, when tea was over and she and the doctor were left alone, she did not feel embarrassed after all. Instead, she felt delightfully happy and at home. Dr. Hamilton put one so at ease.

She told him all about Tom's letter and her subsequent revolt. Dr. Hamilton never once made the mistake of smiling. He listened and approved and sympathized.

"So I'm determined I won't go back," concluded Mary Isabel, "unless she asks me to – and Louisa will never do that. Ella will be glad enough to have me for a while; she has five children and can't get any help."

The doctor shrugged his shoulders. He thought of Mary Isabel as unofficial drudge to Ella Kemble and her family. Then he looked at the little silvery figure by the window.

"I think I can suggest a better plan," he said gently and tenderly. "Suppose you stay here – as my wife. I've always wanted to ask you that but I feared it was no use because I knew Louisa would oppose it and I did not think you would consent if she did not. I think," the doctor leaned forward and took Mary Isabel's fluttering hand in his, "I think we can be very happy here, dear."

Mary Isabel flushed crimson and her heart beat wildly. She knew now that she loved Dr. Hamilton – and Tom would have liked it – yes, Tom would. She remembered how Tom hated the thought of his sisters being old maids.

"I – think – so – too," she faltered shyly.

"Then," said the doctor briskly, "what is the matter with our being married right here and now?"

"Married!"

"Yes, of course. Here we are in a state where no licence is required, a minister in the house, and you all dressed in the most beautiful wedding silk imaginable. You must see, if you just look at it calmly, how much better it will be than going up to Mrs. Kemble's and thereby publishing your difference with Louisa to all the village. I'll give you fifteen minutes to get used to the idea and then I'll call Jim down."

Mary Isabel put her hands to her face.

"You – you're like a whirlwind," she gasped. "You take away my breath."

"Think it over," said the doctor in a businesslike voice.

Mary Isabel thought – thought very hard for a few moments.

What would Tom have said?

Was it probable that Tom would have approved of such marrying in haste?

Mary Isabel came to the decision that he would have preferred it to having family jars bruited abroad. Moreover, Mary Isabel had never liked Ella Kemble very much. Going to her was only one degree better than going back to Louisa.

At last Mary Isabel took her hands down from her face.

"Well?" said the doctor persuasively as she did so.

"I will consent on one condition," said Mary Isabel firmly. "And that is, that you will let me send word over to Louisa that I am going to be married and that she may come and see the ceremony if she will. Louisa has behaved very unkindly in this matter, but after all she is my sister – and she has been good to me in some ways – and I am not going to give her a chance to say that I got married in this – this headlong fashion and never let her know."

"Tommy can take the word over," said the doctor.

Mary Isabel went to the doctor's desk and wrote a very brief note.

Dear Louisa:

I am going to be married to Dr. Hamilton right away. I've seen him often at the shore this summer. I would like you to be present at the ceremony if you choose.

Mary Isabel.

Tommy ran across the field with the note.

It had now ceased raining and the clouds were breaking.

Mary Isabel thought that a good omen. She and the doctor watched Tommy from the window. They saw Louisa come to the door, take the note, and shut the door in Tommy's face. Ten minutes later she reappeared, habited in her mackintosh, with her second-best bonnet on.

"She's – coming," said Mary Isabel, trembling.

The doctor put his arm protectingly about the little lady.

Mary Isabel tossed her head. "Oh, I'm not – I'm only excited. I shall never be afraid of Louisa again."

Louisa came grimly over the field, up the verandah steps, and into the room without knocking.

"Mary Isabel," she said, glaring at her sister and ignoring the doctor entirely, "did you mean what you said in that letter?"

"Yes, I did," said Mary Isabel firmly.

"You are going to be married to that man in this shameless, indecent haste?"

"Yes."

"And nothing I can say will have the least effect on you?"

"Not the slightest."

"Then," said Louisa, more grimly than ever, "all I ask of you is to come home and be married from under your father's roof. Do have that much respect for your parents' memory, at least."

"Of course I will," cried Mary Isabel impulsively, softening at once. "Of course we will – won't we?" she asked, turning prettily to the doctor.

"Just as you say," he answered gallantly.

Louisa snorted. "I'll go home and air the parlour," she said. "It's lucky I baked that fruitcake Monday. You can come when you're ready."

She stalked home across the field. In a few minutes the doctor and Mary Isabel followed, and behind them came the young minister, carrying his blue book under his arm, and trying hard and not altogether successfully to look grave.

Afterword: Finding
L. M. Montgomery's
Short Stories

GREAT LITERARY FINDS are not exactly a dime-a-dozen. But even if they were, for the finder they would always be exciting. I had no notion of ever being one of those people who find something interesting in their own or someone else's attic. In fact, I never thought of looking. When a friend and I visited L. M. Montgomery's birthplace in New London, P.E.I., in 1977, we were going simply as tourists, tourists interested in the author of the twenty books that began with *Anne of Green Gables*. It was my friend who called me over to a glass-fronted display cabinet to look at a short story pasted in a scrapbook. Did I know it? Silly question. Didn't I know all her twenty novels and four short-story collections almost off by heart by virtue of constant re-reading since the age of eleven? Of course I would know this story. But I didn't.

Luckily, the ladies in charge weren't particularly busy and were pleased to get the scrapbook out of the case for me. It was full of short stories by Montgomery, none of which I had ever seen before. "Well, if you're really interested, there are more upstairs," they told me. Up the stairs, in one of the tiny bedrooms, was a cardboard box, the floor around it sprinkled with Mouse Feast. There were eleven other scrapbooks in the box; all contained clippings of published stories and poems by L. M. Montgomery. A feast indeed, but for mice? Were these collections safe, kept in a cardboard box, in a frame house, surrounded by Mouse Feast? I found out much later that the stories only visited the birthplace in the summer and were carried off to the Confederation Centre archives at the end of the season. But at the time my only concern was that they survive until I could come back with more time and read them all.

That was my original focus. I wanted to read them. Unlike most young women who had read *Anne* and the other novels in their teens and then put them aside as childish things, I never stopped reading them. I read them year in and year out, again and again. I never tired of their apparent simplicity, finding them more complex than they seemed, their emotions true and believable. They were part of my innermost being. But there weren't enough of them. Only twenty novels and forty-eight short stories.

Now here was a collection of hundreds. How many, I had not time on that visit to discover. But I knew that I must make sure they were safe, and that I must get permission from someone to look through and read them all and, if possible, copy them so I could go on re-reading them too. Still, it took me a while to get up my courage to do anything about it. Surely, I thought, it must be just my ignorance that I didn't know about these collections; probably everyone in the field (was there a Montgomery field in 1977?) knew about them. And might I tread on academic toes?

One thing I did know was that Montgomery's younger son, Dr. Stuart Macdonald, lived in Toronto, but I thought that he was probably constantly pestered by Montgomery fans and that I should not intrude on him. Without contacting him, I went back to P.E.I. the next summer and spent a happy couple of days making a list of every story and poem in all twelve collections. Only about half of them, by the way, were bound scrapbooks, into which were pasted the pieces Montgomery had clipped. The other half were sewn gatherings of full pages from magazines. I even read a few of the stories, but again, time was short.

Back home in Toronto I put together a typed pamphlet

called "A Listing of Scrapbooks and Gatherings in Montgomery's Birthplace," put a spiral binding on it, and called it a private publication (1978). This seemed rather respectable (it was 27 pages long and contained over 700 entries, half of them poems, the other half stories), so I summoned up the courage to write to Dr. Macdonald. He answered most kindly. He had been unaware of the existence of the stories and, once I had proved my sincere intentions, was willing that I should have access to them. He arranged that his friend Father Francis Bolger, a professor at the University of Prince Edward Island and a trustee of the birthplace, have them photocopied. (Father Bolger was familiar with the collection of scrapbooks because he had used their contents for his book about Montgomery's early publications, *The Years before "Anne."*) The process of copying took about a year, because only one scrapbook at a time could be removed from the collection. Father Bolger made two copies of the scrapbooks, keeping one for the University of Prince Edward Island archives and sending one to me; on receipt of the second copy I made a set for Dr. Macdonald, which went to the University of Guelph archives on his death.

What a feast of reading I had that year! I revelled in every new story, whether it was good or not so good. Some stories were exceptional; some had obviously been churned out at top speed. Several seemed familiar; they were the originals of vignettes in some of the novels. ("Mrs. Skinner's Story," published in *Westminster Magazine* in 1907, was adapted for Chapter 30 of *Anne of the Island* in 1915; "A House Divided against Itself," published in *Canadian Home Journal* in 1930, became one of the strands in *A Tangled Web* the very next year; *Anne of Windy Poplars* and *Anne of Ingleside* are made up almost wholly of stories that had first seen the light of day previously.) Some stories appeared more than once, having been sold, with few or no alterations, to different magazines. Some had Montgomery's own handwritten corrections of typographical errors and stylistic adjustments. All were interesting to me as showing the range of her talent and her ability to keep at it. Does one today assume that a newspaper writer will produce gems of stylistic brilliance in every column, every day? Of course not. And that is almost the way Montgomery was writing: at that speed and at that volume. But more of the volume later.

There was just enough publication information (magazine names and dates) attached to the stories in the sewn gatherings to make me want to produce a bibliography. The 360 stories of which I now had copies had been published in 134 different magazines and newspapers, running from the *Advocate and Guardian* to *Zion's Herald*, and covering most of the rest of the alphabet in between. Of course I couldn't find all these magazines. Some were tiny affairs, long since deceased. Some were ephemeral Sunday School publications. But in the Library of Congress in Washington, D.C., in the New York Public Library, the Toronto Public Library, and a few other regional libraries, I tracked down many of them. They had no indexes, of course. No tables of contents. I spent many hours in the stacks of the Library of Congress leafing through enormous bound volumes of *Boys' World* and *Girls' Companion*, freezing my bottom on cold marble floors and covering my top with decaying leather. And every so often, in the midst of keeping track of dates and page numbers, I would find a story not in the scrapbook collections. Eventually my filing cabinet contained over 400 items.

You might think that, with 400 items, I must surely have a complete collection. Not so. Dr. Macdonald let me borrow and copy a ledger Montgomery had kept, in which she listed every dollar she had earned from her publications: stories, poems, and novels. Her list of stories reached No. 517. Reading the list carefully, I discovered that some of those 517 were chapters of books: *Magic for Marigold* and *Emily of New Moon*, for instance, came out serially (the former before, the latter after, publication as a novel), and Montgomery listed those chapters as short stories in her list. To add a little confusion, sometimes Montgomery's numbers got out of order: she would misread a seven as a one and continue with two rather than with eight, thereby repeating numbers already used, or she would do the opposite, jumping from one to eight, having misread the one as a seven. Some of the stories I had were not on her list; others she did list were not in the scrapbooks and I had not found them. Still, when I completed the bibliography in 1985, listing the found and unfound stories, there were 506 titles, and copies of 400 of them were in my collection. I will probably never find the other 106 stories.

All this time, Mary Rubio and Elizabeth Waterston of the University of Guelph had been comforters and sustainers. They had published my first article, a preliminary bibliography of the stories, in *Canadian Children's Literature* in 1983. They had encouraged me, nay, ordered me, to apply for a Canada Council grant to complete the bibliography. Now they leaned on me again: "Get the stories out to the public." Dr. Macdonald had died since my work began, but he had often expressed his hope that I could get some of the stories published. And so I approached McClelland and Stewart in 1985. They accepted my proposal for the first collection of stories, and *Akin to Anne: Tales of Other Orphans* came out three years later. The next three followed year by year: *Along the Shore: Tales by the Sea*, *Among the Shadows: Tales from the Darker Side*, and *After Many Days: Tales of Time Passed*. A fifth, *Against the Odds: Tales of Achievement*, appeared in the spring of 1993; *At the Altar: Matrimonial Tales*, the sixth, in 1994, and now *Across the Miles: Tales of Correspondence* in 1995. I hope there will be at least two more collections.

I have often been asked why the collections have been grouped thematically. As I was reading over the stories to choose those worth publishing they seemed to fall naturally into certain categories, and although it makes for some sameness to have nineteen stories all about orphans, it is also interesting to note the changes Montgomery is able to ring on such a theme. A chronological presentation or a "best of" collection would pose other problems, so the theme decision was adhered to.

I mentioned before that I had been struck, on first reading the scrapbook photocopies through, at finding stories that I recognized from the novels. But even when Montgomery repeats a story or recycles a plot from one story to another she finds ways in her use of character and setting and point of view to vary it. She was, after all, a professional writer; she wrote in order to earn money; and she produced stories in a quantity that is somewhat staggering. Her output of novels is just as amazing, considering that, as she was producing them, she was a minister's wife in a small Ontario community, with all the concomitant duties that position used to entail. And if there is a distinct falling off in the last two *Anne* books, written at her publisher's insistence, when she was sick of Anne, *Jane of Lantern Hill*, her last book, is one of her best.

Montgomery's first poem was published in 1890; her first story in 1895. In 1901 13 stories and 28 poems appeared; in 1903, the high point for poems, 32; in 1905, the high point for stories, 44. By 1910, when her novel-writing began to take precedence, her output of stories was down to nine (but another 22, previously in print, were re-published); 12 new poems and five re-publications of poems came out that year. An amazing record, and an amazing woman.

Since the publication of her journals, for which we are all eternally grateful to Mary Rubio and Elizabeth Waterston, Montgomery seems much more interesting as a person and worthy of attention as a writer. Is it because we now know of the occasional despair that lay behind the sweetness and light of most of her writing? There are depths to Montgomery, as scholars, critics, and readers are increasingly coming to discover.

Editorial Note

The stories in this collection were originally published in the following magazines and newspapers, and are listed here in alphabetical order. Dates in square brackets are conjectural. Where the original illustrations accompanying the stories are available, they have been included. Obvious typographical errors have been corrected, spelling and punctuation normalized.

Anna's Love Letters, *National Magazine*, January 1908, 441-45.

At Five O'Clock in the Morning, *National Magazine*, July 1905, 405-11. Also in *MacLean's*, September 1914, 8-9, 132-34.

Aunt Caroline's Silk Dress, *East and West*, 7 September 1907, 285-86.

Aunt Susanna's Birthday Celebration, *New Idea Woman's Magazine*, February 1905, 30-31.

A Correspondence and a Climax, *Sunday Magazine*, 20 August 1905, 13-14, 17. Also in *Family Herald*, 27 September and 4 October 1905, 6 and 6, "reprinted from New York Tribune."

Cyrilla's Inspiration, *Epworth Herald*, 25 November 1905, 673-75.

A Fortunate Mistake, *Girls' Companion*, 23 January 1904, 4.

The Girl and the Photograph, *MacLean's*, May 1915, 36-38. Also as "A Girl and a Picture," *Farm and Fireside*,

10 August 1907, 13, 17. The two versions of this story differ slightly. The copy in Montgomery's scrapbooks is from 1915, so I have chosen it as being the last version to leave her hand, although there is no way of telling whether she revised it for the second publication or whether a *MacLean's* editor did.

The Growing Up of Cornelia, *Pictorial Review*, October 1908, 8-9, 15, 65.

The Jest That Failed, *Household Guest* [1901]. Also in *Presbyterian Banner*, 16 March 1911, 1330-31.

The Letters, *National Magazine*, November 1910, 119-26. Also in *MacLean's*, December 1915, 23-25, 89-91.

A Millionaire's Proposal, *Amulet Magazine* [1907].

Miss Madeline's Proposal, *Modern Women*, September 1904, 103-4. Also in *Westminster*, December 1913, 633-36.

Miss Sally's Letter, *Canadian Courier*, 26 November 1910, 13, 24-25, as "Aunt Sally's Letters." Listed in Montgomery's ledger as "Miss Sally's Letter."

The Old Fellow's Letters, *Blue Book Magazine*, April 1907, 1246-49.

Our Runaway Kite, *New Idea Woman's Magazine*, October 1903, 44-45.

The Promissory Note, *Zion's Herald*, 20 September 1913, 1170-72.

The Revolt of Mary Isabel, *Blue Book Magazine*, December 1908, 318-25.

The Schoolmaster's Letters, *Sunday Magazine*, 4 June 1905, 7-8, 12-13. Also in *Holland's Magazine*, August 1914, 14, 39.

The Understanding of Sister Sara, *Pilgrim*, August 1905, 11-12. Also in *Holland's Magazine*, October 1907, 20-21.

Acknowledgements

The late Dr. Stuart Macdonald gave me permission to begin the research that culminated in my collection of Montgomery's stories; Professors Mary Rubio and Elizabeth Waterston encouraged and advised me; C. Anderson Silber gave his constant support. Librarians were unfailingly helpful.

L. M. Montgomery

For the most complete listing, see Russell, Russell, and Wilmshurst, *Lucy Maud Montgomery: A Preliminary Bibliography*, University of Waterloo Library Bibliography Series, No. 13 (Waterloo: University of Waterloo Library, 1986).

The "Anne" Books (in order of Anne's life)

Anne of Green Gables, 1908
Anne of Avonlea, 1909
Anne of the Island, 1915
Anne of Windy Poplars, 1936
Anne's House of Dreams, 1917
Anne of Ingleside, 1939
Rainbow Valley, 1919
Rilla of Ingleside, 1920

The "Emily" Books

Emily of New Moon, 1923
Emily Climbs, 1925
Emily's Quest, 1927

Other Novels (in chronological order)

Kilmeny of the Orchard, 1910
The Story Girl, 1911
The Golden Road, 1913
The Blue Castle, 1926
Magic for Marigold, 1929
A Tangled Web, 1931
Pat of Silver Bush, 1933
Mistress Pat, 1935
Jane of Lantern Hill, 1937

Collections of Short Stories

Chronicles of Avonlea, 1912
Further Chronicles of Avonlea, 1920
The Road to Yesterday, 1974
The Doctor's Sweetheart, and Other Stories, 1979
Akin to Anne: Tales of Other Orphans, 1988
Along the Shore: Tales by the Sea, 1989
Among the Shadows: Tales from the Darker Side, 1990
After Many Days: Tales of Time Passed, 1991
Against the Odds: Tales of Achievement, 1993
At the Altar: Matrimonial Tales, 1994

Poetry

The Watchman, and Other Poems, 1916
Poetry of Lucy Maud Montgomery, 1987

"Anne of Green Gables" and "Diana Barry" are trademarks of the Anne of Green Gables Licensing Authority, Charlottetown, Prince Edward Island, and are used under license from Ruth Macdonald and David Macdonald, who are the heirs of L. M. Montgomery, by arrangement with the Authority.